the
pretty
one

ALSO BY CHERYL KLAM

Learning to Swim

the
pretty
one

cheryl
klam

DELACORTE
PRESS

Published by Delacorte Press
an imprint of Random House Children's Books
a division of Random House, Inc.
New York

Delacorte Press and colophon are registered trademarks of
Random House, Inc.

Visit us on the web! www.randomhouse.com/teens
www.cherylklam.com

Educators and librarians, for a variety of teaching tools, visit us at
www.randomhouse.com/teachers

Library of Congress Cataloging-in-Publication Data is available
upon request.
ISBN: 978-0-385-73373-1 (tr. pbk.)
ISBN: 978-0-385-90388-2 (lib. bdg.)

The text of this book is set in 12-point Goudy.

Book design by Kenneth Holcomb

Printed in the United States of America

10 9 8 7 6 5 4 3 2 1

First Edition

For my sister, Jenny Guttridge—forever the pretty one

Thanks to Esther Newberg, who will always be the first person I pick for my team. Thanks also to the amazing Claudia Gabel, whose energy, enthusiasm, and talent never fail to inspire and astound me. And mega-thanks to Brian Klam, the funniest writer in the world.

one

starstruck (adj):
captivated by famous people or
by fame itself.

The rodent is staring at my sister Lucy.

In the rodent's defense, it's hard not to stare at Lucy. Actually, it's a phenomenon similar to rubbernecking; only in this case people don't stare at my sister because she looks like a car wreck. Men, women, children, animals, and zygotes (I'm guessing) can't take their eyes off Lucy because she is absolutely, undeniably perfect. Like airbrushed "men's interest" magazine kind of perfect.

"Herbert?" I say, since his real name is Herbert Rodale and I only refer to him as the rodent behind his back.

The rodent doesn't answer. He's either ignoring me or so deep in fantasyland he doesn't hear me.

"Herbert!" I shout.

This not only gets Lucy's attention, but the attention of the techie geeks who, like me and the rodent, have gathered to help Lucy turn the gym into a "magic apple orchard" for the fall festival. We attend the Chesapeake School for Performing Arts in Baltimore (otherwise known as CSPA), and the fall festival is the school's lame imitation of a homecoming dance. But unlike in a real high school (where I've heard everyone goes to the dances regardless of their position in the high school popularity hierarchy), only the drama, dance, music, and art majors (well, about half of the art majors) attend the fall festival. Us techies stay home and watch *Mythbusters* on the Discovery Channel.

"Herbert," Lucy says sweetly as she puts her thumbs in her belt loops and hikes up her low-rise Sevens. "Megan wants you."

The rodent looks as if someone has just slapped him out of a trance. "What?" he says, wrinkling up his long, pointed nose as his little beady eyes dart around the room.

"This needs to be hung from right there," I say, shaking a "magic apple" (also known as a red-sequined Styrofoam ball) and pointing to a spot on the wall behind him.

"Yeah, okay," he mumbles. And then he goes back to staring at my sister again.

I should be used to guys ogling my older sister as if she were a Victoria's Secret model holding the newest Sony PlayStation. It happens no matter where we go.

Lucy and I are the only kids in our family and she's the oldest, born eleven months before me. Since Lucy is tall (think model), gorgeous (think bathing suit edition of *Sports Illustrated*), and blond (think bathing suit edition of *Sports Illustrated* model with golden flax hair spun by silver-winged fairies), I like to joke that she used up all our mom's Scandinavian genes, leaving me with Dad's Mediterranean ones (think bushy-eyebrowed president of some country you've never heard of). But although my heritage may explain my stature, thick dark hair, and olive complexion, it's not responsible for my oversized hooked nose, my nonexistent cheekbones, my oversized chin, and last, but definitely not least, my buck teeth.

Life is so unfair. Which is why I toss rodent the ball, hitting him in the head.

"Ouch," he says, rubbing the place of impact.

"Sorry," I grumble.

My aggressive behavior and sour expression have not escaped the notice of my sister, who takes me by the arm and leads me away from the group. "What are you doing?" she whispers.

Even her voice is melodic. Jesus.

"It was an accident," I say defensively.

Lucy peers into my eyes (brown with a little hazel mixed in, my one and only reasonably good facial feature), and I can tell she's trying to read my mind. In spite of our physical differences, we grew up as twins: wearing the same blue pinafore dresses Aunt Erma sent us every year for Christmas, getting our pictures taken together at Honeygo Photo Studio, and being toted around in a double stroller. As a result, we have a brain connect that is sometimes downright eerie, if not bordering on psychic. (Or psychotic.)

"I know you weren't crazy about this whole decorating thing," she says finally. "But I appreciate your help."

"No problemo." I turn away and begin chewing on my right thumbnail. I don't want Lucy to see inside my head, mainly because I'm not exactly proud of what's going on in there. I love my sister, I do, but this idol worship gets to me sometimes. I really shouldn't care that my fellow tech majors have spent the past three hours decorating for a dance that none of them have any intention of attending, all the while acting as if Lucy is doing them a huge favor by *allowing* them to help her. I should be downright delirious with happy-tude that my sister is getting what she wants, even if she always seems to get what she wants without putting in any real effort. But deep down, I just wave that proverbial white flag of surrender.

"I didn't have anything else to do anyway," I add, commending myself on my graciousness.

"That's true," Lucy says absentmindedly, pulling the proverbial flag right out of my hands.

"I could've gone to Spoons," Simon announces, not even bothering to look away from his illustration. Simon is an excellent artist who has been given the task of painting the giant backdrop for the dance floor, a life-size illustration of an apple tree. As my official best friend, Simon is the only one of my peers who's actually here because of me. Simon is short and skinny, but with his big brown eyes and ruffled wavy brown hair, he's definitely one of the best-looking techs (not that that's a huge compliment; as anyone with one good eye could see, we are not an attractive bunch). Not many people realize this though, because they're too distracted by his thick, circa nineteen fifties horn-rimmed glasses; his black, paint spattered T-shirts; his brightly colored Bermuda shorts (that he wears year round—even in the winter); his neon socks; and his silver sneakers.

"I could be drinking an iced mocha cappuccino right now," Simon says, referring to my favorite beverage, as he uses his paintbrush to sweep a brown line across the canvas. "Or I could've gone to see that new Jennifer Aniston movie."

I smile widely. Simon hates iced mocha cappuccinos about as much as he hates chick flicks, maybe even more (I caught him looking at a Sandra Bullock DVD at the mall once). The message is clear: he would prefer either of those to decorating the gym. Not that I haven't been thinking the same thing myself, but I can't help but feel protective of Lucy, and I don't want Simon to hurt her feelings. I narrow my eyes and flash him a look that sends a message equally as clear: put a lid on it.

But it's too late. Lucy is on to us. "Why don't we call it quits for today," she says, reaching toward me and pulling my thumb out of my mouth the way a mother would.

I wipe my thumb on my corduroys, embarrassed to have been hacking away at my nail like an eager puppy attacking a furry slipper. As a kid, I sucked my thumb, which is why my two front teeth resemble those found on a walrus. Somewhere near my eighth year, I made the transition to just chewing on my nail and cuticles, but it hadn't seemed to help my teeth much. My sister never had that problem, of course. She was gifted with two rows of straight white piano-key teeth and entered puberty looking like a poster child for Ultrabright toothpaste.

"This looks great, Lucy," Catherine says, as if Lucy, not me, were responsible for the floor design. Nearly six feet tall and with an almost constant scowl on her face, Catherine Bellows is an intimidating figure. And the flannel shirts and overalls she is so fond of only make her seem more intimidating, in a Paul Bunyan, lumberjack kind of way.

"Thanks, but you really should be complimenting Megan," Lucy says. "It was her design, and you guys are the ones who provided all the elbow grease. Bravo!"

Bravo, Simon mouths with a roll of his eyes. Mocking Lucy isn't a very nice thing to do, but Simon is an ornery guy. It's just one of the reasons I like him so much. "It does look great," I say to Simon. "In fact, it doesn't even look like a gym in here." What I really mean is: Even though it still looks like a gym, it looks a lot better than it did three hours ago when we walked in.

Our school was built as a private Catholic school. Even though its two stories have been remade to accommodate the CPSA (complete with a dance studio, an art gallery, a theater, and a production room for us techs), some remnants still remain: the giant, stained-glass window behind the old sweeping marble staircase; small, dark classrooms; a bunch of lockers that look like they're from the Druid period; and a dark, windowless gym.

"I think we should celebrate," Lucy says. "I'm treating everyone to Slurpees at the Seven-Eleven."

"Slurpees?" Catherine says excitedly. It was as if Lucy just offered her a new blade for the four-hundred-and-fifty-dollar table saw she got as a gift from her parents last Christmas. "Your sister's great!" she says to me.

"I'll meet you at home," I tell Lucy, obviously underwhelmed by her greatness.

"You don't want a Slurpee?" Lucy asks nonchalantly, pulling her sleek black sunglasses out of the quilted leather purse that she paid two hundred dollars for on eBay. Lucy always dresses for the occasion, and today she looks like she's dressed for a glamorous hayride: skin-tight jeans, her new combat trooper boots, and a red T-shirt accessorized with a red-plaid scarf that is looped casually around her neck. Lucy has the looks of pre–Chris Martin, movie star–era Gwyneth Paltrow, but that's not what she wants to be.

Although more than one teacher has suggested she become a model or do some commercial work, Lucy is a total theater snob. She claims she might eventually consider doing some "film work," but only after she's established herself as a serious actress. And no one doubts that she will. She's that good. Lucy's refusal to "sell out" and cash in on her beauty only added to her goddess-like status at the school. As for me, key-grip status is as good as it gets.

"No thanks," I say.

The truth of the matter is that I want a Slurpee more than the rodent wants two minutes with Lucy in the backseat of his

'97 Honda Accord. But I don't think I can stand watching him and the rest of the techies fawn over my sister any longer.

There's only so much my diplomatic, bushy-eyebrowed heritage can take.

"Simon and I will stay and finish up. I'll meet you at home."

I watch as Lucy tosses her silky hair and heads out of the gym like she's working the red carpet in front of adoring fans and hungry paparazzi. I look over at Simon, who's still diligently painting away.

"What was that?" I ask Simon.

"What?"

"I loooove Slurpeeeeeees," I say in a really low voice as soon as everyone is out of earshot. "I didn't think Catherine loved anything except that table saw she keeps bragging about."

Simon half-shrugs. "Yeah, well, Lucy's popular and nice to everybody."

"Too nice." I sit down and my cords feel tighter than they had last week. "Did you see the way the rodent was looking at her? If I were Lucy, I would've . . ."

Simon raises an eyebrow. "Would've what?"

I try to imagine what it would be like to have someone staring at me in awe, or at just a part of me, like my boobs for instance. In fact, my boobs are twice as big as Lucy's. Unfortunately, so is everything else.

"I would've told him to keep his perverted little eyes to himself," I say adamantly.

"Please, it's pathetic," Simon says. "He's obsessed with Lucy, and the closest he'll ever get to scoring is helping her hang sequined balls."

As soon as Simon says the word *obsessed,* my mind flashes to Drew Reynolds, the guy/divine being I've been secretly in love with since I saw him on the first day of school my freshman year. I was looking for the production studio and had wandered down the wrong hall, which was crammed full of drama majors, laughing and sauntering along in a cool, because-I-said-so manner. As I stood outside the door to the auditorium, I tried to get up the nerve to ask someone where the production studio was, but I was too intimidated to approach even the lesser-known drama kings and queens. I was praying that Lucy would suddenly appear when I heard a deep voice say, "Lost?"

He was by himself, sitting on a window ledge away from the crowd, an open book in his hands. He had short, black licorice–colored hair, sparkling blue eyes, and was wearing black combat boots, washed-out jeans, and a black T-shirt. He looked older than the rest of the kids, more sophisticated, like he'd traveled in Europe for two years. Immediately, it felt as though there was a knot tightening in the center of my chest.

Ever since Drew pointed me in the right direction, the mere glimpse of him is enough to make my heart beat faster and my hands shake. Even though I know a divine being like Drew will never be interested in someone like me, there's not a doubt in my mind that if he asked for volunteers to scrape old gum off the bottom of the gym bleachers for the fall dance, I'd be the first in line, even if I had to challenge the entire drama queen population in a kickboxing match in order to get there.

The realization that I might have something in common with the rodent depresses me so much that I heave a big sigh. And I sigh even harder when I notice that some of my flab is hanging over the front of my cords. And the sides. And possibly even the back. "Simon," I say, as I start chewing on my nail again. "Do you ever think about changing majors?"

"No."

"You could get into the music program." Most of us are techies because we wanted to attend CSPA and production is the only major that doesn't require a grueling audition. But Simon has taken music lessons for years and he not only has a great singing voice, he can play the clarinet as well as the piano. He was even in the chorus of *The Music Man* last year (because the director begged him to do it).

"Why would I want to change majors?" Simon asks. I'm not surprised by Simon's response. I've always thought Simon enrolled as a theater production major just to tick off his wealthy mother who is totally annoyed her only child, Simon Winston Chase the fifth, is attending a *public* Baltimore school, especially one that is a school for the arts and especially when he is not even enrolled in the performing arts program.

"I don't know," I say. "Don't you ever get tired of the way everybody around here treats us? We're second-class citizens."

Simon puts down his brush and eyes me intently. "Are you

thinking about changing majors? I bet you could get into the visual arts program."

In fact, I would love to change majors—but not to visual arts. No, there is only one major I want, and that's theater. I fantasize all the time about what it would be like to be Lucy, the star of the show, the beautiful ingenue. I dream about a world where Drew not only notices me, but *likes* me.

But instead of saying this to Simon, I decide to give him a little demonstration of my (albeit limited) talent. I clear my throat as I get up and walk to the front of the gym, which has been roped off as a make-do dance floor. "If you cared about me," I begin, melodramatically reciting the monologue my sister is doing in the senior productions. I have run Lucy's lines with her so often that I know them by heart. "You would've remembered him, remembered how he used to smile at us." I look to Simon for approval and see him trying to hold back a grin as he pretends to ignore me.

"Remember the way he used to tousle his hair?" I continue, only louder. "The way he would run his fingers through it when he was tired or upset? Alas, no! You don't! You've forgotten!" I close my hands and hug my chest, just like Lucy does when she says the line. I'm so in the moment (as Mr. Ted, my drama instructor, would say) that I'm close to tears. "I lost myself and my soul a year ago today." I place a hand on my forehead and swoon. "When God carried away our son."

And then I hear it.

Clap, clap, clap.

I open my eyes slowly and look at Simon. But he's not clapping. The applause is coming from the back of the gym. It's coming from Drew Reynolds.

"That was great," Drew says.

Oh my God. OH MY GOD!

How long has Drew been standing there? I glance at Simon, the only person in the world to whom I've confessed my secret love. Simon has stopped painting and is giving me a look that can only be described as pure sympathy with a dash of cringe-worthy embarrassment thrown in for kicks.

"Thanks." Suddenly I let out a giggle that sounds like an AK-47 machine gun. Simon's face turns bright red.

"You should try out for a play," Drew says. A devastating smile follows, which renders me totally powerless.

So I just stand there and gawk at him like the techie geek everyone knows and expects me to be.

"Have you guys seen Lucy?" Drew asks when he realizes that I'm so mentally challenged, I can only utter the word *thanks*. "I was wondering if she wanted to go over this script."

Drew, like Lucy, is starring in the senior productions, a total coup for a junior.

"She's at the Seven-Eleven buying Slurpees for the common folk," Simon pipes up and rescues me.

Drew lets out a chuckle and scratches the back of his neck. I practically gasp when the bottom of his shirt creeps up. "There's a Seven-Eleven around here?"

Although our school is a charter school, it is still technically a Baltimore city school, which means that most of us live in Baltimore. The ones who don't (like Drew, who lives in Towson, so I hear) have to pay to attend. And drive. (Unlike me and Simon, who live about two minutes away by foot.)

"There's one on Cross Street," Simon says impatiently. "A few blocks away from the market."

"Ah, the Cross Street Market," Drew says, raising his eyebrows in recognition. "I love that place. Especially the kielbasa at Mr. Sausage."

Simon throws me an odd look, probably because he has been thinking about becoming a vegetarian (to piss off his mom, of course).

I, however, think it's adorable that Drew likes the Cross Street Market and kielbasa and immediately add it to his ever-growing list of attributes and reasons why (besides the fact that we both have a penchant for black) he's totally perfect for me. "Me too!" I say enthusiastically. "Have you ever tried the extra spicy Polish sausage? Oh my God! Amazing!"

Simon looks at me in horror, sending me a telepathic message: *Warning! Warning! Fat unpopular girls shouldn't talk about loving any type of sausage with cute popular boys!*

I glance nervously at Drew, who just smirks and says, "I'll have to try some next time I'm there." And then, instead of leaving, he walks toward the dance floor.

Toward me.

Okay, this is one for the journal. It has already been established that Lucy is not around, so why is Drew still here? Any other guy in his league would have been long gone. It's especially surprising because Drew isn't exactly the chatty type. Although he's respected by everyone for his talent, and all the girls think he's really good-looking, he pretty much keeps to himself—but not in that creepy neighbor who's secretly a child predator kind of way. Anything but, actually.

I sigh and make a deal with God, listing all the things I would be willing to give up forever if I could kiss him. Just once. Brownies . . . Oreos . . . Coke Slurpees . . . extra spicy Polish sausage.

"Wow," he says, admiring Simon's work in progress. "This is incredible. It looks so . . . real."

Twizzlers, Twinkies, Doritos . . . sweet Italian sausage.

"Thanks," Simon says. I can tell from the glint in his eye that he's proud of himself. As he should be.

Drew continues to wander around as though he was in a gallery. I think about what it might be like to walk hand in hand with him through the American Visionary Art Museum, gazing at paintings and photographs and talking about the difference between the imagined and the real.

"You guys are doing all this for the fall festival?" he asks.

"Yep. I'm going to be painting the apples," I announce proudly, as if that tidbit will so impress him that he'll ask me to marry him and have his children.

"Megan can draw a great apple," Simon says a little too loudly, obviously trying to help me score some points. Other than the pity ones, of course.

"Are you guys going?" Drew asks as he puts his hands in his pockets.

I'm looking at his eyes, even though his gaze keeps shifting around the room. I had thought they were just blue, but up close they're a blue-green, slightly more blue than green. If I were going to paint them, I would use a combination of colors, beginning with a sky blue before adding a tinge of emerald green. "You mean to Mr. Sausage?" I mutter.

"To the fall festival," Simon says in a labored tone that translates into *Snap out of it, dork! This is your big break! You're talking to Drew. Don't blow it.*

"No, we're not," Simon once again responds for me.

A curious expression emerges on Drew's face. So freaking adorable. "Why not?"

Simon picks his paintbrush back up and twirls it in his left hand. "We owe it to the techies who have wandered these halls before us to stay home and watch our *Battlestar Galactica* DVDs."

Drew laughs. It's not a sarcastic laugh, but a nice, relaxed, hey-you're-funny laugh. Listening to it is as exciting as watching the curtain go up on opening night. "I don't blame you. I'd stay home, too, if my mom wasn't making me go."

Any other teenage girl, including my sister, would think Drew's statement is a giant red flag. Not only did he admit that he'd rather be home on a Saturday night than at a school function with his friends, but he also kind of admitted to being a mama's boy. But I don't see this as a bad sign at all. In fact, I want to take out my trusty proverbial white flag and surrender to Drew over and over again. But then I remember something.

Lucy already took it from me.

two

extra (noun):
a member of the cast with no speaking
role who provides background interest in
a crowd scene.

By the time Lucy is finished with her salad, she's on to me. "You're awfully quiet," she says.

Lucy and I are eating dinner alone. This isn't unusual because our dad travels a lot for his job (he's regional manager for Lucky Lou's Burgers), and our mom is a lawyer and doesn't get home until eight or nine at night. Lucy and I have our own little domestic routine, independent of Mom and Dad. Every day we take turns making dinner and eat it at the table together.

"I'm eating," I say. "It's really good. I love the . . ." I stab a piece of salad and hold it up to the Tiffany (looking) lamp Mom found at a garage sale and is convinced is worth a million dollars. "The lettuce. What kind is it?"

"That look on your face is not due to radicchio," she says.

I put down my fork. It's obvious I have no choice but to confess. "I can't stop thinking about what Drew said."

"About trying out for a play?" Lucy asks.

"Yeah," I say, nodding. "I mean, I know he was just being nice and all."

"Drew's not that nice," Lucy says. "You have talent. I've told you that a million times."

I sit up straight and smile at her. I'm still not a hundred percent certain she is telling me the truth because, quite frankly, Lucy is too nice to tell me if she thinks Drew is full of crap, but still. "Really?" I ask.

"Really," she says with determination. "Let's see," she says, thinking. "Allan Silberstein is producing a play in December. He talked to me about doing it. There might be a part in there for you. It would be fun if we could be in a play together."

I think about the last play my sister got me into. I should have known something was up when I heard the name of my character was Arse McDoody. Unfortunately, by the time I found out I had been cast as the backside of a horse, it was too late to bow out.

"No thanks. Besides, Simon said he'll never do that again." Simon had been cast as the front, so I'm not sure what he was still complaining about.

"No," Lucy objects. "I'm talking about you having a role. A real role."

"Like a person?"

"I can't make any promises, but I'll talk to him."

"Remember the way he used to tousle his hair?" I bark out suddenly, attempting to impress Lucy with my ability to get in the moment just like (finger snap). "The way he would run his fingers through it when he was tired or upset? Alas no! You don't! You've forgotten!" I slam my hand down on the table for emphasis, smack into the tub of butter.

"Oh . . . ," she says calmly, totally unfazed by my melodrama. "Speaking of Drew, guess who he asked to the fall festival?"

Drew asked someone to the fall festival? Not that I ever expected him to ask me, but I still feel a little winded, as if I just found out my beloved boyfriend of the past two years has been cheating on me.

"Who?" I manage. I pick up my napkin and begin wiping off my hand.

"Lindsey McKenna," she says.

Good grief. *Lindsey McKenna?* He was cheating on me with a giant, bubbleheaded, Barbie doll? A girl who drew smiley faces and hearts on all her notebooks and once passed out cards giving people a "free smile"?

"Apparently she's liked him a long time," Lucy continues, oblivious to my discomfort.

Drew is the first and only secret I have ever kept from my sister. I haven't told Lucy about my crush because I know what she would do if she found out. Lucy is extremely protective of me and she would hate the thought that I didn't have a snowball's chance in hell of hooking up with the guy of my dreams, and so she would go to great lengths to reassure me that I actually have a chance at going out with him. And then any time anyone ever mentioned his name she would turn to me with a look of pity mingled with outright grief that broadcast her sentiment to the world: poor, ugly, lonely Megan.

"I guess they hooked up a couple of times over the summer, but Drew wasn't interested in anything serious. So now Lindsey is totally psyched."

"They *hooked up?*" The thought of Drew, my intellectual hero, in the arms of the vacuous (one of my and Simon's favorite words) girl I once caught walking out of a bathroom stall with Mac Gerard (she must have given him one of her cards because he had a *big* smile on his face) makes me want to woof up my radicchio.

"Yeah," Lucy continues. "He's got a little bit of a rep. Like, he doesn't let anyone get too close to him and keeps to himself. Some people think he's kind of stuck up."

"I don't know about that," I say.

Lucy puts down her fork and looks at me.

I shift my eyes away. "I always thought he seemed kind of sweet."

She sighs long and deep. "It seems like everyone has a date for the fall festival except for me."

I don't, of course. And of course, my sister is aware of this little fact. Normally I would point this out in a not so nice fashion. But not now. Due to the whole twisting Allan Silberstein's arm to get me a part thing, I'm trying to stay on her good side. And so I say, "What about Tommy?"

Although Lucy would never admit to it, she loves guys with power. Two of her past three boyfriends have been the director of the spring musical, the most sought-after assignment in the entire school. The director of this year's spring musical was announced several weeks ago: Tommy Calvino. Coincidentally, only days after the announcement, my sister fell deeply in love.

She rolls her eyes and flips back her long, silky hair. "Who knows?" she says, pushing her plate away even though she has only eaten half of her chicken. "Maybe he doesn't want to go with me." I know Lucy doesn't actually believe that. After all, the whole school knows she's interested in him. And no boy in his right mind can resist Lucy. Lucy reaches across the table and pulls my thumb out of my mouth. "Yuck," she says, examining my thumb. "Look at your nail. You've bitten it down to the quick. And your cuticles are all chewed up. Are you wearing that polish I got you?"

In an attempt to break me of my disgusting habit, Lucy bought me some polish that tasted like puke and was guaranteed to squash my nail-biting habit in two days. Apparently none of the test subjects had been quite as determined or addicted as I am, since I wore it for a week and all I got was a headache from consuming all those gross chemicals.

"It doesn't work," I say, pulling my hand away from her and snagging the untouched chicken leg off her plate. And out of the blue I get a visual: Drew with an inflatable Barbie doll, lip-locked and making out.

I put the chicken down as my thumb drifts back in my mouth.

"What's wrong with you tonight?" Lucy asks, looking at me suspiciously. I rarely leave food behind.

"I got a stomachache from all the vegetables in the salad," I say quickly, thus achieving the impossible. Blaming her for my misery and changing the subject.

"Oh," Lucy says. "Sorry."

Oh great. Now, in addition to being nauseous, I feel like I just washed her favorite white shirt with my indigo Levis. "You know I don't like carrots." There. That's better.

I yank my thumb out of my mouth and stand up. As Lucy walks upstairs, I stack the dishes in the sink, determined not to think about vegetables, Drew Reynolds, his inflatable doll, or the fall festival for the rest of the night.

I wait until Lucy is in our room before stuffing my face with Oreos. They've never failed to settle my stomach in a jiff.

I'm hoping that by the time I get upstairs, Lucy will have forgotten all about the fall festival and moved on to more exciting things, like what's on TV. But as soon as I get upstairs she starts yammering away again. And since our house is only fourteen feet wide (like all the other row houses) and only two floors, there's really no place to escape.

We used to live in a big house in Roland Park, but when I announced I wanted to go to CSPA, too, my parents decided it would make more sense if we moved to Federal Hill so we could walk to school. And despite the fact that we'd have more room in a doublewide, it's worked out pretty well. I like city living. The only problem is that even though our house is long and we have this really cool roof top deck, in the winter or when it's raining, like tonight, and I can't escape up to the deck, there's no place to go for solitude. So even though I would prefer to be suffering in solitude, I'm sitting in the bedroom Lucy and I share and working on my latest project, an extra-credit project for my English class, a diorama of the living room of the great Gatsby himself.

"Look at this," Lucy says. She's in front of the computer in our newly renovated bedroom, sitting at the blond-wood desk I designed especially for our room. In fact, I had pretty much planned out and designed almost every aspect of our room, from the style of the bookcases and placement of the beds (Lucy said she would defer to me since I had a year of set design under my belt). For the carpet I chose a soft, plush green shag (that left footprints when you walked on it), and for the walls I concocted my own creation, a creamy yellow that I named Dijon-lite. Lucy (who loves mustard) said it made her feel happy just by looking at it.

The only thing that Lucy insisted on was that she be able to display her signed headshots of her favorite actors. They were all guys, all Broadway, Tony award–winning stars: Kevin Kline, Matthew Broderick, Michael Cerveris, and her favorite, the guy I knew she was totally head over heels in love with and had seen not once, not twice, but thirteen times: John Lloyd Young, the

Tony award–winning star of *Jersey Boys*. So I made a huge bulletin board to hang over her bed.

I place Gatsby's velvet couch in front of his fireplace and carefully set the diorama on my bed. I walk toward the computer and peer over Lucy's shoulder so I can get a better look at the computer screen.

```
From: Andy Strout
Subject: fall festival

Hi, Lucy,
Do you want to go the fall festival
with me? It would be fun.
Andy
```

"Ugh," she says. "I hate this."

Andy Strout is a senior. He's tall, cute, and a drama major. "Hate what?" I ask, rereading the note.

"Well, I can't go with him. Have you seen his hands? They're kind of long and slender, like the hands of a woman."

"What?" I ask, annoyed. "Who cares about his hands? He's totally sweet. And he kind of looks like John Lloyd Young."

"John Lloyd Young?" she gasps, as though she can't believe I would dare to make such a comparison. "Hardly!"

"Well, more than Tommy does, that's for sure. Tommy has blond hair!" And an upturned schnoz. Not that I'm in any position to point fingers. Especially when it comes to noses.

"Andy's fine. It's just that there's no . . . no *spark*," she says, snapping her fingers for emphasis.

"So tell him no."

"It's so awkward," Lucy groans melodramatically. "And what do I say: No, I don't have a date but I'm holding out, hoping someone better might ask?"

"Tell him it's nothing personal but you only date directors." I flop down on my bed, cross my arms across my chest, close my eyes, and brace myself for Lucy's reaction.

But she doesn't get mad. "What's wrong?" she asks softly.

"I don't understand what's so awful." I cover my face with my hands even though my eyes are still shut. "A really cute guy asked you to the dance and you don't want to go with him because another really cute guy will ask you the minute he finds out you want to go with him."

I can hear Lucy start typing her response. For some reason, I'm finding her seeming nonchalance about this whole thing extremely annoying. I open my eyes and swing my legs off the bed as I perch myself on the edge. "I hope you're telling the poor guy no so he can ask someone else. Do you know how many girls out there would love to go with Andy? Who would kill just to have someone, *anyone at all*, ask them to the dance? Huh? *Huh?*"

Lucy spins around in her chair so she's facing me. She gives me a gentle smile. "You know, you could go to a dance, too. You've just never wanted to."

I roll my eyes in disagreement as I begin to nibble on my thumb cuticle, fighting back a tsunami-sized wave of self-pity.

"What about Simon?" Lucy asks.

"He doesn't want to go. He hates these things."

"Maybe he doesn't know that it's important to you."

Be brave, I tell myself. "It's not a big deal."

"And so what if he doesn't want to go? You'll go with someone else."

"Yeah, right," I say sarcastically. Just to demonstrate that the conversation is truly over, I walk to the closet and open the door. But before I can pull out my pajamas, Lucy's dollhouse falls out and lands on my foot.

The tears swell in my eyes and the tsunami hits the shore. "Ouch!"

"Are you all right?" Lucy asks, jumping up and rushing to my aid.

"You need to get rid of that!" I angrily kick the dollhouse. It lands in front of the full-length mirror on the inside of the closet door. "It's not like you're ever going to play with it again."

"I'll figure out a way to fit it in there so it doesn't keep falling out," Lucy says, as she hurries inside the closet and begins rearranging her shoe boxes.

My sister loves that silly old dollhouse. My grandfather made it for her, and since he died before I was born it is a one-of-a-kind original. Lucy was the first and long-awaited grandchild, so my grandfather went all out, sparing no expense. It has porcelain sinks, is wired for electricity, and has built-in tables, beds, and chairs. Unfortunately, we had kept it in the basement of our old house, and when the basement flooded, the dollhouse did, too.

Now it looked like it had been hit by a hurricane, complete with mildew stains, peeling paint, and warped floors. My parents wanted Lucy to get rid of it when we moved, but it was agreed that as long as we kept it in our closet and out of the way, she could keep it. Because there is no room whatsoever in the house and our closet is stuffed with Lucy's clothes, every time we open the door we have to keep the house steady with one foot so it doesn't fall out. For the past two years I have been a good sport about it, but my patience is wearing thin.

Lucy is inside the closet, shoving boxes around in a desperate effort to appease me. I glance at my reflection in the mirror on the inside of the closet door. I look from my bulbous nose down to the roll of fat peeking out under my gray hoodie and flopping lazily over the top of my brown cords that, until now, I actually thought looked okay on me. I step away from the mirror. It's not the dollhouse or my foot that has upset me. Nor is it my sister. It's my lousy life. "It's okay," I say. "Just stick it back in there. I should've remembered to put my foot up."

Lucy smiles at me appreciatively. "You know what," she says, stepping over the dollhouse and taking my hand. "I'm thinking this whole going to the dance with a guy thing is pretty stupid. Friends go with friends, right? Why not sisters? Let's just you and me go together."

Lucy and me? Of course!

I imagine myself entering the dance, basking in the warm and bright glow of my sister's magnificent aura. And then I imagine my sister looking at me with the same tight, miserable smile she had when Mom made her take me to the eighteen-and-under club. And who can blame her? Friends only went with friends and big sisters only took their little sisters when their little sisters were too loser-ish to be asked by anyone else. And as tempted as I might be to drag my big sister down to my level, can I really do that to her?

Why yes! Yes, I can!

Lucy's phone rings. She looks at the caller ID and mouths, "Tommy."

Oh crap.

"Tell him yes," I say, as gently as I can.

"You sure?" she asks, wrinkling her nose in a cute, little girl sort of way.

"I'm sure." I wrap my beefy arms around her size-two body and give her a quick squeeze before she answers her phone. And then I sit on the bed and chew on my thumbnail as I listen to her accept Tommy's invitation to the fall festival.

At lunch the next day, Simon is staring at me. Not that this is unusual, since Simon and I always sit by ourselves at lunch, so there's really no one else to look at. "Is everything okay?" he asks. "You seem distracted or something."

I haven't told Simon I am obsessing about this whole Drew thing, but I'm pretty sure he knows anyway. He can read me like a book. He and I have been inseparable ever since our first day of high school when we met in the nurse's office, both using the same lame excuse to escape the scene in the cafeteria: a stomachache. We immediately launched into a conversation about the difference between Ding Dongs and Ho Ho's and my stomachache miraculously disappeared. By the time the nurse informed Simon that his mother wasn't answering her cell phone, it no longer mattered. We have sat across from each other at lunch every school day since.

"I'm thinking about what Drew said yesterday," I say, putting down my sandwich. I can't stand the awful-tasting glop they serve in the cafeteria, so I always bring my lunch. "About trying out for a play."

"And?" he asks.

"I was thinking it might be more fun if you tried out, too."

Simon laughs. "Not this again."

I play with the strings on my hoodie as I look behind Simon, toward the corner of the cafeteria where Drew is eating lunch. He never eats lunch in the cafeteria. In fact, this is the first time I've ever seen him in here. He's sitting next to Lindsey and has his arm draped casually around her shoulders.

"I just think it might be fun," I say.

"No thanks, Arse," he says. "Or do you prefer Mr. McDoody?"

The thing about Simon is that he really possesses an amazing sense of self. Unlike me, Simon has a life completely separate from school. Every summer he attends band camp, where, according to his stories of all the girls he has made out with, he is the campus stud.

"Miss McDoody, if you please," I say mechnically, as I continue to stare at Drew.

"What *are* you looking at?" Simon asks. He twists around in his seat, following the direction of my gaze. "Oh," he says, "dream boy."

Dream boy. Ha-ha. I get it. Like it's just a dream that I'll ever be able to go out with him. How hilarious. Slap my knee and hold me back.

I know Simon isn't trying to be mean, because although he's ornery he's actually very sweet (in a kind of bitter, cranky grandpa sort of way), but I still feel like I stepped on a jellyfish. "I'm just thinking about what he said about the dance."

"Refresh," Simon says, turning back to face me. "What did he say about the dance?"

"Just that we should go."

"And that's why you want to go? Just because of some offhand comment Drew made?"

"No," I say, as the jellyfish becomes a piranha. "I want to go to the dance because I think it'll be fun. And also . . . because . . . because I'm tired of sitting home alone."

"Alone? Excuuuuuse me! I thought we were going to watch *Star Wars*, with Portuguese subtitles this time. In fact, I just bought you a Princess Leia costume online. I was going to surprise you."

I do my best to crack a smile as I keep my eyes focused on Drew. "I told you I want to be Luke."

Simon tucks the rest of his cheese and guava jam (his mom

has it shipped from Brazil) sandwich into his bag. "All right. If it means that much to you, fine."

"Fine what? I can be Luke?"

"Fine, we can go to the fall festival."

"You'll go?" I ask excitedly. I suddenly see myself making the grand entrance, complete with new eyebrows and physique-shrinking dress. "Thank you," I say.

"On one condition," he says, taking off his glasses and cleaning them with his napkin. "I get to be Luke."

That's the thing about Simon: He always knows the perfect thing to say.

three

bleed-through (noun): transformation from
a scene downstage to another scene
upstage by adjusting the lighting of a thin
piece of gauze draped across the stage.
Depending on the direction of the light, the
gauze can either appear solid or can
disappear altogether.

Lucy is beside herself when I tell her that Simon and I are going
to the dance. And then she tells me the supposed good news:
Dad, not Mom, is taking us shopping for our dresses.

This does not make me happy.

Not that I don't love my dad, but my relationship with him
has always been a bit, well, stiff. The problem is that I've always
had the feeling that he's embarrassed about the way I look. He's
never come right out and said it or anything, but there are subtle
things that I've noticed over the years. Like when he opens the
kitchen cupboard and can't find the cookies or something, he'll

always ask me (in an accusatory sort of way) if I know where "they went." The "hey, fatso" is implied.

And he's always pointing out the benefits of exercise when he thinks I'm being a slug, like when I'm watching TV. Which is really pretty nervy considering my dad, with his double chin and big belly, is not exactly an Adonis. He oversees all the Lucky Lou restaurants on the East Coast, which has him eating tons of hotel food and the burgers Lucky Lou is known for, not exactly a great job to have if you love food, particularly greasy food. And my dad loves food even more than I do. He was downright fat as a kid, and even though he lost a ton of weight a million years ago, these days he's not exactly thin enough or fit enough to be doling out advice. And in my defense, I'm not fat. At least, not *that* fat. But he doesn't see it that way.

Naturally, he never, ever asks Lucy if she masterminded the cookie's escape or if she finished off the container of ice cream or if she agreed that Jennifer Love Hewitt probably works out. Fortunately, my dad is hardly ever home. Which is good, since my mom has never once suggested that I had seen the cookies hop on the last train out of town.

Still, despite my apprehension, on the morning of our father-daughter bonding day, I arrive downstairs dressed and determined to be cheerful. Lucy is sitting at the table reading the newspaper and Dad is at the stove stirring a giant batch of scrambled eggs with cheese. The fact that Mom has gone grocery shopping at nine in the morning and is not there is extremely suspicious. I must say, this whole father-daughter-shopping-for-fall-festival-dresses has her stamp all over it. Every now and then my mom decides we're in desperate need of some father-daughter bonding time, and realizing that both Lucy and I would prefer to be with her, she conjures up some excuse, creating a situation where it's either my dad or nothing at all.

"What is that thing?" my dad asks, motioning toward my diorama, which happens to be in the center of the table, with his spatula. Even though I've been working on my diorama almost nonstop for two months, it figures that this is the first time he's noticed it.

"That *thing* is Jay Gatsby's living room," I say, annoyed.

I did my first diorama last year for a set design class and it has become a sort of hobby for me. I make at least one every other month, usually based on the books we are reading in school. Since I can wield a circular saw with ease (even though I pretty much just use hand tools for my diorama creations), they are pretty elaborate, with real wood paneling, dollhouse furniture I pick up on eBay or make myself, and, as in the case with *The Great Gatsby*, wallpaper I design and paint with tiny little stencils. Mrs. Bordeaux always said she was giving me extra credit for them, which was kind of a joke between us, since I always got an A in English anyway.

"Well, it doesn't belong on the table," he says, totally unimpressed by Mr. Gatsby's varnished wood floors, heavy tapestry drapes, Oriental rug, miniature potted palm, and velvet furniture.

"Well, there's really no other place for it," I say defensively.

My dad stops stirring the eggs. "*Find* a place," he says in a tone that lets me know he's about to blow.

Lucy looks up from the paper and shoots me a nervous look like, *Please don't get him all upset on our shopping day!*

I grudgingly take the diorama upstairs and set it in the middle of my bed.

By the time I get back to the kitchen, the table is set and Dad is dishing out the eggs.

"None for me, thanks," Lucy says, waving them away. "I'm just going to have toast."

"You feel okay?" he asks, concerned.

That's another thing. If I said I didn't want any eggs he never would have assumed I was sick. Instead, he would have assumed I was dieting and congratulated me on my willpower.

"I just don't want to be all bloated when I try on dresses," she says.

My dad glances at the eggs he has already dished out on my plate, like, *Uh-oh.*

I'm half expecting him to rush back over and spoon some off my plate, so I take my seat and (even though I'm not hungry in the slightest) shovel a giant forkful in my mouth. What he doesn't know is that, unlike Lucy, I don't have to worry about bloat. Yesterday I stopped at the mall in the Inner Harbor and purchased some SPANX Power Panties with Tummy Control. Desperate times called for desperate measures.

———

After breakfast I wedge myself into my father's convertible Cabrio and we drive to the Towson Town Center. Both my dad and I follow Lucy through the mass of stores and into Lucy's favorite, Mein-U. Lucy flips through rack after rack like a cranky Simon Cowell dismissing contestants before finally yanking out a bright fuchsia silk dress with spaghetti straps. I can tell it's for me, since Lucy's dresses involve just enough material to dry a wet dish. I can also tell that I already hate the way it looks on me, even though I haven't tried it on yet. "What do you think?" she asks.

"I'm not sure about the color," I say, chewing on my thumbnail. Actually, I love bright colors, but everyone knows that they're not slenderizing, so I prefer to stick with basic black.

"I like it," Dad says from behind us.

I accept the dress from Lucy and hug it to my chest and stand there waiting patiently while Lucy pulls several pastel-colored dresses for herself and two more for me, one black and one red. Finally, she takes her seven dresses and I take my three and we head toward the dressing room, where, even though it is really crowded and Lucy sees me naked every day, I still insist on getting my own room. I don't want Lucy to know about the SPANX, and besides, I have a feeling the dress Lucy chose for me isn't going to work out and I have no intention of humiliating myself any more than necessary.

I walk into the dressing room and lock the door behind me. I take the SPANX out of my purse and step into it, yanking it up slowly. It feels like my butt is in an iron vise and a rubber band is wrapped around my belly. I can't help but wonder if it will even be physically possible for me to wear it more than two seconds. What if I pass out from loss of oxygen?

I start with the black dress first, since it's my official color, not to mention it's the only size thirteen. (The other two are elevens.) I undo the zipper and step into it, pulling it up over my shoulders. So far so good, but the zipper is not up yet. Because of the SPANX it's impossible to suck in my stomach, so I hold my breath as I twist my arms behind me to pull up the zipper. It gets halfway up and stops. This is a size thirteen? Have I gotten too big to fit into a size thirteen? Even though I suspect the answer is a big fat yes, I'm not ready to admit defeat since that would mean having to take a size fifteen off the rack (although it's doubtful it even comes that big) and having to deal with my father's look of shock and horror.

I scoot the dress off my shoulders and tug it down. I twist it around and pull up the zipper. I then wrench it back around, hold my breath one more time, and slowly pull it up. I get it up to my boobs and surrender. It's not even close.

I hear Lucy's door open. "Megan," she says, "come out when you're ready. I want to get your take on this dress."

I refuse to ask for a bigger size. I've accepted the fact that I'm six sizes bigger than my willowy, slightly taller than me sister, but seven is simply one too many. I stick my head out, hiding my body behind the door. I catch a quick glimpse of Lucy in a pink slinky silk dress, holding her golden hair on top of her head and slam the door again. "Love it!" I yell over the door.

"You don't think it makes my stomach look, well, bloated or something?"

"No." In truth, I hadn't had time to notice. I had opened and shut the door so fast my poor overtaxed brain barely had time to register the color of her dress. Still, I found it impossible to believe she could ever look bloated, and even if she did, even if she had a butt that jiggled like two overfilled water balloons, it wouldn't matter. With her beautiful eyes, her button nose, rosebud mouth, and high-sculpted cheekbones, who cares about a little blubber?

"What about you?" she asks through the crack in the door. "Any luck?"

"The black one made me look really washed out," I say, even though the color is not my problem. Neither is the size. The problem is my face.

I glance at the other dress. I appreciate Lucy giving me the benefit of the doubt and assuming a size eleven might have a snowball's chance in hell of fitting, but I'm not sure it's even worth the effort. I give a big sigh, yank it off the hanger, and step into it. I manage to pull it up over my belly button before giving up and abandoning ship. I stare at the last dress on its hanger, the fuchsia one with spaghetti straps.

I think about the book with the magical jeans, the ones that look great on every girl in spite of their figure. Maybe, just maybe this is a magical dress. I take the dress off the hanger and right away notice one good thing: no zipper. I feel the material and realize it's got some rayon in it. Rayon definitely has more give than silk. I suck in and yank it over my head.

The dress is on. I open my eyes and look at myself in the mirror.

Oh my God! It is magical!

"Look at this one," I yell excitedly, throwing open the door.

My sister inhales deeply at the sight of me and smiles. "Fab-U-Lous!" she agrees.

"I know," I say. I realize that it might sound a little conceited but I don't care. This never happens to me. Ever!

I turn to the side, admiring the view. The SPANX is working perfectly, making my stomach look as if I do fifty sit-ups a day. The dress reveals just the right amount of cleavage, making me look sexy but not in a Pamela Anderson sort of way.

"It didn't look like much on the hanger, but it really looks great," Lucy says. "If I were you I wouldn't even bother trying on anything else."

I grin from ear to ear as I sweep my hair off my shoulders, trying to determine if I would look better with my hair up or down. But when I see how round my cheeks are and how big my nose is, no matter what I do with my hair, I feel my enthusiasm take a sizable blow to the chin.

"Wait till Simon sees you," Lucy says.

"I'm not really worried about what Simon thinks," I say, letting my hair back down.

Okay, try focusing on the dress and not your face, I tell myself. This perks me back up a bit.

"Not even a little?" she asks with a smile.

"Ew," I say through a gigantic laugh. When Simon was in the chorus of *The Music Man,* he was changing in the dressing room when I accidentally walked in on him in his underwear. It was a big deal for me, since the only guy I had ever seen in his underwear until that moment was my dad. I can still picture Simon's skinny legs sticking out of his thick white briefs, his scrawny arms, and the sterling silver peace necklace dangling over his hairless chest. "That's like, incestuous."

Lucy just shrugs and turns toward the three-way mirror behind her. "So what do you think of this one?" she asks, spinning around.

"It's perfect," I say. Unlike before, this time I actually look at her. Lucy is stunning as usual. "You should definitely get it."

"You like it better than the other one?"

"Yes."

Lucy grabs my hand. "Isn't this fun? Dress shopping together?"

"Sure." The amazing thing is, even though this originally had as much appeal to me as a dentist appointment, I am enjoying this time with my sister.

"Any luck?" Dad asks when we reappear with our chosen dresses in hand.

"Megan found one but I can't decide," Lucy says, lining the dresses up on the rack. Lime green, teal blue, hot pink.

"You found a dress?" he asks me.

Is it my imagination or does he sound surprised?

"It's a size eleven," I say proudly, showing it to him.

"Great," he murmurs, as if he could give a crap. He barely looks at it before turning back toward Lucy's display. "They're all beautiful," Dad says. "Don't you think, Megan?"

My heart drops. "Yeah," I say. I fight the urge to shove my dress in front of his nose and demand that he show some excitement for my choice.

"I think I'm leaning toward this one," she says, picking up the pink.

"I liked the blue one better," I say.

"Oh," Lucy says, but she's still staring at the pink, not even pretending to consider the blue. It's clear she couldn't care less what I think.

"Whichever one you want," my dad says, smiling at her like she just got into Harvard or something.

"I'm going to take the pink," she says finally.

"How about lunch?" I suggest, as we follow Dad to the cashier. In spite of my dad's less than enthusiastic reaction to my dress, I'm still excited and feel as if a celebration is in order. The restaurant next door to Mein-U makes a sandwich called the California Grill—turkey, bacon, avocado on toasted and buttered bread—that is totally dee-lish.

"You just had breakfast a couple of hours ago," my dad says as he hands me my white-plastic-wrapped dress. "Don't tell me you're already hungry?"

His insult catches me by surprise. I fight my initial reaction (which is to cry) and my second reaction (which is to grab the gold chain around his neck, rip it off, and slap him silly with it).

There's a third reaction, too (feed him to a tankful of piranhas), but the pet store is all the way on the opposite end of the mall. "Okay, I won't tell you I'm hungry," I say quietly.

"I think lunch is a great idea," Lucy says, supportively looping her arm through mine. "I'm starving."

And even though I know Lucy isn't really hungry and will order a salad of which she will only eat half, I still appreciate the effort.

four

black comedy (noun): a comedy with a
distinctly disturbing quality.

Saturday night. I'm sitting across from my mother at one of my favorite restaurants that just happens to be a couple blocks from our house, the Blue Agave. Although Simon claims the only people who come here are tourists, I think the food is superb and my dad, who is practically an expert on these matters, agrees. "What are you going to get?" my mom asks, peering at me over her menu.

Although I have a reputation as an excellent orderer, I must admit I'm never quite sure what to get here because I've had almost everything (except the lamb since I just can't deal with eating baa baa black sheep), and it's all good. "I'm going to get the pecan-encrusted chicken with the fried plantains. And maybe the fried calamari for an appetizer." I snap my menu shut with authority.

"Mmm," my mom says, raising her eyebrows as if intrigued. "That sounds good."

I have a standing date with my mom every Saturday night. Dad is usually at work and my sister has an incredibly busy social life, so Mom and I usually go out to eat or see a movie. I always look forward to it because my mom is totally cool. Even though she works a lot she still finds time to pick up cookies at the bakery to sell at the bake sales, and she'll rearrange her schedule rather than miss a school performance. That's not to say we don't have our occasional issues (for example, I got grounded once for forgetting to lock the front door), but they're few and far between.

As I place my order I'm reminded of yet another good thing about my mom. Even though she is totally skinny and can fit into my sister's jeans, she (unlike my father) never *ever* comments on my food choice or intake. At all.

"So I love the dress you picked out for the dance," she says after the waitress leaves.

"Thanks, Mom," I say, grinning. I tried my dress on for her when I got home and her ecstatic reaction couldn't have been more perfect. It was almost enough to make up for my dad's lackluster response.

"Dad said you guys had a lot of fun," she says.

"Oh," I reply. The mere mention of my father reminds me of my diet. Why did I just order fried calamari?

"You're chewing your nail," my mom says quietly. She is convinced I bite my nail when I'm upset about something. And she's right. Unfortunately, I also bite it when I'm bored, happy, or distracted. Or when we run out of Oreos.

"You didn't have fun?" she asks suspiciously, still looking at the thumb that is now on the table where it is going to stay, just so I can keep an eye on it.

"It was okay." I suddenly realize my thumb is inches away from my mouth, ready to sneak back in. Damn. I tuck it under my rear end.

"Just okay?"

I hadn't really planned on getting into all the Dad stuff with my mom, mainly because I knew it would upset her. I also knew she would probably take his side since she likes to do the whole your-father-and-I-are-a-united-front thing. (My dad's no walk in the park, so I give Mom credit for dealing with him. He likes to fly off the handle for the stupidest things. Last week he was cooking and a spoon fell on the floor and he screamed "JESUS #$%^ CHRIST!" like he was bit by a rat.)

"It was just . . . you know," I say casually. *Be cool*, I remind myself. "The usual."

"What do you mean the usual?"

"Um . . ." The words I know she wants to hear pop into my head, one right after the other: Nice. Enjoyable. Entertaining. Amusing. "Lousy."

"What?" my mom asks.

Oops.

Now I have no choice but to lay my cards on the table. "I so obviously annoy him."

"Your father?" she asks, like I just told her I had proof I was born with three heads. "What would make you think something like *that*?"

"It's the way he looks at me. Like I'm repulsive or something." I know I should've stopped at lousy, but I'm overwhelmed by my own laundry lists of complaints as well as a veritable avalanche of self-pity.

"That's ridiculous. He adores you."

"So why is he always making a big deal about what I'm eating and stuff?"

"Does he?" she asks, in a kind of you-must-be-mistaken sort of way.

"Come on, Mom," I say, zipping up my hoodie even though it's about ninety degrees in the restaurant. "Every time he can't find the cookies or something he always asks *me* where they are—not Lucy, not you. He's always comparing me to Lucy and I'm always coming up short."

"He doesn't compare you to Lucy!"

I can see that my normally calm, cool, collected mom is getting more horrified by the second, and I'm really wishing I hadn't brought all this up. In an effort to make things better, I keep my mouth shut. I just heave a dramatic sigh and roll my eyes.

"Look," my mom says finally. "He just . . . he sees Lucy going out to all those parties and, well, having fun, and he just wants the same thing for you. He worries about you, that's all. He wants you to be happy."

"Happy?" I snort, in a not so attractive way. (Not that snorting is ever attractive. Or sexy, for that matter.) "You can tell him it doesn't matter how many cookies I eat or don't eat. It's not going to impact my social life one way or the other."

"I know how you feel. When I was in high school I was kind of quiet, too, and my brother was tremendously social. He was always going out and doing things . . ."

"This doesn't have anything to do with whether or not I'm *social*. I could be the friendliest most *social* girl in the world, and it wouldn't make any difference."

"What are you talking about?" my mom says quietly.

The waiter arrives with my plate of fried calamari and a salad (with the dressing on the side) for my mother. I suddenly realize my thumb is almost in my mouth. Damn again! I take one look at my appetizer and push it away.

"Look, Mom. I'm not blind and I'm not dumb. *I* know, *you* know, and quite frankly, *everyone who has ever laid eyes on me* knows why I spend my Saturday nights with you while hoochie-mama sister is out partying her butt off. We all know why, even though I'm a *sophomore*, I've never been invited to a single party, why I've never once had a boy like me . . . never had a boy try to kiss me . . . never even had a boy notice me . . . nothing!"

My mom is staring at me. She opens her mouth as if to say something and then shuts it again. Not that I blame her. What can she say? What can anyone say?

"You're beautiful," my mom says adamantly.

I sigh.

"You are," she says, taking my hands, "a beautiful young woman with big brown eyes and long, curly hair with natural streaks that I would just kill for."

I can tell she's serious, that she really does like the way I look.

And for that I love her even more. But even a mother's love isn't enough to change the fact that I'm ugly. And to be honest, I could probably afford to lose a few pounds, too.

Monday afternoon. Fortunately for me there is one cure-all for depression: Drew Reynolds. And he just happens to be sitting next to me in English class. His hair is kind of tousled in a bad-boy sort of way that makes me want to run my fingers through it, and he's wearing jeans that have a little tear on the right knee. I think about my beautiful fall festival dress and wonder if he will even notice, and if he does, what he will think when he sees me. I know it's a total long shot, but I can't help but fantasize that it will somehow make a difference.

As I walk into the gym, the crowd parts. No one can believe the transformation. Drew steps out from the crowd. "Holy crap! Megan?" he mouths. I smile (regally) and nod as I walk toward him. He shakes Lindsey off his arm. As she sprawls ungracefully across the floor, he walks toward me (accidentally stepping on her face), his eyes reflecting pure and total adoration. . . .

Suddenly, Drew turns around in his chair and looks directly at me.

"Yoooo-hooo! Miss Fletcher?" Mrs. Bordeaux is saying.

"Huh?"

She sticks her nose in my face. "Welcome back."

"I was just . . . I thought I saw someone outside." I motion to the window, which is miraculously on the other side of Drew.

"I was just paying you a compliment," she says. "It's a shame you were so distracted you didn't hear it."

Smirks and quiet giggles.

"In any case, I'm willing to repeat it. I've finished grading the pop quiz and you, Miss Fletcher, are the only one to get an A. I have come to the conclusion that either you're simply smarter than the rest of the class or you're the only one who actually bothered to keep up with the reading."

I stare at my desk and chew on my thumb cuticle as the smirks and giggles are replaced by annoyed, irritated stares, as if I had done well on the test just to teach them all a lesson.

"Perhaps *Miss Fletcher* is the only one who has *time* to keep up with the reading," Nancy Abercrombie says snidely. "Most of us are so busy with senior productions and . . ."

"No excuses," Mrs. Bordeaux replies, raising her hands to silence her. "Everyone in this school is busy with extracurricular activities."

I sink even further into my chair as I roll my eyes toward the dirty white plaster ceiling. Nancy Abercrombie has a lot of nerve. For one, she's a sound person, so all she needs to do is flip a switch and hand out the microphones. But still, I can tell from the approving nods that most people agree with her. If I weren't such a loser and had more of a social life, maybe I wouldn't be such a star student. It's enough to make me wish that I hadn't gotten an A. I wonder if this is how Carrie felt before she got the bucket of blood dumped on her.

After class, I'm standing beside my desk pulling a tiny piece of nail out of my mouth when I see Drew walking toward me, his eyes cast over my shoulder in such a fashion that I can almost see why someone might think he was stuck up. But for some reason, I can sense that this is a defense mechanism, like he averts his gaze so he can seem aloof instead of . . . afraid.

When this thought sinks in, I whip my thumb out of my mouth. Then my heart speeds up and my hands start to shake, because Drew is standing right in front of me, but not quite looking me in the eyes.

"Thanks for making us all look like idiots," he says, smirking.

My witty retort is "Ha!"

Thankfully, Drew ignores me and pulls a manuscript out of his binder. "You should read this."

"What is it?" I'm acting as though he just gave me a ring-shaped box tied up with a bow.

"Chris Vicker's play. He's going to start casting next month. I thought you might be interested in reading for it."

"Auditioning?"

"Yeah. Maybe if I get you busy enough, you'll bring down the curve." He gives me a nod and grins before turning on his heel and walking down the hall.

"By the way," I call out after him. "I've decided to go to the fall festival."

"Oh," he says, glancing back over his shoulder at me as he continues to walk in the opposite direction, heading toward the steps.

I look down at the script in my hands. If I weren't intending to frame it, I'd smack it right on my forehead. Why would I think Drew might care that I'm going to the fall festival?

After lunch, I'm on the first floor heading toward production class when I see a small crowd gathering across the hall from the production studio, outside the auditorium. I've always found it a little cruel that the production studio is tucked away in a dank corner of the school, right underneath the cafeteria kitchen and directly across the light-filled hall that leads to the auditorium. I know it makes sense since we're building the sets, and the farther we are from the theater the farther we have to drag what in some cases are pretty heavy set designs. But it's torture.

There we'd be, covered in sawdust and splattered with paint, walking out of what resembled a giant, cold, windowless garage, practically gasping from the Salisbury steak fumes radiating through the ceiling, and there would be all the drama majors, leaning against the sun-drenched windows looking freshly scrubbed and glamorous, reciting their lines. To make matters worse, the bathrooms where we washed our hands were down the hall, past the dance studio where all the fit little dancers were swirling around in their tights, and past the art studio where all the painters were sketching their Picassos.

I make my way through the crowd of drama majors and have my hand on the door to the production studio when, out of the corner of my eye, I see George Longwell drop to his knees in front of pretty senior drama major, Michelle Berkowitz. George is one of Lucy's friends. He's a natural comedian who loves the limelight, breaking into song at the strangest times, like in the middle of a fire drill or after an exam. George takes Michelle's hand and begins to sing a cappella:

Oh, Michelle, you are divine,
Please, please, say that you'll be mine.
Your beauty continually haunts my mind,
You are, hands down, one of a kind.
Say you'll go the festival with me
And so, so happy, I will be.

"What the hell is going on?" Simon loudly whispers, nodding toward George as he sticks his head out of the production studio.

"George is asking Michelle Berkowitz to the fall festival," I whisper back. I swipe some sawdust off the top of Simon's head and move closer to the hubbub to get a better look.

I get there in time to see Michelle nod yes and the small crowd, all ten or so of us who have gathered to watch, erupt into applause. All except Simon, that is.

"How pathetic," Simon says, doing a little jig in an attempt to dislodge some of the sawdust coating his T-shirt.

"I think it's sweet," I say. "He wrote a song just for her."

Simon rolls his eyes at me as George gets off his knees. George blows Michelle a kiss and pats his heart twice. Michelle says something that I can't quite make out and the two of them begin walking toward us. I move out of their way as I say, "Hi, George."

But even though George has been at my house with Lucy and has met me a million times, he doesn't acknowledge me. He just walks right past me, like I'm invisible or something.

"Asshole," Simon says, when George is out of earshot and past the dance studio down the hall.

"Maybe he didn't hear me," I say. A definite possibility. After all, it was kind of a quiet hello. Still, it doesn't feel good to be ignored. I glance down at the script Drew gave me earlier that day, the script that I've carried with me everywhere since, and remind myself that my days of being invisible are almost over. Everything will change once I become a drama major.

"Right," Simon says sarcastically, seeing through my tiny white lie. "I don't understand this. Michelle's a nice girl. Why would she go out with that jerk?"

"He's cute."

"You think he's cute? He's got girl hair."

Although I have never thought about it before, Simon has a point. George's hair is thick and silky straight, and it's cut in an unusual style, like someone put a big bowl over his head and trimmed around it. "Lucy says he's really funny. And that song thing was sweet."

"I'll never understand women," Simon says, throwing his hands up in the air for emphasis.

"You understand me."

"Most of the time."

Most of the time? What does that mean?

But before I have a chance to say anything, the auditorium

door opens and Simon's eyes light up like a Christmas tree. It's Marybeth Wilkens, Lucy's best friend. If I had to describe Simon's ideal woman, Marybeth would be it. She's tall and lanky, pretty but not intimidatingly so. She's a little quieter and more reserved than the rest of Lucy's friends, and according to Lucy, she's a Trekkie, just like Simon.

I wonder if Simon would have asked Marybeth if I hadn't made him ask me. As much as I want to go to the dance, I know I can't let him make that sacrifice. "You know, Simon," I say quietly. "You don't have to go to the fall festival with me."

"What's that supposed to mean?" he asks, as he turns back toward the production studio.

"I just mean if there's someone else you'd want to take . . . like Marybeth . . ."

"Look, Megan," he says, as I follow him inside, "the only way I'm going to that dance is if you and I go together." And then just to make his point, he picks a hammer up off the work bench and, using it as a microphone, begins to sing loudly and totally off-key, "Megan, Megan, you are diiiiiiiiviiiiine. I am so glad that you will be miiiiiiiiine."

As usual, Simon knows just the right thing to say. Or sing, as the case may be.

five

dramatic irony (noun): a dramatic device
whereby the audience knows
something that one or more characters
are not aware of.

"Megan?" my sister says from outside the door. "Are you almost ready?"

"Just a minute," I call out excitedly. It's the day of the fall festival and our house is in a hubbub. The entire upstairs has become official dance headquarters, with makeup and clothes tossed everywhere. I carefully (so as not to mess up my elaborate updo) take my dress off its hanger and shimmy it down. I once again admire the way it clings to my flat, SPANX-covered stomach before I glance back at the mirror, tucking a loose piece of hair behind my ears.

I smile at my reflection. And for the first time in my life, I think: *Damn, I look good.*

Lucy and I have spent the past four hours getting plucked and primed at the salon, and the results are incredible. My hair is done up in the same elaborate style as Lucy's, with soft ringlets framing my face. My eyebrows have been tweezed into a defined arch and my makeup has been professionally applied.

I open the door and head into the bedroom, where Lucy is admiring her reflection in the full-length mirror on the closet door. She looks like a heroine in one of the romance novels our mom buys at the grocery store: *The soft silk of her pink dress cascaded to the ground, clinging to her slender yet supple body in all the right places. Her hair was done up in a tight chignon and her beautiful face radiated the subtle knowledge that her every wish would soon come true. . . .*

"You look amazing," Lucy says, nodding approvingly at my refection as she moves away from the mirror so that I can get a better look at myself. I take my place in front of the mirror and touch my fingers to my stiff, sprayed hair as I give the mirror the closed-mouth smile I've been practicing. (My openmouthed smile makes me look like a donkey.)

"Mother-@#$% camera! To hell with you!" my father yells from downstairs. Even though I shouldn't be surprised, Lucy and I both jump in surprise. Lucy begins to giggle and her laugh is so infectious I begin to laugh, too. My mother appears in the doorway.

"What's so funny?" she asks, smiling.

"Sounds like Dad is enjoying his new camera," I say. Lucy starts to laugh again.

Mom just ignores us. "You girls look beautiful," she says, smiling at us proudly. Her reaction makes me feel even more excited. I don't know about beautiful, but for the first time in my life, I actually feel just a little bit pretty.

"Come on downstairs when you're ready." Mom holds up Dad's old camera and winks. "I have a backup."

After Mom leaves, Lucy turns back toward the mirror, smoothing the imaginary wrinkles out of her dress before spinning back toward me. Unlike when she usually dresses up, I have no desire to push her in the mud. She puts her arm around me and gives me a big hug. "Isn't this great?" she says. "We're doubling to the fall festival."

I look once again at our reflection in the mirror. I wonder if George would sing to me if he saw me looking like this. I'm too excited to worry about my closed-mouth smile. I answer my sister by giving her a toothy smile and a tight squeeze.

Simon shows up right on time, dressed not as Luke Skywalker, but in a very stylish and expensive-looking black tux with black bow tie. Although he's still wearing his thick black-rimmed glasses, he looks really good. In fact, I'm pretty sure he was wrong about Marybeth. If he asked her to the dance looking like that, he would've been pinning a corsage on her chest instead of mine.

Since it's raining (a cold, steady drizzle that is undoubtedly capable of destroying even the simplest of hairstyles), I'm glad Lucy asked us to ride in the limo with her and Tommy, even if Simon and I had (privately) made fun of them for renting a limo when the school was only six blocks away. Simon signals for me to wait while he pops open his umbrella. Even though I'm taller than him by a good three inches in my bare feet and I'm wearing three-inch heels, he somehow manages to hold the umbrella over the top of my head, minimizing my hair damage. During the ride to the school, Simon bends over backward to be nice to Tommy, engaging him in a discussion over their favorite Shakespeare character even though I know Simon can't stand Shakespeare (and neither can I, but I would never admit to it). I don't chomp on my thumb a single time, although at one point I come close but stop when Lucy smiles at me and winks as she takes my hand, like, *Isn't it great our fellows are getting along? Maybe we can have a double wedding!*

Two limos are already parked in front of the school, so our driver pulls up in front of the church next door. I adjust the black shawl that I borrowed from my mother and take a deep breath to calm the butterflies doing backflips in my belly. Tommy grabs Lucy's hand and Simon and I follow them into the school and turn to our left, heading in the opposite direction of the production studio, toward the gym. We enter behind Lucy and Tommy and stop, giving ourselves a moment to digest the scene around us. My sister has arranged for the lights to be dimmed, which pretty much means that the janitor had to unscrew every other fluorescent lightbulb. The sparkly balls that we made spin and reflect the scenic apple orchard backdrops. In spite of everything though, it still looks (and smells) like a gym. A gym with hanging, glittery Styrofoam snowballs and full of dressed-up people.

Almost immediately, a crowd of ravishing drama majors envelops Lucy and Tommy. As everyone comments on how amazing the other looks, Simon and I step away from them, shuffling backward as we slowly but surely make our way toward the perimeter of the gym.

"Are you okay?" Simon asks me quietly. He's staring straight ahead and he looks like he's on high alert, as if he had just managed to give a pack of violent criminals the slip and is concerned they might return at any moment to finish us off.

"Uh-huh," I murmur, taking another step backward, so that my butt is actually touching the wall. I'm scared and excited at the same time. I feel like I'm on the ledge of a building and one wrong step may send me plummeting into either a giant vat of fudge ripple ice cream or boiling oil. "What about you?"

"Yeah, sure."

We stand side by side for a minute, neither saying a word as we stare at the action around us. The DJ is playing a Beyoncé song and the dance majors have flocked to the dance floor, contorting and spinning around like six-year-olds high on Halloween candy.

Simon and I spend a couple more minutes holding up the wall, watching the dancers. The music turns into a slow song and the couples pretty much fling themselves into each other's arms. When the song ends, the DJ changes gears once again, lighting up the room with an old disco tune. "Should we dance?" Simon asks. He asks this as if he's really wishing and praying I'm going to say no. Like: "Should we take a hot poker and stick it in our eyes?"

I look at him and flash him a courageous smile. "We've come too far to turn back."

I drape my shawl over the back of a chair and Simon and I walk to the dance floor and bravely plant ourselves in the middle of the action. And suddenly I realize something: Simon and I have never actually danced with each other before. In fact, the only time I can ever remember touching him was when we were fighting over a box of Famous Amos. "I'm not a very good dancer," I say, which is putting it mildly.

"You just shake it," Simon says, wiggling his rear end. "And imitate animals." He begins flapping his arms and sticking out his neck like a chicken. I laugh, which only seems to encourage him. He jumps up and down as I stand back, laughing and shaking my head, watching him goof around.

Suddenly, the obviously schizoid DJ throws us a curveball, changing the music back to a slow song. The couples meld together, their hips pressed against each other as they sway back and forth. Simon and I both take a step back. Simon looks at me and says, "How about some punch?"

Good thinking. Even the stale, chalky, vanilla-flavored boxed cookies they always serve at school events sound good right now.

Out of the corner of my eye, I see Drew with his arm around Lindsey's waist, heading to the dance floor. He's wearing a black tux and a crisp white shirt. His hair is slicked back, curling up over the sides of his jacket, and his blue eyes look irresistible, almost dangerous. My hands begin to shake as I stand there, unable to take my eyes off him. It's just like in my fantasy. The crowd parts as he begins to walk toward me. He looks up and . . .

He doesn't notice me.

Not so much as a flicker of recognition, a *don't I know you from some place*, nothing. Nada. Zilch. *Niente.*

"Megan?" Simon asks. "Are you okay?"

My brain cranks into overdrive. They're heading right toward me and even though there's a chance Drew might actually notice me when he gets closer, the chance of him not noticing me, the thought that he could be right next to me and still not see me, is more than I can bear. I have to get out of there. Fast!

"I have to go to the ladies' room," I say to Simon.

But I'm too late. I have no choice but to walk right past Drew. Even though I'm tempted to throw myself at his feet and confess my love, I force myself to look away from him as I pick up my pace, determined to make this as painless as possible for both of us. Or at least for me.

"Hey, Megan," Drew says, greeting me.

I whip my thumb out of my mouth as I stop still, stunned.

"So?" he asks, bringing Lindsey to a stop so he can talk to me. "What do you think of the dance? Did I steer you wrong?"

He remembered. He remembered that he told me I should come to the dance. "No," I say. And suddenly everything is all right again. Everything is great.

"Come on, Drew," Lindsey says, as she tugs on his hand, signaling her impatience.

"See you around," Drew says, before following Lindsey to the dance floor.

As I watch him walk away my insides get warm and gummy as a surge of happiness pumps through me. The crowd may not have parted and he may not have tossed Lindsey across the gym and stepped on her face, but for reality, it was still pretty darn good.

I practically float the rest of the way to the bathroom. Even though I don't really have to go, I figure I might as well try since I'm halfway there already. I go into the last stall in the empty bathroom and slide the latch over the door. I have my SPANX around my ankles when the bathroom door opens.

"I just feel sorry for her," I hear a girl say. I recognize the voice. It's Alicia Tucker, a senior drama major and a friend of my sister's. "It looks like she poured herself into that dress."

"I know," I hear Lucy respond.

I'm about to call out to Lucy when I hear her say, "She could've used a bigger size but I didn't have the heart to tell her."

The euphoria I felt only seconds earlier disappears, replaced by a queasy uneasiness. Is Lucy talking about me? I yank my SPANX back up and peer through the crack in the door. Lucy and Alicia are standing with their backs to me, admiring their reflections in the mirror as they apply lip gloss.

"She looks like a giant watermelon," Alicia says, smacking her lips.

A *watermelon?* I glance at my dress. They can't be talking about me. Watermelon is red and green. My dress is fuchsia, kind of a purplish red, nothing like the red in watermelon. And there is no green on me whatsoever.

"Actually, I'm surprised she's not wearing a hoodie," Alicia says. "I don't think I've ever seen her without it. It must just reek."

That settles it. They are definitely not talking about me. Although I wear a hoodie every day, it is not the same one, for God's sake. They're not even the same colors. I have five hoodies. *Five.* Two navy blues, two black, and one gray.

"Truth of the matter is, it's not the dress. She could be wearing the most beautiful dress in the world and it wouldn't make any difference. Not when you look like *that.*"

"A nose job would help," Lucy says. "But she doesn't seem to have any interest."

A *nose job?* Say what?

"It's not just the nose," Alicia says. "What's the deal with the teeth? Why didn't she ever get braces?"

I stare at the back of my sister's blond-streaked head. I think about how I felt when the hairdresser told her how beautiful she looked with her hair pulled up. *That's my sister,* I thought. I was proud to share her DNA.

"The dentist wouldn't give them to her because she sucked her thumb forever," Lucy says. "He said it was a waste of time until she stopped."

I take my thumb out of my mouth as I put my hand on the stall to steady myself. "Well, she doesn't *still* suck her thumb, does she?" Alicia says as she starts to laugh.

Lucy begins to laugh along with Alicia like, *you guessed it!* Like I still suck my thumb.

I flush the toilet, open the stall, and step out.

Lucy stops laughing and her eyes grow wide at the sight of me. "Megan," she breathes.

I try to keep my head held high as I walk past her and Alicia on my way to the door.

"Wait," Lucy says as she grabs for me, attempting to stop me. At my sister's touch, something inside me snaps. I push her away with all my might, causing her to topple into the bathroom sink. As tears fill my eyes and sobs wrack my body, I slam myself into the bathroom door, knocking it open. I need to get out of there, away from the stupid gym, the stupid dance, my stupid sister.

I run through the gym, barreling my way through the crowd as I head for the door. Students are still arriving but I don't acknowledge anyone. I make my way against the crowd, pushing past them, escaping outside into the darkness and pouring down rain. *How could I have been so stupid as to actually believe I looked good? That a pretty dress and some makeup would make a difference?*

As I stumble down the school steps, the wind whips my skimpy dress around my legs as the rain pelts my face.

Nothing will ever make a difference because I will always be ugly, ugly, ugly. . . .

I run down the crowded sidewalk and past the limos. Within minutes I'm blocks away from the school and alone on the sidewalk as cars speed past me, making their way toward the heart of Federal Hill.

Ugly, ugly, ugly . . .

By the time I get to Cross Street my elaborate hairstyle is sprayed across my face and over my eyes like some sort of helmet. My dress is soaking wet and clinging to my body. I barely look for cars as I dash into the street, determined to get home as quickly as possible.

Ugly, ugly, ugly . . .

I hear a horn and the squeal of brakes and twist toward the sound, just in time to see the headlights bearing down on me.

Ugly, ugly, ugly, ug . . .

"Megan," I hear Lucy say. It's as if she's whispering in my ear. "Can you hear me?" she asks.

Everything feels heavy, as if I'm weighted down.

"Megan, it's me. Lucy."

I slowly open my eyes. Lucy is leaning over me. "Can you hear me, Megan?" Her hair is all messed up and her eyes are red and puffy. She's still wearing her pink princess dress, but it's spattered and smeared with something red, like ketchup.

I can barely breathe. It feels like there's cotton in my mouth, cotton in my nose. Cotton everywhere.

"I'm so sorry," she's saying. "This is all my fault."

I scan the room with my eyes. Everything looks unfamiliar.

Shiny blue walls. Machines. Weird cotton curtains hanging from the wall.

"What . . . ," I begin, but I stop. I taste something horrible in my mouth, something so salty it makes me gag. Blood.

"You were hit by a car. On Cross Street."

"Mom . . ." I mutter. I want my mother. I need my mother.

"She and Dad are talking to the surgeon but they'll be right back. He said that you're lucky Megan, that we're lucky. It could've been so much worse. But you're going to be okay. The doctors say that the worst damage is cosmetic, and they can fix that."

Cosmetic . . . doctors . . . lucky . . . The words float in the air, empty and meaningless. "They're going to make you look great, Megan. I promise. You're going to be okay," my sister says with a sob.

As I look at my sister wailing beside me, her tears spilling down over her beautiful face, I suddenly remember. I remember Lucy laughing. I remember the nose, the teeth. The watermelon.

I'm ugly, ugly, ugly . . .

"I'm so sorry," Lucy whispers through her tears, squeezing my hand.

I close my eyes and the world once again fades away.

intermission (noun): a short interval between the acts of a play or a public performance, usually a period of ten to fifteen minutes, allowing the performers and audience a rest.

Six

overture (noun): an introductory piece that contains many of the musical motifs and themes of the score.

Ten Months Later

The smell of chemical-infused bubble gum floats through the air as Lucy smacks her perfectly shaped pink and glossy lips together, admiring her reflection in the mirror. "Your turn," she says, stepping away from the mirror.

I inhale deeply and take my sister's place. I look into the medicine cabinet mirror that I've been brushing my teeth in front of for the past two years and give a big (openmouthed) smile at the stranger staring back at me. "Hellooooo Frankenstein," I say.

I'm not sure why Frankenstein popped into my head. I know he is a mishmash of cadavers, and (to my knowledge at least) my new face is constructed solely from my own skin, but I can't help but feel camaraderie with him. A new face will do that to a girl, I guess.

"Hardly!" Lucy says. "Frankenstein is ugly. You're a babe!"

I suck in my cheeks and turn from one side to the other, attempting to evaluate my new face objectively, as if I'm trying it on for the first time. "Really?" I ask, even though Lucy has told me this before. In fact, everyone keeps repeating the same thing: "You're beautiful." And then they smile proudly as if they were personally responsible for my transformation and add, "It's a miracle."

They got that part right.

It is an unbelievable, incredible, bizarre miracle that I have a face at all considering that I got sideswiped by a car and slammed face-first into the asphalt, leaving my nose and three of my front teeth behind. After the accident I looked so bad the hospital's trauma team called in a social worker to help prepare my family for the worst. First they told them that I had been severely brain damaged (due to the fact that I kept repeating "watermelons, red, green"), so when they found out that in spite of the fact that I had three broken ribs, a broken arm, and a broken leg, the worst damage was cosmetic, my parents were relieved. They didn't really hear the part about their daughter resembling a monster from late-night TV, so awful-looking that she would remember her plain old ugly days with a sense of nostalgia.

As soon as all the major medical issues were cleared up and the ear, nose, and throat doctor had constructed a "nose" (in quotation marks simply because it didn't look like any nose I'd ever seen before), my parents went to work, researching plastic surgeons. They settled on one in New York and thus began the rehabilitation of Megan Fletcher.

I spent the remainder of my sophomore year shuffling (literally, due to my leg and my ribs) between doctors' appointments and surgeries and meetings with my tutor (so I could keep up with my classes). Along the way I had four reconstructive surgeries, had my jaw realigned and wired shut, got the braces taken off, had three bone grafts (in my mouth), and received four teeth implants. I asked for new eyeballs, too, something in a turquoise, but apparently they haven't figured that one out yet.

"You really think I'm pretty?" I ask Lucy.

"No," Lucy says. "I think you're beautiful."

My final operation was in the beginning of the summer, and the swelling finally went away a couple of weeks ago. I've spent a lot of time since then staring at myself in the mirror, trying to figure out what it is exactly that makes me look so different. My eyes are the same brown eyes that I've had since I was born. But that's where the similarities end.

My nose is now small and delicate, almost perfect with the exception of my right nostril, which is almost indiscernibly smaller than the other. A faint scar is visible at the base of my nose, but because of the shadow, it's hard to see. Gone are my chubby, inflated cheeks and in their place are the sculpted cheeks of Pocahontas, Native American princess. Even though they didn't do anything to my lips, they look different, too, fuller or plumper or something. But maybe my new straight white choppers just make them stand out more.

"It's so weird, isn't it? My nose is different. And this," I add, sucking in my cheeks.

"The doctor said you lost a lot of bone in your mouth. Maybe that's what did it. The loss of those front teeth of yours. And the new ones they put in . . . well, they don't stick out. Plus you lost a ton of weight when your jaws were wired shut," she says simply, handing me some blush.

This is new, the sharing makeup thing. Before my accident I hardly ever wore makeup. But lately it's been different. I like wearing makeup. It helps to acquaint me with my new features. *Hello, eyelashes, how long are you today? Hello, cheekbones, there you are!*

"Now you need lip gloss," she says when I'm done.

I recently came to the earth-shattering conclusion that I can't stand lip gloss. Why would anyone want to put a sticky paste on their mouth? But still, I hand Lucy back the blush and accept the lip gloss. I like to defer to the experts. And Lucy is an expert at applying makeup.

I dab it on my lips as Lucy watches. "Go like this," she says, smacking her lips together again. So I smack my lips together. Why didn't Lucy worry about my makeup (or the lack of it) before my accident? Was I just too hopeless? (Like painting a toilet. What's the point?)

"Perfect," Lucy says, smiling at my reflection in the mirror.

It's Saturday, and since school starts on Monday, my sister decided that she and I should go out together to celebrate. So even though I would prefer to stay home and watch the gross medical reality shows I became addicted to during my convalescence, I'm trying to be a good sport. "Do you think anyone we know will be there?" I ask.

Anyone. Read: Drew. I have thought about him so much this past year. I was able to pry some information about him out of my sister (he and Lindsey dated all year and went to prom together), but she hasn't spoken with him or seen him all summer. I wondered if he ever thought about me or wondered how I was doing, especially when I was scared, like right before surgery, or after, when the pain got so bad I felt like my head was going to explode like the tomato I once microwaved. (In my defense, it was for a science experiment. As in, I will see if the act of exploding this tomato in the microwave alleviates my boredom and/or causes me to go blind. My conclusion: only temporarily.) I would think about Drew and wonder if all these surgeries might make me look good enough to get his attention; that it might all be worth it in the end. And then I would imagine him pulling me into his arms and sweeping me off my feet as he laid a big wet one right on me. And then I would think, *Hell yes. What's a little asphalt up your nose for a guy like Drew?*

"No," Lucy says. "It's too far away." Lucy and I went to this club once before, about six months before my accident. Although she has wanted to go back ever since (sans yours truly), my parents had refused since they didn't want Lucy driving all the way through the city at night and they said it was too far away and too much of a hassle for them to take her. But when Lucy suggested taking me there tonight, they practically jumped up and down for joy, calling it a "great idea!" They still didn't like the idea of us driving through the city by ourselves, so they were taking us and dropping us off. They were going to go to dinner, see a movie, and pick us up afterward.

I finish applying my mascara and turn back toward my sister. "All done," she says, smiling from ear to ear. She hurries over to the top of the stairs. "Mom! Dad!" she calls out excitedly, peering down. "Are you ready?"

Considering the fact that my dad is at home *and* using the camera that he only used once before (the night of the accident), his silence is remarkable. Chances are slim that he figured out how to work it, but he's obviously trying to behave, which only adds to the weirdness. I would much rather have him swearing his head off than this Mr. Cleaver/*Leave It to Beaver* routine.

Lucy waves me over.

"Taaa-daa!" she says, moving out of the way as I take my place at the top of the stairs.

"Would you look at that!" Dad exclaims as he practically blinds me with a camera flash.

"Oh Megan," Mom says, holding her hands to her mouth, as if in shock.

Now I know how my sister feels when she's playing a role. As I walk down the stairs, I wonder if my parents can see my new pink thong. Ew. I try to wipe the thought from my mind as I adjust the short skirt my sister picked out for me and self-consciously pull my snug shirt over my bra strap. I'm baring much more skin than normal. I have lost nearly fifty pounds over the past year, and my parents insisted on buying me a whole new wardrobe (thus explains the thong), all purchases supervised by my sister (also thus explains the thong). All my old clothes are stored in the back of my closet in a big black Hefty bag marked SALVATION ARMY.

"Now one of you together," Dad says, waving Lucy over. Lucy and I stand side by side as we wrap our arms around each other. She looks over at me, beaming sisterly love. I smile back, even though there's something about this whole thing that is giving me the major heebie-jeebies. And for some strange reason, I'm tempted to muck it up a bit. Maybe give my sister, who has been nothing but nice and sweet, a big old kick in the ass. Or perhaps I could just take my dad's camera and, oops, drop it smack on the floor as in: I'm still *me*, people. I know I look a little (to be fair, a lot) different but WHY ARE YOU MAKING SUCH A BIG DEAL OUT OF THIS? YOU SAW ME EVERY DAY FOR SIXTEEN YEARS!

I must be a really terrible person to even think about kicking my sister or dropping my dad's camera, considering the hell we've all been through the past year. After all, it wasn't just me who went through the ringer; it was every single person in the room, particularly Lucy. Lucy originally blamed herself for what happened to me (What a coincidence! So did I!), saying that if it wasn't for her I never would've been upset and blah, blah, blah.

Amazingly enough, like some beneficent religious figure coming into town on my white horse, I took the high road. And although I managed to convince myself that I alone was responsible for my accident, I never really managed to convince Lucy, who put herself into purgatory. She broke things off with Tommy, and although she performed in the senior productions, she didn't even audition for anything else all year. She claimed that she didn't want to commit herself, preferring to stay flexible so that she could accompany Mom and me to New York for the surgeries. At first I was kind of happy to have Lucy as my own little servant or magic genie, but by spring it started to make me feel mildly guilty to think of all the fun Lucy was missing, and all because I had stupidly run into the street without looking.

"Wait a minute," Lucy says, her eyes flashing concern. "Megan needs a tissue."

This is the worst side effect of my surgeries: my runny nose. It wasn't horrible, like the gushing of a waterfall, but more slow and steady, like a leaky faucet. At first the doctors were concerned I had a "cerebrospinal fluid leak" (that is, my brain was leaking), but they tested me and ruled it out. The doctors said it was due to either the misplacement of the glands that secrete mucus, or because the cells that handled the flow of mucus were destroyed, or both. To make matters worse, due to the "sensoral" nerve damage, my nose and the entire area underneath it to my mouth are totally numb. End result: I can blow a lung through my nose and still not be aware that I need a tissue.

Fortunately, the doctors gave me some nasal spray that they said would turn off the faucet in my runny nose. And it pretty much does, except for when my eyes get watery, like if I'm crying, or like now, if my eyes are watery from a flash. None of the zillion doctors I've seen can figure out for sure why this is happening, but they think it's due to a "misplaced" tear duct. (Gee, I wonder who misplaced it: perhaps the doctor who was poking around back there with a scalpel?) One thing is certain: I now possess the remarkable and annoying trait of being able to cry through my nose. Beat that, Zippy the bike-riding chimp!

Lucy takes the tissue and dabs my nose for me, like she's my mom.

"God, I'm not five!" I say.

She pulls the tissue away and smiles at me. "Perfect!"

Then Lucy hands the tissue to my mom and the flash goes off once again. I grab another tissue and wipe my own nose. (Just to show my adoring fans I'm more than capable.)

"Look girls," Dad says, showing us the picture. "Look how great you both look."

He scans through the pictures, stopping at the last one we took before my accident, the one with Simon and me in front of the fireplace. My father quickly turns off the camera, as if the reminder of my previous appearance is too painful. Even though I don't look anything like I used to, I'm still irked by his rejection. I'm privy to info no one else seems to realize: this new face of mine isn't truly me. That's right. The real me is the one in the old photo, the one my dad still can't stand the sight of. The one that wants to kick him in the shins. Really hard.

My parents drop Lucy and me off in front of the club a few minutes later, and we make it inside rather quickly. (Let's just say, two girls can budge the line if the bouncer likes what he sees. Given how Lucy holds my hand and plays with my hair, I'm pretty sure the bouncer has seen lots of late-night Skinamax.) I survey the crowd as my eyes slowly adjust to the darkness. There are a few tables here and there, but most people are either on the dance floor or standing in groups, talking or laughing with friends. Everyone looks like they eat lunch at the popular table during daylight hours.

"Let's get away from these speakers and find some place to sit down," Lucy yells, motioning toward the bar. "Do you want something to drink?" This place has a bar (just like a regular club), but instead of alcohol it's stacked with soft drinks and a Slushee machine.

I nod as I follow her over, putting my hand on my purse, ready to pull out my wallet. Lucy puts her hand on mine and shakes her head. "Put that away," she says, stopping by a table filled with guys.

"I thought we were going to get something to drink."

Lucy locks eyes with a guy at the table and smiles. "We are," she says.

"I don't know about this, Lucy," I say nervously. "Maybe we should just find a place to sit by ourselves."

"There aren't any seats," she proclaims, still maintaining eye contact.

"But I don't know how to do . . . to do . . . *this*," I say, stepping out of the way as a studious-looking guy with braces leads a pretty brown-haired girl to the dance floor.

"All you have to do is talk to them," Lucy says. "Ask them questions about themselves. All guys *love* to talk about themselves."

"Questions," I repeat. "Like where they live and stuff?"

"Anything at all. They love it. And you just need to sit there and open up your eyes really wide and nod your head, as if you're interested."

"Really? That works?"

"Definitely. Oh—and guys love to be teased. They eat it up."

"This seems like a lot to remember."

"And if you really like them, you touch them."

Um, excuse me? "What do you mean, I *touch* them?"

"Just like a little flirty touch, like if they have something in their pocket you lean over and pull it out, something like that."

"What?" I am utterly and totally confused. *"Hey, what's THIS in your pocket . . . why . . . it's a . . . a RABBIT!"*

"You girls want to sit down?" eye contact guy asks, waving us over.

"Sure," Lucy says to them. She gives me a little smile of encouragement as she nods toward the table.

Gulp. It's showtime.

"What if I say something stupid?" I nervously whisper as I hover behind Lucy.

"Hah! Like they'd even notice." Lucy turns back toward the guy-filled table. She motions for me to take the seat next to her, right smack next to the cutest boy in the group.

"What's your name?" she immediately asks the one sitting next to her.

"Alex Neumer," he says.

"Alex Neumer," she repeats, offering him her hand. "I'm Lucy Fletcher. And this is my sister, Megan."

"Hi, Megan," he says, giving me a wave. "That's Ben, John, and Ron," he says, pointing around the table.

"John and Ron . . . cute," Lucy says, and they all laugh. "You guys aren't brothers, are you?" This is how my sister memorizes names. Right after she meets someone, she makes a little comment about his or her name and just like that, poof, it's committed to her memory for life. She could run into them ten years later and she'd be like, "Hey, Ron, remember me, Lucy Fletcher? We met at that club back in . . . blah, blah, blah." I, however, had none of those skills and had instead committed this to memory: right next to Lucy, "pouffy-haired cute guy"; next to him, "red-haired guy"; next to him, "braces guy"; and next to me, "cute, skinny guy."

"No," red-haired guy chuckles.

"I guess that would be a little much." Lucy grins.

They all seem to lean a little bit closer to her, as if hanging on her every word. It has taken Lucy about one second to have them eating out of her hand.

"Do you guys want something to drink?" braces guy asks.

Lucy shrugs and looks at me. I can tell it's my turn to speak.

"A Diet Coke," I mutter timidly.

"Make that two . . . *John*," she says. Braces man blushes (as if flattered she remembered his name) and the rest of the table laughs as if she just cracked a joke. "So where do you guys go to school?" Lucy asks.

Question. Always ask them questions.

"Gilman," pouffy-haired cute guy says.

"Cute boys school," Lucy whispers to me, just loud enough for the guys sitting on either side of us to hear. I know she did this intentionally, but I can feel the heat rise up my cheeks as my hands start to get a little sweaty.

"What about you?" Pouffy asks, responding to her compliment by putting his arm over the back of her chair.

Lucy nudges me under the table.

I'm up again? Already? "CSPA," I spit out.

"Chesapeake School for Performing Arts," Lucy explains.

"I've heard of that school," red-haired guy says. "I saw that dance movie that was filmed there."

"So in a couple of years you're going to be famous?" cute, skinny guy asks.

I laugh nervously. I've never received attention like this before and I'm baffled in a total fish-out-of-water sort of way.

"What time is it?" Lucy asks suddenly. "Is the game still going on?"

"You mean the Orioles?" braces guy asks, returning to the table and setting Diet Cokes in front of Lucy and me.

Lucy nods and takes a sip of her free Coke. Even though the stadium is about four blocks from our house and we could see it from our rooftop deck, until this moment I would've sworn Lucy didn't know who the Orioles were, or even that they had a game today.

"Four nothing, bottom of the seventh," cute, skinny guy says, putting his hand over the back of my chair and leaning over me.

"Yes!" Lucy says enthusiastically, clapping her hands, as if she actually gave a crap.

"Are you a baseball fan, too?" cute, skinny guy asks me. He has blue eyes, like Drew, but even though they're a similar color, they don't have nearly the same intensity and depth of Drew's.

"Nah. What a waste of time."

Cute, skinny guy looks stunned and a little offended, like I just made a joke at his mother's expense.

I make a face at Lucy. Oops.

I think about what Lucy instructed: *Ask questions.* "What about you?" I ask.

I wonder if I can remember all of this for when I see Drew. *Questions, tease, touch, questions, tease, touch. . . .*

"Orioles and Ravens, baby," he says.

"My dad says the Ravens are a bunch of thugs," I volunteer. "No, wait, I think he calls them hoodlums."

He gives me a blank look. I give him a blank look.

I glance back at Lucy. I'm stumped.

But Lucy's not paying attention to me. "Oh my God! Is that a Popsicle stick in your pocket?" she asks, touching Pouffy's back pocket.

"This?" he asks, leaning forward as he pulls out his wallet. "It's my wallet."

No offense to Lucy's technique, but there's no way that wallet looks like a Popsicle stick. Claiming that she thought it was a Popsicle stick had to be, hands down, the most idiotic, obviously stupid thing anyone had ever said.

Lucy nudges my leg under the table and I know she wants me to say something.

"I thought it was a Popsicle, too," I announce. The whole table begins to grin and smile right along with us, which is all I need for encouragement. "I was like, why does that guy have a Popsicle in his pants!" I exclaim, inwardly wincing since it came out sounding way more perverted and stupid than I had intended.

But Lucy is right. No one seems to mind. I look around the table as they all continue to laugh, not *at* me, but *with* me. I rest my eyes on my sister, who's smiling at me, sending me a look of pure and total adoration. And suddenly I realize that this is right out of my fantasy moments. Cutting in front of a crowd, free drinks, a ratio of four boys to two girls, being able to say any stupid thing at all (to cute boys who would never have even noticed me before), and still have everyone think that I'm great . . . it makes me feel powerful, as if I can do anything. And it's all due to my new face. I once again remember what the doctor said as he handed me the mirror for the first time: "You're beautiful now, Megan. Everything is about to change. . . ."

I turn to the boys and say, "Everyone thinks Yo-Yo Ma is such a great cellist. I think he's just a total spaz."

They look at me, smiling, like I've just told them I want to go skinny-dipping with them. It's almost too good. It's like a reality show made just for me. So I say, "Why do you think they call it plutonium? What's wrong with Goofy? Why didn't he get his own element?" I'm thinking about saying something nasty about Harry Potter, but I decide to quit while I'm ahead. I take a sip of my drink, then I say, "Why do superheroes always wear underwear outside their pants?"

As the guys start to laugh, I give Lucy a big smile and toast her with my glass.

seven

curtain time (noun): the time at which a play or other performance is scheduled to begin.

It's my first day back at school. I've been up since five, so excited that I'm practically hyperventilating. The potential effects of my new appearance hadn't really registered until the other night at the club. But ever since then I've been feeling like a kid counting down the days until Christmas. I'm ready to burst into school and embrace my new life. Megan Fletcher, admired, adored, and appreciated.

I shower and blow my hair out straight and go back into my room, where I dress in the outfit I picked out weeks ago (with Lucy's help, of course)—short-sleeved, snug-fitting bright pink shirt, one-hundred-dollar jeans (size two!), and black flip-flops that have sparkly sequins glued to the top.

We always walk to school but since it's hot (and neither Lucy nor I want to risk pit stains on such a big, important day), my mom drives us. Mom pulls up directly in front of the school and Lucy and I climb out of her Buick Lucerne. She beeps the horn and blows a kiss as we walk away.

We're about a foot away from the steps leading up the main entrance when I stop dead in my tracks.

"What's wrong?" Lucy asks.

Unfortunately, I don't have an answer for her. All I know is that I can't feel my toes. Or my legs. Or my hands. All I can feel is my heart racing in my chest and the Cheerios I had for breakfast bubbling in my belly.

"Come on," Lucy says, encouraging me. She loops her arm through mine, practically pulling me toward the school. I'm walking with a stiff-legged gait I associate with the Boris Karloff Frankenstein. "I'm so excited for you," she says. "Wait till Simon sees you. He was so miserable without you last year."

Simon. Just the mention of him makes my knees unlock. I've missed the little bugger. Although he visited me whenever he could, I was in New York a lot over the past year, and even when I wasn't, a lot of the time I was just feeling too sick to be social, even if being social just meant watching *Battlestar Galactica* DVDs. The last time I saw him was right before he left for camp in June. I still had my braces on and a huge bandage on my nose from surgery.

Lucy and I walk past Ali Hankey, a wannabe stage designer I've known since middle school. She's sitting smack in the middle of the steps, drawing a skateboard on the cover of her notebook. "Hi," I say.

"Hi, Lucy and um . . . hi," she says, looking directly at me.

"Ali," Lucy says, as we stop. "You remember Megan? My sister?"

Ali's mouth drops open.

Her reaction makes my heart beat even faster. Lucy grabs the door for me and motions for me to enter. A group of her friends (obviously alerted by Lucy that we were on our way) are waiting for me and begin clapping as I walk in the door.

As I step inside the clapping quiets down almost immediately as Lucy's friends take me in, inch by inch. There are stunned gasps and a lot of *"Oh my God. Look at you . . . you look amazing . . . you look totally different. . . ."*

Through the crowd I see Simon (who undoubtedly was alerted of my impending arrival by Lucy as well). He's standing at the end of the hall over by the production studio, staring directly at me.

"Megan?" he mouths, as if he's not quite sure.

I'm so happy to see him I break through the crowd and run to him, nearly knocking him over as I throw my arms around his neck. He laughs nervously, and jams his hands in his pockets as he takes a step back.

"I'm here!" I announce, just in case he hadn't noticed.

"I see," he says, still staring at me.

"I look weird, don't I?" I whisper.

"Not weird," he says. "Just different. Holy crap."

"Exactly," I say with a nod and smile. Standing before him, being so close to him, makes me feel one hundred percent better.

"I, ah . . ." He stops talking.

"I'm totally freaking out. I wish you could just stay with me all day." I glance at the familiar cowlick flipping over his glasses. The black T-shirt that says "Joey's Bar." The purple Bermuda shorts. The red socks and silver sneakers. It all combines to make me so happy that I throw my arms around his neck once again and rub my nose against his sawdust-smelling T-shirt. But he doesn't return my hug. He stands stiff as a board.

My sister puts her hands on my hips and leans around me. "I better get going," she says happily. I can tell Lucy is thrilled to have me back in school again. "Call me if you need me."

"I guess I should get going, too," I say to Simon, checking my watch.

"Sure," he says. "Maybe we can get together for lunch—unless of course you have other plans, which I completely understand . . ."

"Of course I want to have lunch with you," I say. "Who else would I eat lunch with?" I suddenly remember that Simon has practically a year of solo lunches without me under his belt. Maybe he has a new crowd he sits with. "I'll see you before lunch anyway, remember? Lucheki's class?"

Last year Simon and I had almost all of the same classes. Although I have kept up with my academic courses while I was out, I still have to make up the set design classes that I missed last year, which, according to the deal my parents had worked out with the school, was going to entail summer school at NYU, which was totally cool and exciting. In the meantime, though,

Simon and I only have one class together, Mr. Lucheki's Sound and Light Management.

"Yeah," Simon says grinning from ear to ear. "Right."

I do a double take, looking at him an extra moment, wondering why he's so smiley about a class where you learn how to point spotlights. I climb up the marble staircase, smiling at everyone even though there's a ton of people I don't recognize. I can't help but feel I'm in the twilight zone. I hadn't really had a chance to get to know the freshman crowd before my accident, and with the graduation of the seniors and the arrival of the new freshman class, there's been a lot of turnover.

From across the hall I see a familiar face: Catherine Bellows, the lumberjack who was so thrilled to help my sister decorate for the fall festival. She's wearing her trademark oversized overalls with her dirty brown hair pulled back in a plaid bandanna.

"Hey, Catherine," I call out, giving her a friendly wave. She looks at me, and although she nods, acknowledging me, I can tell she's confused.

Out of the corner of my eye, I spot the rodent walking toward me, his eyes shifting nervously back and forth as he clutches his backpack to his chest. "Hey, Herbert!" I say cheerfully. He glances in my direction as he walks smack into an open locker.

"Are you okay?" I ask, helping him up.

"Uh, great," he says, staring at me.

"It's good to see you again," I say. And surprisingly enough, I honestly mean it. Not that I have missed the rodent, but I'm happy to be back, happy to see at least some people I recognize, happy to get back to life as normal.

"Do I know you?"

The rodent doesn't recognize me either.

Even though Lucy told me that no one would recognize me, I'm still surprised to find that it's true. "It's me," I say. "Megan."

"Megan?" he repeats, searching my eyes for some familiarity.

"Fletcher," I add.

"Wild," he finally murmurs. "Megan Fletcher."

I leave the rodent and head to my locker. I must admit that all this excuse-me-do-I-know-you crap is beginning to wig me out. I open up my locker and discover that someone, namely Lucy, has been hard at work. All of my old pictures of Lucy and Simon and me have been taken down and in their place is a big "Welcome Back—We Love You" red Sharpie–printed sign that runs down the length of the door and is signed by so many people the signatures all blend together.

My first class is history, so I pull out my eight-hundred-page *Essential World History* book and brand-new spiral notebook and slam my locker shut just as George Longwell turns the corner. I stare straight ahead, determined to avoid rejection on my first day back. But this time, instead of ignoring me, he stops in front of me.

"Whoa there! I'm George," he says, smiling at me and sticking out his hand. "George Longwell."

He's introducing himself?

"Now's when you shake my hand," he says as he continues to smile. I stick out my hand and he takes it in his. "Let me guess. Drama major, right?"

I shake my head. "Tech."

"Tech?" he laughs. "Well, you'll certainly be a stand out."

Oh crap. Does he not know who I am either?

"I just wanted to tell you that if you have any questions or anything, well, I'd be more than happy to help. This school can be a little intimidating at first. Do you know how to get to your first class?"

Well I guess that answers my question. "I'm not a freshman," I say.

"Transfer student?"

And then I see him. *Drew.* My heart slams against my chest as he turns the corner, heading right toward me. As per usual, he's dressed in black from head to toe. His black, licorice-colored hair is just a tad longer than I remember, but his deep blue-green eyes are every bit as mesmerizing.

"Hey, Megan," he says, nodding in my direction. "Welcome back."

"Megan?" George says. "I love that name!"

But I don't acknowledge his compliment. I'm too distracted by Drew, who continues down the hall as if everything is exactly the same as it was before my accident. As if I still have the same old face and body.

And that, I decide, is not so good.

After school, Simon and I go to Spoons, our favorite coffee shop. Before my accident, Simon and I used to come here almost every day. Everyone, even the part-timers, knew that Simon always ordered a hot black tea and I had an iced mocha cappuccino and a chocolate chip cookie. But today, I don't recognize the person behind the counter. Not that it makes any difference. As I'm beginning to realize, she probably wouldn't have recognized me, either.

"Here's to your first day," Simon says, toasting me with his cup. I gently knock his cup with mine. "Did it get any better?" he asks.

Simon is talking about a comment I made at lunch, when I told him that the hubbub over my new face was driving me crazy. It was nothing like my night at the club. For one, the only person I had hoped to wow by my new appearance (Drew) barely noticed me, and everyone else made me feel like a three-eyed monkey at the zoo. All day long people kept telling me how different I look and what an "amazing job they did." After the fifty-millionth ohmyGodyoulookamazing I couldn't help but start to feel a little defensive because no one, not a single person, seemed even mildly upset by the fact that they would never *ever* see the old me again.

"Welcome to the Megan Fletcher freak show," I say.

"What are you talking about?" Simon asks. "You're not a freak. Look at you! You're, well, incredible."

"You look so different," I imitate in a high-pitched, annoying

voice. *"You were so awful-looking before. Were you even human? You were like this twisted creation of monkey parts and cadavers, but now you look like a million bucks. The sight of you used to make my eyes bleed. Want to be my best friend?"*

"It wasn't like that. Seriously. The whole school was talking about how hot you are now."

I give him one of Lucy's big, dramatic sighs. "I'm not fishing for compliments. It's just, well, today wasn't exactly what I expected."

"What'd you think would happen?"

"I don't know. When Lucy and I went to the club I felt, well, pretty. No one saw me as a former warthog made pretty by mad scientists. They didn't realize what everyone at school knows. That my parents didn't give me this face, the doctors did."

"Megan," Simon says. "No one was looking at you like a freak today. Believe me."

I take a sip of my iced mocha cappuccino, my first one since my accident, and let it linger in my mouth before swallowing. But surprisingly, it doesn't taste as good as I remembered. It's more bitter than sweet.

"I'm just glad you're as good as new again," Simon says. "Even better."

"I may look different, but I'm not exactly better than I was before. I have to take that nose spray every day so that my nose doesn't run. And even then it still runs when my eyes water and stuff. And I have to sleep with a nose stent for the rest of my life."

"A what?"

"I showed it to you before. It's that little thing that looks like a piece of rigatoni . . . the thing I have to stick in my nose at night."

Although my nose before was extra large, most of the tissue was so embedded with gravel it was unusable. They had to cut out all the damaged parts and make do with what was left, pulling the skin so tight that I have to stretch out my nose every night just to make sure it keeps its shape. Otherwise my nostril will just close up tighter than an unroasted pistachio shell. I'm thinking about sharing all this with Simon, but I just don't feel like saying the word *nostril* out loud. Or *pistachio*.

"I'm sick of talking about my face." I push my drink away from me. "Let's talk about something else. Tell me about band camp."

This year they didn't allow the campers to send e-mails, so Simon could only communicate by snail mail. To make matters worse, I had barely spoken to him while he was at his dad's. I had hoped to catch up at lunch, but with all the people stopping by to gawk, we never really got a chance.

"It was all right," he replies.

"All right?" I repeat. I can tell from the way Simon is shifting his eyes that all right means fantastic, which means some physical activity involving a member of the opposite sex. "In your letters you said you were having a great time."

"I guess."

I lean over the table and grin as I whisper, "What's the story that you wanted to tell me?"

"What story?"

"When you wrote this summer you told me you had a wild story for me, but that you had to tell me in person."

"Oh," he says, shifting uncomfortably in his seat. "It was nothing."

Okay, if he wants me to twist his arm a little, I'm more than happy to comply. "Does it have to do with Susan?" Susan was the girl he had hooked up with the previous year.

"She's nothing," Simon says defensively. "Just a friend."

The little twerp is lying to me. But why? I pick up a fork and poke him in the wrist. "Did you guys hook up again?" I ask, determined.

"I told you, we're just friends."

"So you mean you didn't hook up?"

"I mean we're not seeing each other or anything like that. We're both, well, single." Simon is looking at me in a way that makes me feel as if my bra strap is showing. The truth of the matter is Simon has been acting weird all day.

"It's amazing," he says. "It's like a whole different you. Does it feel that way, too?"

"Yes and no," I say with a shrug. "I felt different at the club the other night, that's for sure."

"I remember when I came to see you in the hospital, right after . . . *it* happened. Your face was all puffy and swollen and you had stitches all over and I thought that, well, I didn't think they'd ever be able to fix you. And here you are. *Tu sembles parfaite.*"

"What?" I ask, even though I have taken enough French to translate. What I really mean is, Who are you and what have you done with my best friend?

"You look perfect," he says softly.

I crunch down on something hard and vaguely familiar. With horror, I realize that I've bitten off part of my thumbnail.

eight

On Wednesday I stay after school to talk to my pre-calc teacher, Mrs. Pritchie. Students weren't allowed to take pre-calc unless they achieved a B or higher in Algebra 2 and even though I had finished the textbook with my tutor, Mrs. Pritchie is concerned I might not be able to keep up with the class and has loaned me a tutoring book in case I need it.

I finish tucking *Tutoring for Precalculus* into my backpack and I'm standing at my locker, staring at the sign and trying to make out the two signatures that are smeared together on the bottom, when I hear a familiar voice say hello. My blood pressure suddenly spikes because I know who it is before I turn around.

Drew.

We don't have a class together this semester, so we've not

really spoken besides an occasional hello in the halls. I have however, learned two key details:

He and Lindsey broke up over the summer.

He spent his summer working as a counselor at a camp for the arts. (Not exactly key, but I'm always happy to get any details on Drew, no matter how trivial.)

I'm so nervous standing so close to him after all this time that I step back up against my open locker, nearly toppling inside.

"Hi," I reply, grabbing onto the edges of my locker and pulling myself upright.

"Are you coming out or going in?" he asks, nodding toward my locker.

"What?" I ask.

"Narnia. You know, the magical door that leads to the other world. My guess is you were coming out."

Drew is making a Narnia reference? I had no idea something this dorky would make him even hotter. "Ha, ha," I say stiffly. "I loved that movie, too."

He brushes a lock of his thick hair out of his eyes. "Oh yeah, I heard there was a movie. I'll bet it wasn't as good as the books though."

My smile fades away. I suddenly feel the need to say something really, really smart. I think of Albert Einstein and for some reason I think of his closet, which I once read was filled with set after set of the same shirts and the same pants.

"I've been meaning to see it, though," he adds quickly,

for what I'm hoping is my benefit. "So what are you doing here so late?"

How do I weave Albert Einstein's clothes into that? Suddenly, I can't remember what he just said. And so I say "What?," which I don't think helps me seem more intellectual.

"You're here late. I was asking why."

Oh yeah.

"I had a meeting with Mrs. Pritchie. Even though I took precal with my tutor, she's worried that I won't be able to keep up with the class." Um, hello? Did I really need to share that tidbit? What happened to sounding intelligent?

"I see," he says politely.

I glance back at my locker, not trusting myself to speak.

"Nice," he says, nodding toward my sister's sign. The tone of his voice is hard to read and I can't tell whether he's being sarcastic or complimentary. I wouldn't blame him for being sarcastic. The sign *is* a little stupid. I only left it up because I'm not sure what to replace it with. Last year I coated the inside of my locker with pictures of me and Simon and Lucy, but it seemed weird to put them back up when I don't look anything like that anymore.

Drew leans up against the locker next to me, as if he's planning on staying a while. This is strange. Didn't Lucy say a long time ago that he "didn't let anyone get close to him" and that he "kept to himself"? Maybe Drew has changed since last year. Not like I have of course, but still. I'm curious.

"I haven't had a chance to talk to you since you came back. How has everything been going for you?"

"Okay, I guess."

Drew kind of raises his eyebrows like he (a) doesn't quite believe me or (b) he wants me to elaborate. In either case, I intend to deliver. "Actually, not really. Things have been really weird."

"Yeah?" he asks.

"Everyone says hello to me now."

"And they didn't before?"

"I'd say the number of friendly hellos has increased about ninety-five percent."

"Wild. You're quite the celebrity."

Did I just imply that I think I'm a celebrity? "No, no," I say quickly, forcing myself to look away from his eyes. "It's not just the hellos. Everything seems, well, different. I don't know. Maybe it's just my imagination."

"I doubt it," he says. "The accident, the surgery, missing all that school. That's a ton."

Wow. Ever since I got back to CSPA, everyone has been telling me how different I look with my new face and body and how happy I must be about how everything turned out. Drew is the first person who seems to get how overwhelming this situation is. This settles it. There is a definite, almost otherworldly connection between us. In other words, we're meant for each other. It's kismet.

Then suddenly Drew does something familiar. He averts his gaze and glances down at his beat-up black boots. I follow suit, looking at them, too. His feet must have stopped growing a long time ago because I'm pretty sure his boots are the same pair he was wearing at the beginning of last year. I recognize some of the scuffs.

"I guess I should get going," he says finally, a hint of awkwardness in his voice. "It's nice to have you back."

Drew takes a few steps away from me without saying another word, like he's trying to keep his distance.

What? He's leaving? Already?

I slam my locker and hurry to catch up with him. "So I hear you got into the senior independent study. That's great. What's your play about?"

"It's called *The End*," he says, as we walk down the marble staircase. I look at his hand grasping the polished wooden banister and wonder how it would feel to hold it. "It's a pretty simple one act about a guy who's breaking up with a girl. At least, he's trying to."

"Sounds interesting," I say. Quite frankly, he could've told me it was about a girl feeding her dog and I would've said the same thing.

"It's not really about a breakup. It's more about how sometimes we don't see people for who they really are until it's too late."

"Wow," I say. Wow? Did I just say *wow*? Smart, Megan. Think smart! "Sounds good!" Ugh. Just as bad as wow. I am only hoping it doesn't get worse, that I don't suddenly start picking my nose or yodeling.

Drew gets to the door first and holds it open for me, just like Simon did the previous day. Only this time, instead of being annoyed, I'm flattered. As I walk past him, my arm brushes up against his chest and a tingle runs down my spine.

"I haven't forgotten that you still owe me an audition," he says, after the door slams shut behind us.

He remembered. Almost one year after the fact and he still remembered that he had asked me to audition. Once again: kismet.

"Are you up for it?" he asks.

"Auditioning? You mean for your play? For your independent study?"

He nods, but his eyes keep darting around like he's distracted.

"Yes," I say, a little too enthusiastically.

"Great. We're holding auditions next week."

"Yeah, okay." I follow him down the steps. It rained earlier and the marble is still slick and wet.

"Are you parked around here?" he asks.

"No. We live a couple blocks away."

"That's right. I forgot. I drove Lucy home one day last year." Silence.

The corner where we will part ways is quickly approaching. He will go to the left (toward the parking garage) and I will go to the right (toward my house). I have about 200 seconds left to wow him with my sparkling conversation—199 seconds . . . 198 seconds. Think. What were Lucy's instructions again? Question . . . tease, touch! What's a good question? Why can't I think of a good question? 195 seconds. 194 . . .

"I wish I lived around here," he says. "Towson's a hike."

I forget all about asking a brilliant question as Drew grins at me. Even though I'm so excited to be with him that my heart is banging a million miles a minute, there's something about his smile that makes me feel relaxed and happy at the same time. "Whenever my mom can't find a parking spot she talks about moving to suburbia," I say. "But I think she's afraid that all the women out there wear Lilly Pulitzer and spend their time squeezing melons at the grocery store."

"What does she have against melons?"

I laugh. "She's always been antimelon. She's in therapy, but it doesn't seem to help."

His grin turns into a smile, enough to give me another tickle in the base of my belly. We're at the corner. Our time together is over.

"Well," Drew says. "I guess I'll see you around."

"Sounds good!" Once again, I'm displaying extraordinary enthusiasm. Sheesh, I'm pathetic.

Still, as I watch Drew walk up the street toward the parking garage, I realize that this is the first time since my accident that I'm also happy.

When I get home I practically bound up the stairs and into our bedroom, looking for Lucy. She's sitting on her bed, a manuscript in her lap. She has changed out of her school clothes and into her study-at-home ones, a pink Juicy sweat suit.

Her long blond hair is twisted back in a bun, held in place by a pencil.

"How was your meeting with Mrs. Pritchie?" she asks.

"Fine," I say excitedly. "But guess who I saw after school? Drew Reynolds!"

"Drew?" Lucy tucks a strand of hair behind her ear. "Oh my God, that's so funny! I was just talking to Annie about him. Did he tell you the good news?"

Annie Carmichael is one of my sister's closest friends, but I can't really stand her. Not only is she a notorious gossip, she dyes her hair platinum blond, wears a ton of makeup, and talks in this really fake, baby doll voice. I shake my head as I continue to practically dance around the room.

"Annie overheard Mrs. Habersham saying that he's been chosen to direct the spring musical."

I stop still. Mrs. Habersham is the head of the drama department. Considering Lucy's rep for dating the directors of the spring musical, this is not good news. Not good at all.

"Drew?" I ask weakly, hoping and praying that she'll say something like: *Drew? You thought I was talking about Drew? Hah! That's a laugh!*

"He's so talented," she says, looking all starry and goo-goo eyed, the way I used to get around Frosted Flakes.

"He doesn't seem like the kind of guy who should be directing the spring musical." Read: He doesn't seem like the kind of guy who should be going out with *you*. "All the past directors have been so . . ." I think about Lucy's previous spring musical director boyfriends, Tommy Calvino, Warren Masters. "Preppy."

"Well, he's not preppy, that's for sure," Lucy says with a laugh. "But he's got . . . I don't know . . . charisma. And he's a lot less stuck-up and antisocial than last year."

I breathe in deep. Maybe it's not as dire as I think. After all, she's not talking like someone who has just found the man of her dreams.

"I'm reading his one act right now."

I look excitedly at the manuscript in her lap. "Is it good?" I take a seat next to her and rest my head on her shoulder in order to get a better look.

"Amazing. The part of the heroine is incredibly juicy. And guess what?" she says, putting down the manuscript and raising her eyebrows at me. "Annie told me that he wrote the part of the heroine for me."

Say what?

I pick my head up off her shoulder. "For you?"

"I know," she says with a smile. "Isn't that cool? I'm totally psyched. I've never actually had someone write for me before."

I scoot a little farther away from her. "How many parts are there?"

"Just two," she replies. "A boy and a girl."

Wait, if there is only one girl, and Drew wrote the part for Lucy, why did he ask me to audition?

"Are you chewing your thumb again?" she asks, her brow furrowed.

I whip my thumb out of my mouth and look at it as if I've never seen it before in my life. Oh crap. "No," I say weakly.

"Megan! It's such a nasty habit," Lucy says, focusing her attention back on her script. "And you didn't do it for almost a whole year. You can't start up again."

I tuck my hand under my rear end and say, "Are you sure he wrote the part for you?"

Lucy looks at me. "What do you mean?"

I stand up and kick off my shoes. "I was just . . . curious."

"Well, that's what Annie says."

Annie, Annie, Annie. She is really beginning to get on my nerves.

"She and Drew carpool sometimes," Lucy continues. "She said she thinks Drew likes me."

My heart drops into my belly. *Drew?* My Drew likes *Lucy?*

No, no, no, no!

"Surprising, isn't it?" Lucy continues. "He's so quiet and standoffish. I mean, I always thought he was really cute, and of course everyone always talks about how talented he is and everything, and then today, I was looking at him and I couldn't take my eyes off his chin."

"His chin?"

"It's so well defined, so strong. It's quite unusual."

I summon up a visual of Drew. Lucy's right. He does have a very nice chin. But the fact that she is zeroing in on this tiny detail is totally disconcerting. It can only mean one thing: Lucy is in love with my future husband.

"What about that guy from the club?" I ask. "Pouffy. He's so, so cute! And he seemed to really like you."

"Pouffy?" she repeats, like she has no idea who I'm talking about.

"The guy who was sitting next to you, the one who e-mailed you the next day . . ."

"Alex?" she asks, like *you've got to be joking*. "Those guys were cute, but they were totally GU," Lucy says, using her acronym for geographically undesirable. "I think they lived in Hunt Valley. And besides, they were no Drew Reynolds."

Why even bother? It's hopeless. My wannabe relationship with Drew is over, gone, kaput. No guy possesses the strength to resist my sister's giggly, wiggly, touchy, smiley, blue-eyed, question-asking tractor beam.

I take a seat beside her, my heart broken. I have no choice but to play my last card. It's desperate, potentially foolish, and almost surely disastrous, but I honestly don't know what else I can do. I have to tell her how I feel about Drew. "Lucy, there's something I need to tell you . . ." I begin.

But before I can spit out the truth, Lucy's phone rings. She raises a finger as if telling me to wait a minute. "Marybeth," she says, looking at her caller ID. "I'll tell her that I'll call her right back."

As Lucy answers her phone I sit on the edge of my bed while I silently practice what I'm about to say. Something like, *You know what's funny? Ha ha! Listen to this: I like Drew! Isn't that a riot? That's right, me! Megan Fletcher, your sweet, loving sister who just spent the past year recovering from a horrible accident that proba-bly never would have happened if you and Alicia hadn't been talking about how ugly and grotesque I was but hey, that's all water under the bridge, right? Forgiven and forgotten. And it will especially be for-gotten when you forget all about Drew and hook up with good ole Pouffy instead . . .*

Lucy is nudging me with her foot. "George Longwell?" she shrieks excitedly, giving me a big smile. "Oh my God. He is so cute!"

My heart lurches. Am I being saved by George Longwell? I lean forward and hold my breath.

"And such a sweetheart, too!" Lucy exclaims, winking at me and smiling.

Saved! I breathe a big sigh of relief and give Lucy a big happy smile. I always knew I liked George Longwell but I really think that at this moment I might just love him.

"Megan's right here," Lucy says. "I can't wait to tell her."

"George Longwell? He is so, so cute!" I blurt out as she hangs up her phone. "And talk about chins . . . does he have a great one or what?"

"I know," Lucy says. "I'm so excited for you."

"And the way he writes poetry for his girlfriends and . . ."

Hold on a second.

Did she say she was excited for *me*?

"Marybeth said she ran into him at the market after school and all he wanted to talk about was you," Lucy says. "She said he went on and on about how cute you are and how sweet and blah,

blah, blah. He even asked her if she thought you would go out with him."

No, no, no. This was not happening.

"She was like, *duh*!" Lucy laughs. "Of course! He's such a great guy."

"But . . . ," I begin.

"You wouldn't believe how many girls like him," Lucy continues. "They're always calling him and asking him out. But he doesn't want them. He wants *you*."

"He doesn't even know me."

"Oh Megan," Lucy says, taking my hand. "Last year I kept trying to be positive by thinking how great everything would be for us both when you got better. And now here you are—here we are. I have Drew, you have George. . . . This is the first time I've actually been happy in a long, long time." She sighs deeply and smiles as her eyes well with tears.

Is she crying? Please tell me she is not crying!

How can I tell her the truth when she's blubbering with happiness? And then, for some horrible reason, a visual pops into my head: Lucy on the day I came home from the hospital, looking all loving and sweet as she helped me out of the car.

"It feels so good, doesn't it?" she says. "To finally be happy again."

Ugh! I'm speechless. Totally, utterly, speechless.

"I guess," I manage.

Well, almost speechless.

———

My head is killing me. I need to talk to someone about this, and since Mom won't be home for another couple of hours, I make my excuses to Lucy and do exactly what I would've done a year earlier if I was upset: I head to Simon's.

Simon lives with his mother on the other side of Key Highway, in a giant fancy high-rise apartment building right on the water. I'm in such a rush to get there that I take the closest route, the highway. I'm pondering my situation when I hear someone yell, "Hellllooo beautiful!"

Suddenly it sounds as if I'm in the middle of the jungle. Monkey noises, shrill hoots, hollers, and whistles fill the air. "Beautiful lady in pink, give us a smile!"

Several men wearing orange safety vests are perched around a giant pothole on the other side of the street, waving and blowing kisses in my direction.

Are they talking to me? I look around, convinced there has to be someone else dressed in pink and risking death alongside the highway, but besides the cars zooming past, it's just me.

"Make our day, beautiful lady!" says a man who is standing next to what appears to be a giant vat of tar. "Give us a smile!"

But I don't feel like smiling. I feel like screaming STOP LOOKING AT ME, YOU PERVERTS! But I don't. Instead, I start to run. Even though I'm wearing flip-flops, I run and run and don't stop running until I reach Simon's apartment building.

I walk through the enormous fern-filled lobby and into the elevator, which opens directly into Simon's mother's penthouse.

I haven't been here since last spring, but it looks exactly the same. Unlike the hobbit hole my family and I live in, Simon and his mom have a huge, cavernous, bright and airy open space with floor-to-ceiling views of the inner harbor. Everything is white—white furniture, white carpet, and heavy white drapes. With the exception of Simon's crap, the entire apartment has that pristine-model-home-no-one-really-lives-here kind of look.

"Come on in," Simon calls out. "Just give me a minute to straighten up." He dashes out of the living room and heads toward the kitchen with an armful of newspapers.

"Simon, I don't care if it's messy."

Simon appears, grinning ear to ear. The smile fades, however, the minute he sees me. "What's wrong?"

I'm relieved that in spite of my new face my best friend can still tell when something is bothering me. "Oh . . . ," I say. "Nothing. Some guys were fixing the sidewalk and they started yelling at me like I'm a . . . stripper or something." I have actually never seen a stripper or a striptease, but I imagine that's how the average red-blooded construction worker might have responded to one.

"Really? What were they saying?"

And suddenly I realize how ridiculous this is. Am I going to complain that they said I was pretty? After all, they were complimenting me. I should be grateful. Right? They noticed me. And it's better than having them yell *"Hey, fatso."*

"Nothing," I say, waving it away. "How about some tea?" I ask Simon, purposely changing the conversation.

"English breakfast or green?"

"English breakfast," I say.

"English breakfast it is." He grins as he turns toward the kitchen. "So how was your meeting with Pritchie?"

"It was okay," I say. "But I ran into Drew Reynolds after school. He said he wanted me to try out for his play."

Simon puts down the tea box. "Wow, that's exciting, right?"

"Yeah, well, I was excited until I got home and Lucy told me that he's going to be the director of the spring musical. You know what that means."

"He's her new boyfriend?"

I nod.

"Well, maybe it won't work out. Maybe *he* won't like *her*."

"Oh yeah, right," I say sarcastically. "You know that part he asked me try out for? Apparently he wrote it for Lucy."

"That doesn't make any sense. Why would he ask you to try out for the same role he wrote for your sister?"

I sigh and fall backward, up against the wall. "Who knows?"

Simon shrugs. "Sounds strange to me, but then again, I'm not really surprised. I know you have a crush on him and everything, but the guy has always seemed a little off. Not to mention full of himself. He never even bothers to look at anyone when he walks down the hall."

"Off?" I stand up straight. "He's not *off* at all. And he's certainly not full of himself either. He's just shy." I know Simon's just trying to comfort me in my time of need, but nobody bad-mouths Drew. Even if he was going to be my brother-in-law instead of my husband.

Before he can say anything else, I turn and walk out. I open the sliding glass door in the living room and step out onto the balcony, shutting the screen door behind me. I've always loved the view from Simon's balcony, and today is particularly clear. I can see far into the Chesapeake Bay, to the shipping barges anchored offshore. Directly across the water are the Galleria and the Baltimore Aquarium, where the line of people waiting to see a bunch of fish wraps around the building.

"Guess what else?" I call out a couple of minutes later as I turn my back to the view and peer through the screen into the living room.

"What?" Simon says, rounding the corner with the tea. He has taken off his glasses.

"Marybeth called Lucy and said she ran into George Longwell at the market. She said he wants to ask me out."

Simon walks directly into the door, causing the tray with the tea to spill on the floor.

"Are you okay?" I ask, opening the door.

"I'm fine," he says. "I just, well, didn't see the screen. It's a fine mesh."

"Fine mess or fine mesh?"

Simon cracks up.

"Where are your glasses?" I ask, following him back into the kitchen.

"I just don't feel like wearing them," he says. "They've been bugging me."

I take a towel from him and use it to dab at the tea stain on his shirt. Simon stops laughing. There's something in his eyes, a look . . . a spark that makes me wonder once again if my bra strap is exposed. I turn away from him and head back to deal with the carpet.

"I hope this doesn't stain," I say, soaking up the tea with the towel.

"I don't care about the carpet," he says quietly, kneeling beside me. "About this George thing. Do you think you might be interested in him?"

It's the tenderness in his voice that makes me realize that my day has just become worse. Is Simon trying to impress me or something? Is that why he keeps taking off his glasses? Because he thinks he looks better without them? I get a pit in my stomach just thinking about it.

"Of course not," I say, annoyed. I can't deal with this lunacy right now. My day has been awful enough as it is. I go back into the kitchen and rinse my towel out in the sink. "So where's your mom?" I ask. I'm desperate to lighten things up a bit and get back on the we're-just-friends track. What better way than a mention of good old mom?

"Palm Beach," Simon says. He's followed me back into the kitchen and is leaning up against the doorway, watching me as I rinse the towel out in the sink. "I have the place to myself for a couple weeks. I'm flying down to visit her this weekend, but maybe next weekend we can do something," he says. "Order in dinner and watch a movie or something."

"Only if you promise to wear your glasses," I say.

Simon starts to laugh and I can tell he thinks I'm joking. But I'm not. And just to let him know I'm serious, I pick his glasses up off the counter and put them on his face. He starts to take them off, and I grab them and try to hold them on, and he is saying "No, really," and I'm yelling "No, really," and we each have both hands on his glasses, which is not an easy thing to do, and finally I say, "Simon, I'm going to pinch you!" and then he stops fighting because if there's one thing I'm good at, it's pinching.

nine

ad-lib (verb): to improvise.

There are some days when it just seems like the stars are lined up against me. And today is turning into one of those days. First, my mom had to be at work early so she wasn't there to make certain Lucy and I didn't sleep through our alarm. (Which we did.) Then, I put on my brand-new blue shirt from the Gap and discovered that it had a big stain smack on my boob from paint that I had dripped on it during production class last week, and finally, Annie called from the school and said she heard it was official: Drew Reynolds was to be the director of the spring musical. Call me an eternal optimist, but as I arrive at school, I'm still not ready to lock myself in my room and call it a day. As I finish climbing the marble staircase, I see something that makes me question my optimism. George Longwell is standing in front of my locker, waiting for me.

The sight of him makes me choke on my charcoal toast. I do

the only thing I can think of. I turn on my heel and head right back down the steps.

But it's too late. He's already seen me. "Megan," I hear him call. "Wait up."

I stop at the landing, turn around, and open my eyes wide in mock surprise. "Oh hi," I practically shout.

"I've been waiting for you," he says, jumping down the steps, two at a time.

"Oh . . . Oh you were? Oh, wow. Yeah. How about that? I was going to go to my locker but then . . ."

But then what? I saw you and I thought how what I really wanted to do was run screaming in the other direction as fast as my feet would take me? "But then I realized I already have my pre-cal book."

"I'll walk you to class," he says.

"That's okay," I say, quickly. He raises his eyebrows and it looks like (at least I think it looks like) he's a little hurt. "I wouldn't want you to be late on my account," I say.

"It's worth it," he says. "Besides, I'm a senior. What can they do?"

"Ha-ha! Right!" I reply. And then even though I totally *hate* it when Lucy giggles, I hear myself make the same sound. Giggle. And then again. And again.

"A group of us are going to the Cross Street Market for lunch today and I was wondering if you wanted to come with."

"Um, I can't. I have . . . plans with Simon."

"How about blowing old Simon off?"

"I brought lunch," I say, motioning toward my backpack. God forbid I waste that great turkey sandwich, especially when Mom told me two days ago I had better finish the turkey up because it was starting to smell.

"Rain check then." He jumps the last step and stands in front of me, blocking my path. "I'm not leaving until I get one."

"A rain check?" I ask.

"Alrighty then," he says with a smile. "It's a date."

Say what?

I'm on my way to English class when I see Drew and Lucy huddled together, deep in discussion. For the second time that day I change directions rather than deal with the consequences. And for the second time that day I'm not quite fast enough.

"Megan," Lucy says, cheerfully waving me over. "Drew and I were just discussing the spring musical," she says.

"Oh yeah," I say, my attention focused only on Lucy. Maybe if I don't look at Drew ever again my heart will stop hurting. Eventually. I hope. "Congratulations," I say politely as my eyes inadvertently glance toward his.

"Thanks," he says, giving me a little smile.

My heart skips a beat.

I glance away. Damn! What was I doing looking at him?

"I'm trying to convince Megan here to audition for my one act."

"You *are?*" Lucy exclaims.

I forget all about my vow not to look at Drew and stare at him, openmouthed.

"Sure, why not?" he asks, opening his folder. He takes out a manuscript and hands it to me.

It's a play. *His* play. "Thanks," I squeak. I can barely breathe, not to mention speak. I glance at my sister as if to say, "Can you believe this?" But it is obvious from the major frown on her face that she doesn't share my happiness.

"All right Fletcher sisters," he says, "I have to get to class."

As soon as Drew is out of earshot, Lucy looks at me like I just sucker-punched her and says, "Why didn't you tell me he asked you to audition?"

I turn away from her, torn between a tiny sliver of guilt at having somehow played a part in upsetting her and a huge wad of excitement over the fact that Drew wanted me to audition. "I don't know," I say, glancing down at the play as if it is a ten-carat diamond. "I guess I didn't think he was serious."

"So are you going to?" Lucy asks, as we begin to walk down the hall.

Is that a tremor I hear in her voice? Don't tell me she's got a tremor!

"Going to what?" I ask, stalling for time.

"Audition for his one-act."

No doubt about it. It's a tremor. The tremor she gets when she's really upset. The one she gets when she's about to cry. This is so unfair. I know she's disappointed, since she thought Drew wrote the part for her and he so obviously did not, but still. "I don't know," I say.

And then I get it. A bolt from the blue.

"What do *you* think I should do?" I'm going to put my future and potential love life in her hands. I'm willing to bet that my sister's good-naturedness and her natural ability to share will put a stop to the tremor.

She looks stunned. "Well, you wouldn't be able to work on the set with all your friends if you were in the play."

No tremor. "Yeah," I say, even though her reasoning is total bs since "friends" really means one person: Simon. And he certainly isn't going to care.

"And besides, Habersham really prefers that the directors cast the senior drama majors."

I'm beginning to get a little nervous. I honestly thought she would have caved by now. "You were cast when you were a junior," I say, as I start walking faster.

"True but—"

"But I guess that was different," I say angrily, forgetting all about my plan to play it cool. I begin to walk really, really fast, so fast, I'm already three steps ahead of her. Ugh. Why had I even given her the power in the first place? So she had a tremor. So what?

"Megan, wait," she says. "Maybe you should try out anyway, just for the experience. And Drew asked you to, so why not," she says with a tiny bit of resolve.

I stop in my tracks. "Really?" I say.

"Really." She nods.

It's family dinner night. Before my accident I wasn't too crazy about family dinner night, because it meant Dad was home and his presence always guarantees a certain amount of tension. Even though Mom makes more money than Dad (and of the two of them Dad is the only one who knows how to cook), on family dinner nights, Mom is the one responsible for dinner. She sets the table and serves the food and then asks him a million times how his dinner is and if he likes it, as if she's slaved over the stove cooking it instead of double-parking the car outside a restaurant and running in to pick it up. Tonight she has picked up dinner in Little Italy, which just happens to be one of my favorite places on earth. Lucy and I help set the table and we all sit down.

"So . . . ," my dad says, helping himself to a gigantic portion of pasta. "Mom says you got asked to try out for a play today," he says, looking at me.

I steal a glance at Lucy. Even though Lucy has given me her blessing to try out for Drew's play, I can't help but feel a little weird. But to her credit, all her hesitancy about me auditioning seems to have evaporated. She's eating her rigatoni, seemingly unbothered by the topic. "Yeah," I say.

"Good part?" he asks.

"It's just for the senior playwright independent study. Not a big deal at all," I say as if I couldn't care less. "Lucy's trying out, too."

"What did you think of Drew's play?" Lucy asks me. As she knows, I read it the minute I got home from school.

"I think it's . . ." I stop myself. What I want to say is that I think it should get a Tony and an Oscar and the Nobel Prize. But instead I say, "Okay."

"Yeah," Lucy says, reaching for the block of Parmesan cheese and the grater. "There's definitely some problems, but I'm hoping he'll be amenable to making some changes."

I get it. *She* will make the changes *when* she gets the part. "The other day you said you thought it was amazing," I point out.

"Did I? I guess it's pretty good, for a rough. But there are some definite problems. Like the fact that the characters don't have names. What's with that? It's so confusing."

"I wasn't confused." There are two characters. One is referred to as "Guy." The other "Girl." Simple.

"These senior productions typically become a real partnership between the writer and the actor," she says authoritatively, ignoring me.

"That's interesting," Mom interjects cheerfully.

"I love the story though, don't you?" Lucy says to me, as she begins grating the Parmesan cheese. "There's kind of an ominous undertone. The heroine is definitely a little unhinged—the way she tries to seduce him into staying with her and stuff."

"She seduces him?" my mom asks.

"There's sex in this play?" my dad practically exclaims.

"No," I say to my parents. "It doesn't say that they had sex. It just says that they hooked up or, well, got together. And I don't think she's crazy."

"Got together?" Lucy says. "You don't think that means they had sex? They totally did."

Lucy has a point, which makes me think about Drew. I know he's a writer and this is fiction and all, but does the fact that he's writing about people having sex mean that he's actually had sex? Read: Did he sleep with Lindsey?

"For two," Lucy continues, "if she's not crazy, why is she sitting in the park by herself at night talking about vampires?"

"Vampires?" Mom asks.

"She's upset," I say to Lucy. "And I think that it's sad, not crazy. She thinks she knows him but she doesn't. She's in love with the, well, idea of him."

"Idea of him," Lucy grunts, ramming the cheese over the grater.

"There's vampires?" Dad asks.

"No," I say to him. "The play takes place at night when there's a full moon. The character of the girl makes a comment about how she's always heard that weird things happen on a full moon. And I think she only says that because she's trying to be wacky just because she thinks that will make her more interesting or something. She really likes this guy."

"She's nuts," Lucy says, grating even more ferociously.

"Lucy!" Mom says, motioning toward her plate.

Lucy stops grating as she looks down at the mountain of cheese on her plate.

"I think that's enough," Mom says. "Since when do you even like Parmesan cheese?"

"I want to hear more about how you're doing in school, Megan," Dad says.

"Well," I say, pausing to chew, "my teachers are a little concerned. I think they're afraid Jan wasn't up to snuff." Jan was my tutor last year. She looked like a smarty, but I think she took one too many whiffs from the glue bottle.

"Are you sure you want to try out for a play?" Mom asks. "Maybe you should just focus on your studies for a while."

Uh-oh. This is a potential complication I didn't expect. "I can handle it," I say quickly.

"Mom's right," Lucy says. "You don't want to overwork yourself. You want to be able to have some fun this year, too."

I give Lucy a look that signals her to mind her own business.

"Yeah," Dad says. "I bet you're going to have quite the social life now that you're—"

"Better," Mom says, interrupting him.

"So is everyone fawning over you now?" Dad asks. "I bet you and Lucy are the prettiest girls in the school!"

Before my accident, I would've loved my dad to say something like that (even though I would've known it wasn't true). But now it just makes me want to chomp on my nail. It's as if he's all excited and giving me credit for something that has nothing to do with who I really am. And it's a reminder of how he felt about me when I was ugly.

"A lot of guys are interested in her," Lucy announces.

"Really?" both Mom and Dad say at the same time.

"Guys?" I say to Lucy.

"George Longwell, one of the most popular seniors. He's a music major."

"Whoopee," I say sarcastically. "*One* guy: a music major who sings in a barbershop quartet."

"Barbershop quartet? Those guys who sing a cappella?" Dad asks.

"Bingo," I say.

"So you think he's weird?" Lucy asks, annoyed. "Is that why you keep avoiding him?"

"I'm not avoiding him."

"He said he could swear that you run away from him when you see him."

A piece of pasta lodges in my throat and I choke it down with a gulp of water. "That's ridiculous."

"He's really cute," Lucy tells my parents. "All the girls have a crush on him."

"If he's so great, maybe *you* should go out with him," I say to Lucy.

She puts her fork down and raises an eyebrow, flashing me the evil eye. "If you don't like him, maybe you should tell him to leave you alone."

"I don't even know him," I say, backing down a little.

"Well, all I'm saying is that it's going to be hard to get to know him when you're constantly running away."

I look at the piece of rigatoni loaded with sauce that I just stabbed and I'm suddenly filled with an overwhelming urge to fling it in my sister's face. "Can I be excused?" I say instead.

"We haven't even had dessert yet," Mom says. "I picked up some cannolis."

"Mmmm," Dad says, looking at me. "Your favorite!"

I put down my fork. For the first time in my life I am turning down a cannoli. I flash my sister a dirty look as I push back my chair. "I've lost my appetite," I say to her.

"What?" Lucy says innocently, looking at me. "What did I say?"

ten

melodrama (noun): a dramatic form that
exaggerates emotion and emphasizes plot
or action at the expense of
characterization.

I'm sitting outside the classroom where Drew's holding auditions. My head is pounding, my hands are shaking, and I'm pretty certain I'm going to throw up. Why in God's name am I doing this? After all, Lucy's right, they usually give the parts to the seniors. So why even bother? Why torture myself? Am I that much of a masochist?

I'm about to run screaming for the hills when Mrs. Habersham comes out to get me. I follow her into the classroom where Drew is waiting. He's sitting in the front of the room, reading his script. I can feel my knees start to shake as if they're trying to keep my shaky hands company. I really do not want to barf up the ham sandwich I had for lunch onto Drew's combat boots.

"Hey," he says with a smile, standing to greet me. "We're going to start on page four." He flips my script to the right page for me and points two-thirds of the way down the page. "With the line that begins with 'I remember.' Okay?"

I look at Mrs. Habersham. What is she doing here, anyway? I thought I would just be auditioning in front of Drew. I didn't think I would be auditioning in front of the head of the drama department. "Okay," I say.

I have to focus. I can do this. I understand this character. We have a lot in common. I'm a girl in love with a guy. And though I'm not as kooky as she is, I might just be as desperate. Besides, I've had the script for a week and I've read it so many times I've practically memorized it.

"Begin when you're ready," Drew tells me.

I take a deep breath and begin to read my first line: "I remember the first time we got together. You told me that I was special . . . that you had never felt like this about anyone before. That you loved me. Remember?"

"I remember," Drew says, reading the part of Guy.

"Was it a lie?" So far, so good. I take another breath.

"Of course not."

"When you first broke up with me I was so devastated, I couldn't sleep. I couldn't eat . . . I couldn't do anything. And then I thought . . . I'll be okay as long as he doesn't date anyone else. As long as I know his heart still belongs to me." I glance up at Drew. He's leaning against the desk, looking at me intently. I shiver as I say my next line. "When I heard that you and Wendy were hanging out, I told myself that you guys were just friends. And last night, when you saw me talking to that guy, I could see the pain in your eyes and I knew you were jealous. I knew you still cared about me. And then you touched my arm. Remember? 'I miss you,' you said."

Drew looks away from me, just like the script instructs. Even though the script calls for me to caress his arm, I'm so caught up in the moment that I grab it instead, yanking him back toward me. "You still love me," I say.

"But that doesn't change how I feel about us," Drew says, locking eyes with me. I feel a sudden tingle. It's no longer Guy who's talking. It's Drew.

"I can't . . . I don't want a relationship right now," he continues.

My lips are inches away from his. I'm thinking about the first time I saw him, the day I got lost on my way to the production studio. I knew right there and then that I wanted his attention more than I ever wanted anything in my life. I wanted him to *notice* me. Well finally, *finally*, he's noticing me. "So we won't call it a relationship," I say with conviction. I'm a girl obsessed, a girl possessed. "It's just about what feels good. And this . . . this feels good."

Time for the kiss. I'm breathing hard, ready to put my lips on his, ready to demonstrate just how much I love him, how much I've always loved him . . .

"Thank you, Megan," Mrs. Habersham says, interrupting me just as my lips are about to touch his. She smiles as she adjusts her glasses. "That was nice. Very nice."

I suddenly realize that I'm clinging to Drew, my arms wrapped tightly around his neck and my boobs pressed up against his chest as if he really is my boyfriend. Holy crap, what am I doing? I drop my hands and step back.

"Drew?" Mrs. Habersham asks.

Drew is standing still, staring at me. He looks a bit off-kilter, as if confused or surprised.

"What did you think?" Mrs. Habersham asks him.

"You were great," Drew says quietly to me.

Great. Drew said I was great. "Thanks!" I reply enthusiastically. I grab my backpack and escape out the door, a Cheshire cat–sized grin on my face. I did it. I read for Drew's play and I didn't pass out or throw up or make a fool of myself. It's all too good to be true.

"Hey!" Drew says, rushing to catch up to me. Although school ended an hour ago the halls are still crowded with students auditioning for the senior productions. I stop in front of the drinking fountain and wait for him.

"I just wanted to tell you that I'm totally impressed," Drew says.

My heart bangs in my chest, and even though I've never done one before, I feel like doing a high kick right here in the hall. "Really?" I ask, smiling so big it actually hurts. "It was your script," I say quickly. "Very powerful." Very powerful? What kind of drama-speak is that? I'm beginning to sound like Lucy.

"Are you ready for me?" Iris Mackler asks Drew, pushing in between us to get a drink of water. She slurps it up and then turns around to face Drew as she slides her thin wire-rimmed glasses back up her nose. Iris scored big-time as a freshman, nabbing the lead in *Medea*. Tall and thin, with long, greasy-looking blond hair, she's one of the best dramatic actresses in the school. It's bad enough having to compete against my sister. I have forgotten about all the other way more talented than me drama majors who are auditioning as well. The wind is going out of my puffed-up sails.

"In a minute," he says to Iris as he touches my arm, steering me away from her. I look down at his hand on my elbow and decide right then and there that in spite of the inevitable rejection it will still be worth it, just for this moment alone. "You read her exactly as I had envisioned," Drew says. "A lot of people have been reading her like she's crazy. You seemed to interpret her as more of a victim."

"I don't know if she's a victim," I say. "But I do feel sorry for her. She's in love with someone who doesn't exist." *Nice*. Smart sounding but not over-the-top enthusiastic.

"I had a feeling you would get it," he says. Drew smiles at me. This time, the tingle goes all the way to my toes.

"I should be getting back," he says. "We have a couple more people to see this afternoon and then we're all going to get together to discuss," he says, walking backward while he continues to face me. "We'll have the cast list up tomorrow."

"Megan!" I hear. I turn around and see George, waving frantically as he heads in my direction.

"I'll talk to you tomorrow, then," I say twisting back toward Drew. *I'll talk to you?* I sound so certain, like of course I'll be talking to him when he tells me I have the part. "Or whenever!" I call out quickly.

"Right," he says, as he and Iris head back into the classroom.

I feel as if I just drank a six-pack of Mountain Dew. I'm wired so tight my head might just implode any minute.

"Hello, beautiful," George exclaims, catching up to me. "Going to your locker?" I can't deal with George right now. I really can't.

"I'll walk you," he says, even though I haven't answered him.

"But first . . ." George grabs the umbrella sticking out of his backpack and poof, opens it right in front of me. Right in the middle of the hall.

"You know what this means?" he asks me.

He either has a tick in his eye or he just winked at me.

"Seven years' bad luck?" I say.

"Hah! Time for a rain check!" he exclaims. He narrowly avoids stabbing Catherine Bellows in the head with the umbrella as we begin to climb the stairs together. I say hello to Catherine but she ignores me, walking right past me without answering. I glance after her. What's up with that?

"Danny Warner is having a few friends over Friday night," George continues. "Come with me."

Danny Warner is a friend of Lucy's. Danny lives in a mansion in Roland Park and is known for his parties. I've been dying to go to one for as long as I can remember.

"I, ah . . . ," I say, reaching the top step. I stop when I see Simon waiting for me at my locker. Simon has made it pretty clear how he feels about George, and I don't relish the thought of getting the two of them together. As Simon looks at me standing underneath an umbrella with George, he rolls his eyes and crosses his arms.

"Come on," George is saying. "I'm not going to leave until you say you'll go."

What can I say? I'd love to go, but not with you? Besides, due to the stupid umbrella, people are starting to stare. There must be some giggly, hand-touchy way to get out of this gracefully, but I have no idea what it would be. "If you leave the umbrella at home," I say.

George pats his heart twice, just like I saw him do the year before when he asked Michelle Berkowitz to the fall festival.

"That guy is so annoying," Simon says, when I get to my locker. "What was that shtick with the umbrella?"

"He said he was cashing in on my rain check from blowing him off for lunch the other day. He asked me to go to Danny Warner's party with him on Friday night."

"What an elitist bum," Simon says, angrily. "He never noticed you when you were, well . . ." Simon stops himself.

"When I was *what*?" Excuse me, but was my best friend about to call me the u-word?

"Did he ever say hello to you before this year?" He shakes his head. "I hope you put him in his place."

"Well . . ."

"You're kidding me," Simon says, reading my reaction as a big, no-I-did-not-put-him-in-his-place.

"He caught me at a vulnerable moment. I panicked."

"All right, fine," Simon says. "So we'll go out on Saturday night."

Crap and double crap. I forgot that I talked to Simon about doing something this weekend. "Saturday night is my date night with my mom."

Simon looks like I just threw his favorite sneakers in the toilet. "So you're blowing me off this weekend," he says.

"No," I say. "I just need to . . ."

"Take a rain check?" Simon jokes. But it's obvious from the look in his eyes that he's not happy. "Anyway, how was your audition with *Drew*?"

Up until that moment I had every intention of discussing it in detail with Simon. But the sneer in his voice when he said Drew's name was unmistakable.

"Okay," I say simply. And amazingly enough, Simon lets it go at that.

When I get home, I go straight to the kitchen and start rummaging through the cupboards, looking for something good to eat.

"Hey," Lucy says, walking into the kitchen with her purse swung over her shoulder.

I find an unopened bag of pretzels and another of Oreos. I decide that I should start with the least caloric snack first. "All right," I say. "I was nervous." I rip open the pretzels.

"Did Drew say anything? Give you any clue as to what he thought?"

"Not really." I practically gag on the dry lump of pretzel as I swallow it. I twist around and grab the package of Oreos. My dad was buying double-stuffed for a while, which I'm not crazy about since I find them too sugary. These are the original single-stuffed, the kind I prefer. "How did yours go?" I ask, as I rip them open.

"Fine," she says. "Great."

"Good," I say, crunching down on an Oreo.

"Well, I guess I'll see you later," Lucy says casually. "Marybeth invited me out to dinner with her parents."

"But it's your turn to cook," I mumble, my mouth too full of Oreos to speak clearly.

"Sorry," she says. "I'll cook tomorrow night if you want."

It's obvious that she is still mad at me. And I feel a little guilty, like maybe her anger is justified. Like I have done something wrong. But what have I done? After all, she gave me the go-ahead to audition.

"Oh, by the way," I say, trying to sound excited. "George asked me out for Friday night."

My telling her about George is a peace offering. After all, I would expect this news to please her since she's been pushing for me to go out with him.

"Oh, that's nice," she says, heading toward the front door.

"We're going to Danny Warner's party."

"Should be fun," she says, opening the door.

I put down the bag of Oreos. "Lucy," I call out.

"Yeah?"

I hesitate. "Is everything okay?"

"Fine," she says impatiently. "I just don't have time to chat. I have to meet Marybeth in twenty minutes."

I don't believe her but instead of tackling her in the doorway and forcing a confession and a sisterly hug, I go back to my Oreos. After all, everything will go back to normal tomorrow when she finds out she has won the part.

I'll be disappointed, but in a way, it'll be a relief.

eleven

upstage (verb): to overshadow another
performer by moving upstage and forcing
the performer to turn away from
the audience.

Even though I try to go to sleep before Lucy, I'm still awake when she crawls into bed. I know Lucy knows I'm still awake because my eyes are wide open, but neither she nor I say a word to each other. Up until two days ago, Lucy and I never went to sleep without wishing each other good night. I didn't really think much of it when we missed the first night, but I was a little bothered by it the second time it happened, and now I find myself extremely agitated by the realization that we might never wish each other a good night again. And that would really stink because what kind of sisters went to sleep without wishing each other good night?

"Good night," I say.

"Good night," Lucy says softly, just like always.

But I still don't feel any better. I lie there, staring at the ceiling, listening as Lucy's breathing becomes more and more regular. I find myself a tiny bit annoyed by the way Lucy so easily drifts off to sleep. She doesn't really seem to be anxious or nervous about the cast lists at all.

I twist around in my bed, push myself up on my elbows, and peek over my white iron headboard at Lucy. She is wearing her pink tank and boxer set pajamas and her long silky hair is splayed out over the pillow. Even when she's sound asleep, she looks like a doll.

I puff up my pillow and flop back down, my arms crossed over my face as I try and breathe through the stent in my right nostril while feeling sorry for myself. Before my accident, I couldn't sleep if my nose felt the least bit stuffy, and now I have to go to bed with what feels like a piece of macaroni jammed up my nose every night.

I spend the next five minutes keeping pace with my sister's long, even breaths, but it doesn't help one bit. I can't compete, not even in the breathing department.

I get out of bed and walk into the bathroom. As I turn on the light, the sight of my reflection in the mirror catches me off guard. The doctor had told me it would take me awhile to get used to it, but it's been nearly two months and I still feel like I stole someone else's face. I raise my head, getting a bird's-eye view of my nostril as I pull the stent out of my nose. I set it on the edge of the sink and lean over it so I can be closer to the mirror. I touch my fingers to my forehead, trailing them down my cheeks to my chin. I look straight into my own eyes and think: *Who are you?*

What would my old face say if it could see me now: wracked with nerves and unable to sleep? It would probably say something smart-alecky like, Boo hoo, cry me a river. But my new face knows something my old face doesn't. So I consider my equally smart-alecky reply as I stick the macaroni back up my nose. Cry you a river? I say to my old face, but before I can make my snappy reply, I burst into tears.

And then the stent shoots out of my nose.

The cast list goes up at the end of the school day. I'm on way to the auditorium to see Lucy's name on Drew's cast list when I pass Lucy's friend Jane Hitchens in the hall. "Congratulations," she says politely.

"For what?"

"Drew's play," she says.

Suddenly, I'm running as fast as I can. I get to the auditorium and elbow my way through the small crowd gathered around the cast lists, frantically searching for Drew's list. And there it is. Right smack in the middle.

THE END.
GUY: DREW REYNOLDS
GIRL: MEGAN FLETCHER

My heart catches in my throat as I turn, glancing across the hall toward the production studio, looking for someone with whom to share my excitement. *I did it! I finally did it!*

"Hey, Megan," Marybeth says. "Congratulations."

"Thanks," I say. *I got the part! I got the part!* I don't think I've ever felt this way before. I feel so full of love, happiness, and joy that I want to scream from the rooftops, draw hearts and flowers on all my notebooks, and throw my money up to the sky.

"Um . . . ," Marybeth says, motioning toward my nose.

I grab a tissue out of my pocket (I always keep a stash, just in case) and swipe it across my nose. I'm so happy, I'm crying through my nose.

"Does your sister know yet?" Marybeth asks.

And just like that, my nose dries up.

I remember how content Lucy looked last night in her sleep. How peaceful. "I don't know," I say to Marybeth.

"She's going to be bummed," she says, half under her breath.

"She saw it," says Maria, another one of Lucy's close friends.

"How'd she take it?" Marybeth says, wrinkling up her nose like she just smelled something stinky.

"She got cast in Russell's play. But she's still pretty upset."

"Have you seen her?" I ask.

"I think she said she needed to get something from her locker."

I hurry back upstairs and toward Lucy's locker. I'm not sure what I'm going to say to her, but I'm hoping it will come to me when I see her. One thing I'm sure of: I have upset the natural order of the world and I'm about to pay penance.

I turn the corner and stop. At the far end of the hall is Lucy. In spite of what I have just heard, she doesn't look upset. In fact, she's smiling. But she has a reason to smile. Drew is with her and she is resting her head on his shoulder.

I quickly turn and head in the opposite direction. How could I think for one minute that I could win in a duel with my sister? Even now with my new face, there's no way I can compete with Lucy's charm and effortless grace. I may have won the part, but she would win the guy.

I'm halfway home when my phone rings.

"Hey, kiddo," my dad says casually when I answer, as if he always calls me that. "Mom said congratulations are in order. It didn't take you long to spring to the top of the heap, did it?"

I'm sure this is meant as a compliment, but this whole my-dad-likes-me-now-that-I'm-pretty thing is very annoying.

"It's not like a big, huge deal. It's for the senior playwriting independent study. There are going to be five productions."

"Don't minimize it," he says sternly. "You've worked hard for this."

Not really. At least, not in terms of studying the craft of acting. The only thing I've done was have plastic surgery to improve my face and lose an inner tube of blubber, which I guess, according to my dad, counts.

"Wow! Must feel great, huh?" he continues, obviously waiting for me to jump up and down or something.

"To be honest . . ." Wait a minute. I'm going to be honest with my dad? I must have leaked a little too much cerebrospinal fluid. "I'm a little creeped out."

My dad is quiet for a minute as if he doesn't know what to make of my reaction. "Yeah, well, good for you. We'll all have to go out and celebrate when I get back."

I think about Lucy. I can't imagine she will be in the mood for much celebration. And after seeing her with Drew, I don't really feel like celebrating, either. "Um, well . . . ," I begin.

"Where do you want to go? Your choice. How about the Bicycle?" he says, mentioning one of the most expensive restaurants around.

"Actually, it's kind of awkward because Lucy tried out for the same part."

"Mom said she got a part in another play, though."

"Yeah, but . . ."

"This is the first time you've tried out for anything. And you got a role. I'm sure Lucy's happy for you."

It's obviously a lot more complicated than that, but I don't feel like getting into it with my dad. And so I say, "Yeah. Sure."

"I'm sure this is just the beginning. All the guys are going to be fighting over who gets to cast you in their play."

When I get home, the house is empty. The first thing I want

to do is eat myself back to fatness to spite my father and bring back some normalcy. Lucy, I imagine, is still talking to Drew, giving him the guided tour of Lucyland, which is something like a Disney creation—she's the cartoon princess with birds chirping all around her, and midgets and mice and orange-faced Oompa-Loompas sing songs about her in this crazy high pitch, and the fat kids end up in the chocolate river. Drew is hers forever, the whole thing tinged with an edge of wicked stepmother cruelty because of the brief bit of hope I was allowed.

And to make matters worse, Simon hasn't called me back yet. And to add insult to injury, it's absolutely freezing in here and I really, really hate to be cold.

I walk upstairs and open the closet door, careful to keep Lucy's stupid dollhouse up with my foot. I glance at my reflection in the mirror on the inside of the door. I think about what my dad said about all the guys wanting to cast me now because of the way I look. I know he meant it as a compliment, but I didn't quite see it that way. I wanted to think that I had won the part because I was the best person for the role. And even though I really, really wanted this part and should probably be kissing the mirror with appreciation (if what my dad said is true), I feel a little embarrassed, like in fifth grade when I used a dictionary for an English test when (unbeknownst to me at the time) I wasn't supposed to and got an A. I gently nudge it back in the closet, holding it in place with my foot as I thumb through the sweaters, looking for something to put on. But they all seem too formal or something, like a costume. I just want something comfortable that I can get swallowed up in. I glance at the black bag marked SALVATION ARMY. I want one of my old hoodies.

Lucy walks in the house about twenty minutes later, carrying a grocery bag. "What are you wearing?" she asks, stopping and nodding toward my hoodie.

Odd. I have just upset the natural order of the world and the first thing out of her mouth was in regard to my choice of clothing? "I was cold," I say simply.

"Did you check to make sure the heat is on?" she asks, walking right past me.

Lucy is acting as if it's just another day after school, which is totally freaking me out. "Um, yeah," I say, following her into the kitchen.

"I got you something at the market." She sets the grocery bag on the kitchen table and pulls out a box of doughnuts.

She got me doughnuts? What in God's name is going on here? "Thanks," I say.

"Congratulations on the part," she says, as she begins to put the groceries away.

"Oh, thanks." I stand still, holding on to my box of doughnuts.

"I'm really happy about the way things turned out. Drew was so wonderful about everything. He explained it all. Apparently Russell was just like insistent that I be in his play." She shrugs her shoulders. "I would've preferred Drew's, of course, but they're buddies so . . . *comme ci, comme ça.*"

I get the gist. It's not like I won the part fair and square. Lucy won both roles and the directors drew straws.

"But this will be fun," she says a bit tightly. "Two sisters, both in senior productions."

Sure, I think. *Fun. Fun like jumping into an ice cold pool of water, fun like tearing off a scab, fun like getting your eyebrows plucked, fun like having a flock of birds pluck out your eyes, fun like being set on fire and shot out of a cannon.*

"Yeah," I say, nodding my head as I open up the box of doughnuts. "It'll be a regular old funhouse around here."

twelve

I have always wondered what it might feel like to be cast in a starring role. I imagined that the minute the cast list was announced I would be immediately transformed into a star, parading through school with an almost halolike glow over my head as a wind machine blew my perfectly straight, blown-dry hair behind me. I'm wearing a shiny sequined outfit and (for some reason) twirling a baton. I'm surrounded by secretly jealous well-wishers who I would immediately charm by my grace and modesty. "Oh thanks," I would say casually. "I was *shocked* to get the role because from what I heard, *you* were fantastic!"

Unfortunately, I don't have a portable wind machine or a flunky to drag it around in front of me. And my hair, due to impending rain, is a giant mass of frizzy curls. And because the jeans that Lucy had assured me were ultracool and extremely flattering are starting to feel tight, I'm at school the day after the cast lists were posted wearing my more comfortable but not nearly as flattering Levis, so maybe it's a good thing—unlike in my fantasy—no one seems to care that I have landed the starring role in Drew's play.

And it's also probably good that I'm not surrounded by well-wishers, because I don't exactly feel full of grace. Maybe it's the three doughnuts I polished off the night before, maybe it's the fact that Lucy acted like Drew had thrown me a bone, maybe it's the fact that Simon hasn't returned a single one of my million messages, maybe it's the fact that I'm not a hundred percent sure I won the part fair and square, maybe it's the fact that I had to get to school early to finish up my work in the production studio and am currently covered in sawdust and wearing protective goggles that cover half my face and make me look like I'm preparing for an underwater expedition (instead of what I am doing, which is cutting a straight edge on a foot-long board with a table saw), but I am pretty much graced out.

"Hey," I hear a voice say as I feel someone tap me on my arm.

It's Drew. I lose my concentration, causing the board to go veering off course and spraying him with sawdust. I narrowly miss my finger and avert disaster by turning off the saw. I turn toward Drew, my heart racing.

"Sorry if I scared you," he says, casually brushing the sawdust off his black, short-sleeved T-shirt. "I guess I should know better than to sneak up on a girl wielding a . . . whatever that thing is."

"Circular saw." I'm staring at the muscles in his arm. They're totally defined but not like the gross guys in the fitness-machine ads who drank one protein drink too many.

"I just wanted to congratulate you, since I didn't get a chance to do it yesterday."

I look away from his muscles and into his deep blue eyes. I wipe my suddenly sweaty hands across the front of my jeans. "Oh, thanks."

"We should exchange e-mails and stuff. Anyway, the first practice will be on Monday. I'm not sure what the schedule is yet for the auditorium, but we're going to be trading off with the other groups. When we're not in the auditorium, we'll be in a classroom. And you're familiar with the performance schedule, right? The performances are the week after the fall festival. There's one play each night, Monday through Friday. We're up first, Monday, October sixteenth."

"Okay," I reply.

He picks up the board I just cut in half. "Wow, that's a pretty intense machine."

"It's good for cutting long straight edges. And those over there," I say, pointing to the next table, "are jigsaws. We use them for cutting shapes."

"Cool." Drew pauses a beat and for a moment I'm afraid he might just keel over from boredom. Why am I talking about saws when he's just trying to be nice?

He holds up half of the board and says, "So, you could make this into a star if you wanted to?"

The board he's holding is actually my homework assignment

(which was to make two five-inch clean cuts), but I couldn't care less. If Drew wants a star, I'm going to give it to him.

I take the board from him and say, "Sure."

He follows me over to the table saw, standing beside me as I turn it on. I haven't actually cut a star before, but I have cut a triangle. How much harder can it be? "Damn," I say, as the blade runs off the wood.

Drew touches my arm, causing a tingle to run down to my fingers. "Don't worry about it."

The tingle only makes me more determined to impress him. I pick up the other piece of wood. "I can do it."

I look from the board to the machine, giving myself a pep talk as I plot out my strategy. I turn the saw on and five minutes later, he has his star. "Here you go," I say, handing it to him.

"Are you always so determined?" he asks, his blue eyes twinkling. I watch as he touches his finger to a sharp point on the star. I don't care that I'll have to do my homework assignment all over. I have impressed Drew, which was well worth it.

Our eyes lock and we both stand there for a minute, just looking at each other. I twirl my finger around a loose strand of hair and pull it across the top of my mouth, like it's a mustache.

"I guess I should get going," Drew says. "I'll see you later, though, right?"

"Later?" I ask, dropping my mustache. I thought he said our first practice was on Monday.

"Danny's party. Lucy said you guys were going."

"*You're* going?" I ask.

"Thought I might," he replies nonchalantly.

"Great," I exclaim. Up until now, I haven't been looking forward to Danny's party, simply because of George. But he no longer matters. What matters is that I'll get to see Drew.

Drew gives me a nod and grins. Only after he's gone do I realize that I'm still wearing my protective goggles. I make a mental note to take them off before the party.

I experience a Drew-inspired high that lasts all the way until third period, Mr. Lucheki's sound production class. Even though it's in the auditorium and there's only twenty of us in the class, Simon and I always sit in the same seats: J 19 and 20. But today Simon arrives late, and instead of sitting in his regular seat next to me, he takes a seat by the exit, directly behind Catherine and her new best friend, Laura, a freshman techie who all the guys are gaga about.

Simon doesn't even look at me and I can tell he's trying to avoid my eyes. What is going on here? No congratulations on the part, no I'm happy for you . . . zilch.

Even though he's been acting weird lately and I probably shouldn't be surprised, I am. After all, he, more than anyone else in this school (besides Lucy), knows how terrible last year was for me. He, more than anyone else, knows how badly I want to act and how much this part means to me. And he, more than anyone else, knows how I feel about Drew.

After class Simon doesn't wait for me. Even though we always walk to lunch together, he takes off like a jackrabbit the minute it's over. And that's when I realize that he's a class-A jerk.

I return my books to my locker and pull out my lunch, growing angrier by the second. I march into the cafeteria where I spot Simon eating by himself in a corner trying hard to pretend like he doesn't see me. I tighten my grip on my lunch bag and head straight toward him. He looks up, surprised.

"What's going on?" I ask angrily.

"I . . . ah . . . well . . ."

"Why didn't you return my messages?"

"Sorry," he says. "I meant to but I just got busy."

Busy. Suddenly my anger is replaced by an ache deep inside and I'm blinking back tears, struggling to keep it together. The last thing I want is to start bawling in the middle of the cafeteria. "I just . . . I was surprised I didn't hear from you, that's all."

"Oh . . . ," Simon says. "Sorry. Congratulations on the play."

"Thanks," I mumble. I take the seat across from him and discreetly wipe my nose with my napkin before opening my sandwich bag and pulling out my breadless "sandwich" (a piece of rolled turkey), a punishment for all the doughnuts I've consumed.

"I volunteered to work on the set," he says.

"You did?" I ask, surprised. From the way Simon has been behaving, I would've thought that he didn't want to have anything to do with Drew's play.

Catherine and Laura pass by our table. Even though I wave at both of them, only Laura waves back. "I'll see you after school," Laura says to Simon as she walks past.

"Laura's going to do the set design with me," Simon explains as he watches them walk away. No wonder Simon volunteered to do Drew's set. He is doing it to be closer to Laura, not to be supportive of me.

"I have to go," he says, making a point of checking his watch. "I have an appointment with my ophthalmologist." He scoops up his lunch and practically runs toward the door.

I'm tempted to chase after him and tell him how he's ruined my whole fantasy. Instead I take an oversized bite out of my one-hundred-calorie apple as I blink back tears and look across the table at the empty space in front of me.

"Lucy?" I call out when I arrive home. "Lucy?" I repeat.

The house is silent. My heart drops as I slowly trudge toward my bedroom. Now I really wish I wasn't going out with George. The only bright spot to my date tonight (besides seeing Drew) was this fantasy I had about Lucy and I getting ready together. I've watched her get ready for parties with her friends a million times and it always looked like so much fun. Up until two seconds ago, I had big plans. Our recent squabbles would be forgotten as we laughed and shared secrets, rummaging through our closet, borrowing each other's clothes and makeup.

I walk into my bedroom and . . .

Ah! *Jesus!*

I jump backward, clutching my chest in fear. But it's not a burglar, nor is it a dead body. It's just Lucy lying on her bed, dressed in yet another velvet sweat suit (blue this time), reading *Backstage*, the New York theater magazine. Even though you could read it online and a subscription to a hard copy costs $195, Lucy had been getting it delivered pretty much ever since she could read.

"Hey," she says casually, not even looking up. "John Lloyd Wright just got cast in another play. I'm not surprised. He's so brilliant."

"You scared the crap out of me! Didn't you hear me calling you?"

"I said hello back," she says.

"You must not have said it very loud," I say.

She just shrugs.

I take a breath. I'm about one hundred percent certain she's lying, but I don't want to get into an argument about something so lame, especially when I was so looking forward to being with her.

"I'm glad you're home," I say. "George is coming over in a couple hours."

"Oh," Lucy says, turning the page in her magazine.

Okay, she obviously isn't feeling very social and so I'm going to give her the benefit of the doubt and assume that she, like me, has a pounding headache. Maybe it's going around.

"So what do you think I should wear?" Even though it's not looking good, I'm still hopeful that she'll come around.

But Lucy just shrugs.

"Any ideas?"

"I don't know," she says, her eyes still glued to the magazine.

Okay, now I'm getting frustrated. "What's the matter with you?"

"I'm reading."

"You were the one who wanted me to go out with George. I thought you'd be happy for me."

"I am."

Ugh. I open our closet door and Lucy's dollhouse falls on my foot. I'm tempted to kick it off but in the interest of sisterly good-will, I bend down and gently place it out of harm's way. "Can I wear your pink shirt?" I ask (in what, for me at least, is a very sweet voice).

"Which one?"

I pull out the T-shirt she found on a clearance rack at TJ Maxx for ten dollars and wave it in front of her.

"That's my Michael Kors shirt," Lucy says.

I try not to roll my eyes. "Are you wearing it?"

"No," she says, as she begins to read her magazine again. "And neither are you."

Ouch. Someone less determined might retreat, but not me. "Why not?"

Lucy sighs long and deep, as if I'm asking if I can borrow her brand-new one-hundred-and-seventy-two-dollar jeans. "All right," she says finally.

"Forget it." I put it back on the hanger. "I'll just wear one of my old hoodies." Lucy *detests* my hoodies and I know the thought of her sister looking like a ragamuffin in front of her friends will inspire her to take action.

"Whatever," she says.

Lucy doesn't care that I'm going to wear an old hoodie on my date with George? "I just didn't think it would be such a big deal," I say, once again trying to bait her. "Wearing that Michael whatever shirt."

"It's not," she says simply.

I walk over to the foot of her bed and cross my arms over my chest. "Is this about the play?"

"What?" Lucy puts down her magazine. I've got her full attention now.

"The fact that I got cast in Drew's play and you didn't."

Lucy sits up straight. She angrily tightens her lips and squints her eyes. I can tell by her fiery expression that she's ready to dress me down. Not that I didn't think mentioning the play would incite a riot. Truth of the matter is that I know exactly what I'm doing. I'd rather have a fight than endure another day of this ridiculous silent treatment.

But I forgot that Lucy isn't the fighting type. "Oh please," she coolly replies. And then hugging her magazine to her chest, she walks out, slamming the door behind her.

I give the dollhouse a kick, causing the balcony to fall off. I throw the balcony in the kitchen and then shove the whole thing back in the closet.

thirteen

audition (noun): a trial hearing given to a
singer, actor, or other performer to test
suitability for employment, professional
training, or competition.

Up until now I have always wondered what the parties my sister
went to were like. One thing is certain. I thought they would be
a lot better than this.

Lucy and Drew aren't here yet so I'm sitting by myself on
a sleek leather couch in Danny Warner's giant house watching
George and a group of music majors belt out Broadway tunes beside a baby grand piano. They're each trying to sing louder than
the other, each trying to be showier and peacockier and practically head butting one another out of the way.

"Megan," George says, waving me over. "Come join us."

"No," I say. "That's okay."

"Come on," George says. He puts his hands together like

he's praying and puckers his lips like a baby. "Please. One song for George."

Ew. I hate baby talk and I especially hate baby faces.

I see him whisper something to Danny, who's playing the piano. Danny begins playing a different tune as George looks in my direction. He puts a hand on his heart as he begins sing: "*You are so beautiful . . . to me—dooooooon't you seeeeeeee? You're everything I liiiiiive for—*"

"Okay!" I exclaim, jumping up and raising my hands as if surrendering. This is worse than Chinese water torture. "I'll sing."

"What do you want to sing?" he asks me.

Everyone is silent, waiting for my answer. They look at me in this impatient sort of way, like they want me to hurry up and sing so they can get back to trying to be the next Hilary Duff or whoever.

"But first," I spit out. "I just have to . . . ah, get some water."

I make a beeline out of there and into the kitchen. I practically sigh with relief when I realize I'm alone. As the crowd in the other room erupts into a rendition from *West Side Story*, I pour myself a glass of water and glance at the bowl of chips sitting on the middle of the table. I was so nervous about my date that I didn't really eat much dinner. I did, however, eat two doughnuts when I got home, but as my father would've been quick to point out, doughnuts are loaded with fat, not protein. I gnaw on my thumbnail as I calculate the calories in my mind.

"Man, I hate these things." I hear a familiar deep voice say.

I yank my thumb away from my mouth and spin around. Drew is standing in the entranceway to the kitchen.

Just the sight of him makes me go weak in the knees. "What things?"

"Parties," he says, as he walks over toward me.

"Really?" My heart is clanging in my chest and the room is starting to spin. "I never heard of anyone who didn't like parties."

"Do *you* like them?" he asks, obviously surprised that some people might disagree.

I swallow back the lump in my throat as I try to think of a response that will totally wow him with my wit and intelligence. "I don't know . . . this one seems a little, well, maybe not so good. But I haven't been to many, to tell you the truth." *That's* the best I could do? That's the response that was going to wow him?

He crosses his arms and leans up against the counter, about an arm's length away from me. "You're lucky. They're all pretty much like this."

I'm breathing again, but after my last lackluster response, I don't trust myself to speak.

"I have a strategy. I try to find one person I can stand and talk to them until I'm bored. Then I wait a reasonable amount of time and I make my getaway."

"How long have I got?" I say, thinking out loud.

A smile forms in the corners of his mouth. "How much time do you want?"

Even though Drew is staring right into my eyes—something

he rarely does—I don't look away. "I don't know. I can be pretty long-winded sometimes."

Holy crap. Am I actually flirting? How can I be flirting when I don't know how?

Over the pounding of my heart I hear the music change gears as George starts to sing, "*Theeeeeeeere's a plaaaace for us, Soooomewherrrrrrrrrre a place for ussssss . . .*"

"You're funny," Drew says, smiling. He sounds a little surprised.

Funny. I'm funny. I try to think of something to say that would prove his compliment is merited, but my mind is a blank. Where's that hilarious retort when you need it? I'm so nervous the glass of water in my hand is actually shaking.

"Maybe we should find a quieter place. How about outside?" Drew nods toward the glass doors on the opposite side of the kitchen.

"Okay," I say breathlessly.

Still holding on to my glass of water, I wrap my arms across my chest in an attempt to hide my shaking hands and deafen the sound of my heart thwacking against my chest wall. He pulls open the French doors and motions for me to go first. I step outside. It's a warm fall night, nearly sixty degrees, but I wouldn't have cared if it were freezing. Drew shuts the door and looks at me. After all the noise inside it seems extremely quiet. Almost too quiet. And dark.

Drew gives me a little grin. It seems like he's still waiting for me to say something, something funny, something that reeks with hilarity, but what? My cheeks grow warm as I pretend to admire the little tiny landscaping lights twinkling in the yard. Funny, funny, funny. The only thing I can think of are the horrible jokes my uncle Stanley likes to tell at Thanksgiving.

"I thought you were long-winded," he says, resting his arms on the balcony railing and surveying the view right along with me. "You seem pretty quiet to me."

I drop my arms and lean over the balcony, balancing my water on the railing. "I'm trying to think of something funny to say," I reply honestly.

"You don't have to be funny on my account."

"That's good because all I can think of are 'your momma' jokes."

He raises an eyebrow. "Your momma?"

"You know, your momma is so fat people jog around her for exercise. Your momma's so old she ran track with the dinosaurs."

"Huh," he says, and goes back to staring into the yard.

Did I just tell Drew some "your momma" jokes from my uncle Stanley's Thanksgiving table repertoire? "I've got some other things, but they're not that funny."

" 'Your momma' jokes are hard to beat." Drew sounds serious, but his smirk is giving him away. "But give it a try."

He's so close I can feel his breath on my cheek. I don't look at him for fear that one more close encounter and I might fall over the balcony in ecstasy, dropping the two stories down and splattering across the stone patio.

"One is your combat boots."

"Go on," Drew replies.

"I noticed they're the same ones you wore last year. Does that mean your feet stopped growing?"

"Seriously, this is your subject?" he asks playfully. "Maybe we better go back to 'your momma' jokes."

It's all the encouragement I need. I look him directly in the eyes and smile. "The second one has to do with plays, since I know you like them. I was trying to think of an intelligent question so I looked through Lucy's playbooks, but I didn't come up with anything."

"You did this before you came tonight?"

I nod.

"You were trying to think of something to say to *me*?"

Uh-oh. I hadn't intended on admitting that to anyone, especially to him. "I just meant, well, we're going to be spending some time together because of the play and all and, well, I just wanted to make sure we had some things to talk about."

"That's sweet," Drew says, grinning again.

A car door slams and we both instinctively turn toward the sound. I can hear kids talking and laughing and even though we can't see them, I have a feeling it's more drama students arriving for the party.

"So what about you?" Drew asks. "What kinds of questions would I ask you if I was trying to make conversation?"

"Food." I immediately cover my mouth. Did I just say *food*? Oh man, I'm hopeless. "I didn't mean to say that. Ask me again."

"No take backs. So what's your favorite food?"

It's so ridiculous that I can't help but laugh. "Sausages."

Drew begins to laugh, too, and I'm filled with a surge of pride. "Can I ask you something?" I say.

"About my boots or my momma?"

"If you don't like parties then why are you here?"

It seems like an obvious question but I can tell from the surprised look on his face he wasn't expecting it.

"Good question. I'm trying to make myself do things because if I gave into my instincts, I would just be a hermit. And also because, well, sometimes I get lucky and find someone I really like talking to."

Drew is looking me in the eyes again. My spirit starts to soar right along with my heart. Is he talking about me? Am I the person who is going to make him lucky? Please God, *please*?

Just then we're interrupted by the sound of the glass door behind us sliding open. "Here she is!" George calls out, bounding outside to join us. He's out of breath and rivulets of perspiration are beading on his forehead. "I didn't want you to think I was ignoring you." George gives me a peculiar look. "Aren't you hot?" He reaches out and unzips my hoodie.

It's an intimate act, a boyfriend-girlfriend thing to do, and from the expression on Drew's face, it has not escaped his attention. Drew glances from George to me, as if he's trying to figure out what the connection is.

"Hey," Lucy says cheerfully to me, stepping out onto the deck. "I was wondering where you were!"

She gives me a big cheeser, like I'm the Mary-Kate to her

Ashley even though I haven't spoken with her since the incident in our bedroom and had no idea that she had even arrived. "Hey, Drew," Lucy says, turning her significant charm on him. "So what are you guys doing out here? Let me guess—shop talk! No more of that!" She playfully wags her finger at Drew.

Drew laughs as the two of them share a meaningful gaze. It only lasts a split second but it still counts.

"Can I have a sip of your water, babe?" George asks me. Drew raises his eyebrows as if to say "Babe?"

I want to push Lucy off Drew and tell Drew that I don't belong to George but instead I say, "Um, okay," and do my best not to look repulsed as I hand him my glass.

"Come on, Drew," Lucy says, giving him a tug on his arm.

"Come on where?" he asks.

"Jane found a Scrabble board. I need you and your dictionary." Lucy looks at me and says rather knowingly, "Drew always carries a dictionary." She turns back toward Drew and leans into him, flirtatiously reaching her hand into his shirt pocket. "Where is it?"

Question, tease, touch. I can barely stand to watch.

"Not there," Drew says with an uncomfortable chuckle.

"Where then?" Lucy reaches behind him and feels up his butt. "I got it," she says, pulling it out of his back pocket and showing it to us.

I think I'm going to be sick.

"All right," Drew says, grinning at her. "I'll be your partner."

I have to do something quick! Question, tease, touch.

Question, tease, touch! "You always carry a dictionary?" I ask. *Question!*

"Always," Lucy responds. "He learns a new word each day."

George takes a few loud and noisy gulps of my water, then wipes the dribble off his chin with his sleeve. "He's a writer. He likes words."

"Here's one," Lucy says, dodging out of the way as Drew tries to get his dictionary back. "Gemeinschaft," she giggles. "A spontaneously arising organic sexual relationship."

"What?" Drew smiles and takes the dictionary back. He holds it up to the light of the moon so that he can see. Even though Lucy was reading just fine in the dark, she leans in on him, her chest resting on his arm as she pretends to read it again over his shoulder. Much to my dismay, Drew doesn't jab her in the boobs with his elbow and knock her off the balcony. Instead he smiles and says, "Not *sexual*. Social. An organic *social* relationship."

"Oops," Lucy says with yet another flirtatious giggle.

She's good, I'll give her that. But it's not over yet. "I think dictionaries are cool," I announce in a really loud, unnatural voice.

Drew, Lucy, and George gape at me. "Oh really?" my sister says, in a smug tone usually reserved for sarcastic replies to our mother. "That's funny considering the only time I've ever seen you use a dictionary is when you put it on the chair and stood on it so you could reach the Halloween candy Dad hid from you in the top cupboard."

I stare at her, speechless. In one fell swoop Lucy announced to the man of my dreams that I was not only stupid but stupid with an eating disorder.

"We should probably get to that Scrabble game," Drew says quickly, as if he's aware that we're on the verge of a major sister slugfest.

"See you guys," Lucy says cheerfully as she follows him out.

George hands me back my water. "Here you go."

Even in the dark, I can practically see his saliva floating around in the remaining water. "That's okay. Keep it."

I follow George back in and sit by myself on the couch taking turns glancing from my sister and Drew playing Scrabble, to George singing at the top of his lungs, to my watch. By the time George asks me if I'm ready to go I feel like I've been sitting on this couch for hours instead of just one. I ignore my smiling and waving sister and shoot Drew a quick salute good-bye as I follow George to the door. I make a mental note to delete the photos my mom took in front of the fireplace when I get home, since I definitely do not want to remember this evening. Nor will I ever attempt to question, tease, and touch again.

During the ride home, George is subdued and quiet, obviously as anxious to get rid of me as I am of him. He pulls up in front of my house and stops the car. I put my hand on the door, but he stops me from making a quick getaway by saying, "Look, Megan . . ."

Even though I've never been broken up with before, I have

watched enough chick flicks with my mom to recognize a breakup speech. But this is totally unnecessary, isn't it? I figure I'll help George along.

"It's okay. I feel the same way."

"I'm glad," he says, grinning. "I don't know what it is . . . this thing between us. But I felt it from the first moment I saw you this year."

Um . . . *what?* This is not a breakup speech. This is a . . .

"I want to see you again . . . soon. Tomorrow night. I want to take you out to dinner."

What?! He is supposed to break up with me, not ask me out again. "No!" I practically shout. "I . . . I'm going out with my mom."

"Can't you get out of it?"

"No can do." Since when do I say *no can do*? I sound like my father.

"All right, next weekend then." Drew leans forward, puckering up.

Fortunately, I turn my head and his big wet one ends up on my cheek instead of my lips.

"Bye," I say, hurrying out of the car.

Minutes later I'm up in my room drafting an e-mail to Simon.

From: Megan Fletcher
Subject: Cancel the caterer

Simon,
Sorry to inform you that your

services as best man will no longer be
needed. The Longwell/Fletcher nuptials
are off.
Sincerely, Megan
P.S. You should probably return the
crystal candlesticks.

Within seconds, he writes back. Just like before.

From: Simon Chase
Subject: Re: Cancel the caterer

So sorry. Will happily cancel caterer
but warn that you may still have to
pay for five-tiered oversized cake your
former fiancé wanted to jump out of.
Or in.
Sincerely, Simon
P.S. They're glass.

fourteen

expressionism (noun): a style of playwriting
and stage presentation stressing the
emotional content of a play, the subjective
reactions of the characters, and symbolic
or abstract representations of reality.

"What are you doing?" Lucy asks.

I'm sitting at the breakfast table, eating my second bowl of Cap'n Crunch while continuing to work on the diorama I began at two in the morning. "I'm redesigning Simon's living room. See?" I swing the diorama around.

"That's not one of my shoe boxes is it?" she says, not even looking at it.

"I'm not sure." In fact, the shoe box had until last night been the home of her silver gray lace-up sandals that she bought last spring.

Fortunately, she's already distracted. "Did you sleep in your clothes?" she asks.

I shake my head. "No."

"You're wearing the same thing again today that you wore last night?"

"It's not dirty."

Lucy wrinkles her nose like she begs to differ and shakes her head as she opens the fridge. "I thought you were getting rid of all those old hoodies."

"They're comfortable." I take another bite of my cereal as I turn the diorama back toward me. I move the miniature baby grand piano (that I painted white to match Simon's mother's furniture) a smidgen to the side. Last spring, I bought a giant box of dollhouse furniture on eBay for thirty dollars. Simon had thought I was crazy to pay so much for it, but I had been putting all the furniture to good use. "That's better," I say out loud.

"So did you have fun last night?"

"Oh yeah," I say trying as hard as I can to make sure each word is oozing sarcasm. Lucy is only asking to be nasty. After all, I think it was pretty obvious exactly what kind of time I was having.

"I had a great time," she offers, even though I didn't ask. She pulls a Diet Pepsi out of the fridge and kicks the door shut with her foot. "Drew and I played like ten games of Scrabble. We annihilated everyone in the room."

My hands shake at the mention of Drew's name and I drop the couch. It bounces off my big toe and lands on the floor.

I bend over and pick up the couch. While I'm down there, I catch sight of my ugly-looking toenails. Yuck. Lucy and I both got pedicures and manicures for our first day of school, and even though I took the polish off my fingernails a million years ago, I haven't touched my toes. My cuticles are overgrown and the bright pink polish is faded and chipped.

"Anyway," Lucy says. "I wanted to tell you that after you left I was talking to Liz Hopkins, and she said she's never seen George so into anyone before."

"George?" I pick up the dental pick that I use as a tool on my dioramas and begin gently pushing back the cuticle on my big toe. "She must be kidding. He was so busy performing he barely noticed me."

"You sound upset," Lucy says with a knowing smile.

"What?" I stop pushing back my cuticle. "No! I'm just saying the whole idea of him really liking me is ridiculous. He doesn't even know me."

My sister shrugs. "Apparently he likes what he sees."

"Eech," I say, making a face as I go back to my toe cuticle.

"What?"

"*What he sees.* What you're saying is that he likes my new face and body. That's so, well, superficial. By the way, do you have any nail polish remover? I have to take this polish off. It's gross."

"It's under the bathroom sink," Lucy says, in her annoyed voice. "Look, Megan. You have to accept that you look different now. You better adjust. You can't keep acting like you used to otherwise people are going to start to hate you."

"What do you mean *acting like I used to?*"

"Don't take this the wrong way, but I just don't understand why you still seem to feel so sorry for yourself. I know that before the accident things weren't all that easy for you. But now you have a whole new you, and all these guys think you're hot, and you got a part that a lot of people wanted and here you are, still eating a million bowls of Cap'n Crunch, sucking your thumb, working on your dioramas, and picking your toes."

Picking my toes? "For one," I reply, sitting up straight as I set down the pick. "I'm taking care of my cuticles. For two, this is only my second bowl of Cap'n Crunch. For three, I don't feel sorry for myself. And for four, I don't suck my thumb!" How dare Lucy even insinuate such things? After all, she's the one who feels sorry for herself. She just can't seem to get over the fact that I, her lowly little sister, beat her out of a part.

But I don't say that. I really don't want to argue with Lucy anymore, and besides, I suspect she might have a small point. I am feeling a little sorry for myself. But I have a right to. After all, my sister and my best friend have recently gone loco. Anyone in my shoes would be upset.

In fact, I'm so certain I'm in the right, I pour myself some more Cap'n Crunch to soak up the leftover milk in my bowl and call the one person I know will agree, my mother. Even though it's Saturday, she left for work before I woke up.

"Hey, honey," Mom says, answering her phone. "I'm about to go into a meeting. What's up?"

Lucy walks back in the room, eyeing me suspiciously as if

she thinks I'm going to tattle on her or something. "I just . . . I wanted to know what movie you wanted to see tonight," I say loudly into the phone. "I can order tickets online."

"For when?" she asks.

"Tonight." I have been looking forward to my date with my mom. I have everything all planned out including where we will eat (Blue Agave) and what I will order (house salad followed by carnitas).

"Oh Megan, I'm sorry. For some reason I thought you had plans. I'm going out with Carol tonight. We're going to the Baltimore Symphony. They're playing Mozart's Requiem."

My mom made plans that didn't include me? "But I've hardly seen you all week," I say, sounding more like a five-year-old than a sixteen-year-old. "I have a lot to tell you."

"Hah!" Lucy murmurs, just loud enough for me to hear her. I roll my eyes at her and she shoots a smirk in my direction before leaving the room again.

"Sounds like we got our connections crossed," my mom says.

I honestly can't believe my mom, the one person who is supposed to be there for me in my time of need, is blowing me off. After a moment of silence she says, "Maybe I should call Carol and tell her I can't make it."

As much as I'm tempted to tell her what a fabulous idea that is, I keep my mouth shut while I think about it for a minute. Can I really ask my mom to cancel her plans just to hang out with me?

"It's okay," I say finally, forcing a smile even though she's not there to appreciate my effort. "I'm supposed to read *Moby-Dick* this weekend, anyway."

If she preferred listening to a funeral procession to going out to dinner with me, fine. I'm not going to feel sorry for myself. No way. I will stay home with *Moby* and read. And I will like it. But before I begin to read, I find Lucy's nail polish remover and use it to take off my toenail polish. Then I clip off all my fingernails and paint them with the rancid No More Nail Biting stuff she bought me last year.

After an hour of alone time with *Moby*, my nails are dry and I'm so desperate for company that I call Simon. I know it's a risky proposition because he was so angry with me for blowing him off, but he did respond immediately to my e-mail last night, so I'm kind of hoping that things have calmed down between us. I call him up and act like nothing weird has transpired between us whatsoever and ask him if he wants to do something. Even though I'm kind of expecting Simon to be busy (even though he's not), he acts totally normal and suggests we meet at the coffee shop at six.

Since I have about five hours to kill, I take my book and walk to the aquarium. *Moby* stays in my backpack while I watch his distant cousins the dolphins perform before heading back to Federal Hill to meet Simon at Spoons. Since Simon has paid the last couple of times we went out, I plan on getting there early so that I can get the drinks before he arrives. I'm feeling pretty good until I set foot inside the coffee shop. Simon is already there and has snagged a premium spot near the window. Even though I'm counting calories, he has an iced mocha cappuccino (with whip) waiting for me. To make matters worse, he's sans glasses and wearing a preppy boy costume.

"Why are you all dressed up?" I say, taking a seat across from him.

"I'm not dressed up."

"You're not wearing your shorts or your glasses."

"I'm not wearing shorts because it's cold and I'm not wearing glasses because I got contacts."

I take a sip of my iced mocha cappuccino. I want to believe him. I really do not want to think that his being dressed up has *anything* at all to do with me, but I have a nagging and mildly horrific idea it does. "I thought you said you couldn't wear contacts."

"I figured it was worth another try. My glasses were . . . beginning to annoy me."

"Well, you look good." I take another sip. I'm not a hundred percent sold, but if Simon says that his glasses were beginning to annoy him, I'm willing to take him at his word. The past few weeks have been totally stressful and I so badly want everything to be back to normal again. If I have to ignore a few things until they blow over, so be it.

"Thanks," he says, reddening. "And so do you . . . as usual."

Ignore it, I remind myself. After all, how could I blame Simon for seeing me a little bit differently these days? I *am* different. I now look like the kind of girl I used to secretly envy; the kind of girl with a face that wins attention and admiration from strangers; the kind of girl who has no idea what it's like to be mocked and despised, or worse yet, invisible. "So what did you do last night?" I ask, quickly changing the subject as I dab about twenty calories of whipped cream off my lips with my napkin.

"Laura came over and we hung out," he says. "She's really funny. You'd like her."

Even though I really don't know her that well, from what I have seen, she's not funny in the slightest. But I don't care about that. What matters is that Simon obviously likes her. And I really want him to *like* her—like her so he'll be happy, and we can get back to normal. "What did you guys do?"

"Not much. She came over and we played Monopoly."

"Sounds fun," I say, although I hate Monopoly. In fact, as Simon knows very well, I hate all board games. So it is probably good that he has found someone besides me to play Monopoly with.

He smiles at me again and glances away, as if he's getting ready to say something. Something uncomfortable. "About the other day . . . ," he begins. "I'm sorry. I'm happy for you about this play thing. I was just being a jerk."

I'm reminded of the scene from *Men in Black,* when the old man's head opens and there's a little alien sitting in there, manning the controls. Simon may be wearing a costume, but the same little alien is at the wheel. He is still my BFF.

"Look what I did last night." I reach into my backpack and pull out the diorama and the plastic bag with the furniture. I set the diorama on the table, place the furniture inside, and turn it around so he can see it. "Look familiar?"

"That's . . . is that my living room with the furniture re-arranged?" Simon asks. "That's great! Let's do it for real. My mom will totally freak. Can you come over tomorrow? We'll rearrange the furniture before she gets back."

"Your mom will kill you if you do it without her permission. But keep this and show her. If she likes it, I'm totally up for it."

He takes the diorama and smiles at me again.

Neither one of us say a word.

"Thanks again," he says, tapping the top of the diorama. "This is really, really great."

"It's not *that* great." His reaction is a little over the top con-sidering I've made him dioramas before and he couldn't have cared less. Like when I bumped my knee on his dresser and de-cided it was in the wrong spot, so I made a diorama of his bed-room with all the furniture rearranged. He looked at it for two seconds before telling me in detail why my design wouldn't work.

"I just want you to know that I'm happy for you—you know, about the play," he says. "I just, well, I missed you last year. I was kind of hoping that when you came back things would get back to normal. The Chase/Fletcher set design team would be in business again."

"I was looking forward to that, too, but this whole acting thing just kind of popped up out of nowhere."

"And it's *great*. Considering how much you used to talk about being a drama major." Even though Simon's trying to be supportive, his insistence is beginning to sound a little insincere. "By the way, I was sorry to hear about your wedding."

"I'm all broken up about it." I take my napkin and pretend to dab my eyes. "Hah! We couldn't even make conversation! It was so awkward it was painful. I only gave him one-word answers."

"Who can talk to that guy?" he asks. "He's so full of himself."

"I don't know. I wasn't any great catch, either. But when he dropped me off, he acted like we were made for each other. Get this: He told me he wanted to see me again and then he tried to give me a big wet one, right on the lips."

"You *kissed* him?" he asks, squinching up his face.

"My reflexes were too good. He got my cheek instead."

"The guy's a little thick," Simon says, picking up a napkin and folding it. "You're going to have to be blunt, otherwise he'll never get the message."

"I don't know if he's thick. He's in all AP classes."

"So what. He's still thick about other things."

"Well, what do I say then?"

"How about no thanks, not interested. Sayonara." Simon has turned his napkin into a little paper hat.

"I'll try," I say weakly.

"Jesus, Megan," Simon says, throwing down the hat in frustration. "You have to learn how to say *no*. Unless, of course, you don't want to." He shakes his head and crosses his arms as he leans back in his chair. "I'm beginning to think you got a little more than just Lucy's nose."

I feel as if he just slapped me. "What's *that* supposed to mean?"

"It means you've never been a girly girl. That's what's so great about you. You're just you. But you're beginning to act like Lucy with all this so-many-men-so-little-time stuff."

"I don't think Lucy has ever been like that. She's always had a lot of guys who liked her, but, still—"

"And now you're the one with the guys," he interrupts.

"Like *who*? George?"

"All the guys notice you now, Megan. Don't pretend that *you* don't notice *them*."

"Yes, I notice them, but I haven't figured out what to do with them yet. What am I supposed to do? I'm still the same inside, but it's like everyone around me has turned into aliens." I yank my napkin to my mouth and spit out the chemicals I just consumed while I was chomping on my nail.

But Simon doesn't say anything. He just sighs and looks away.

fifteen

antagonist (noun): the adversary of the
hero or protagonist of a drama.

After all the recent hubbub, I can really use some peace and quiet. Since Mom has to work (even though it's Sunday), Dad is out of town, and Lucy is not her usual chatty self, it is quiet. Very quiet. At least until I get an e-mail from George.

> From: George Longwell
> Subject: Thursday
>
> Hi B-utiful,
> Had a blast on Fri. Want 2 see u
> soon. Maybe Thurs? Dinner? G

"Oh God," I mutter under my breath.
"What?" Lucy asks. It's her night to make dinner and she has

just returned from picking up some ingredients at the store. She leans over my shoulder to read George's e-mail.

"I don't understand this," I say. "Why would he want to see me again? We had a terrible time."

"I told you he likes you. He wants to give you another chance."

"Ugh," I say.

"So tell him you're not interested. End of subject. Otherwise it's like you're leading him on, playing hard to get. And not only is that mean, it will just make him want you more."

"What am I supposed to say: I don't know you and I don't want to get to know you?"

"Of course not." My sister rolls her eyes as she picks up her brush and begins running it through her hair. Lucy is the only person I know who brushes her hair for no reason whatsoever. "How many times do I have to tell you this? You have to be diplomatic or else everyone is going to hate you. You can't keep acting like you're the same old ugly duckling, because you're not. You have to be extra special nice."

"*Extra special?*" I say, looking at my reflection in the mirror on the vanity.

"All I'm saying is that like it or not, you have something all these people want. And if you don't want them to hate you, you're going to have to turn on the charm."

Lucy is making this all sound so easy, but I know for a fact it's not. I know this because one time Marla Cooper, the prettiest girl in seventh grade, was totally nice to me one day and I found out later it was only because she wanted to copy my math homework. Everyone who looks like I used to look has a million stories like that and views people who look like how I now look with distrust bordering on disdain. And besides, as informative as all this is (not), it's doesn't help me with the task at hand. "So what do I tell George?"

"I don't know." Lucy puts down the brush. "But you'll have to think of something. By the way, I got you a box of chocolate-covered doughnuts."

What? Why would Lucy pick me up a box of doughnuts when we weren't exactly getting along? Not only that, this was like the fifth box of doughnuts she had bought me in the past month. Either the doughnuts were a peace offering or . . . or . . .

"Are you trying to make me fat?" I joke. But my question sounds more angry than funny.

Lucy looks at me, stunned. "You are *such* a psycho."

"I was only kidding."

"Don't worry about it!" she yells, as she stomps down the steps. "I'll just throw them out."

The kitchen is directly under our bedroom and I can hear some cupboard doors slam and then the TV turning on. I know I didn't handle the whole doughnut thing all that well, but in my defense, it is a little weird—she never bought me doughnuts until recently. So I pick up the phone and dial my mom's number, anxious to get her advice on how to apologize to Lucy. My mom doesn't pick up and I hang up rather than leave a message. I decide that it's in my best interest to give my sister a little time to cool down, so I slip on my black hoodie and go back upstairs. As I walk into my room I catch sight of my reflection in the vanity mirror. Why am I acting all wishy-washy about this George thing? I didn't look like the type of girl who needed help with her love life. I looked like the type of girl who should be hanging out with the Marla Coopers of the world, not doing their math homework. I focus my attention back on my computer, determined to deal with the George thing once and for all.

```
To: George Longwell
Subject: Re: Thursday
Dear George,
You are a really, REALLY great guy.
But I'm sorry—I can't make it on
Thursday night.
All best, Megan
```

I press Send and the message flashes off my screen. Totally relieved, I sit down on my bed and pick up *Moby*. But seconds later, I see I have a new message.

```
From: George Longwell
Subject: Re: Thursday
Sorry B. forgot u r busy. Friday or
Saturday. Take your pick.
G
```

Now what am I supposed to do? How can I get out of this without hurting his feelings?

I type a quick response:

```
Dear George,
Thanks, but I can't.
Megan
```

But I don't send it. I really want to get Lucy's take on this whole thing and if that means I have to eat humble pie, so be it. All this turmoil is giving me angina.

Lucy is sitting on the couch with her arms crossed angrily in front of her, obviously still fuming. I take one look at the giant frown on her face and realize she's in no mood for a sisterly hug out.

"What are you making for dinner?" I ask.

"You're on your own," she says, not even looking at me.

I want to ask her what she planned on making, thinking that if she isn't going to make it, maybe I will. "Thanks for the doughnuts," I say instead.

"I threw them out," she says.

I go into the kitchen and open the cupboard where we keep our trash. The doughnuts are there, right on top, never been opened, still perfectly good. I take them out of the trash and open the box. I put two doughnuts on a napkin and climb back up the stairs. I sit in front of my computer, take a bite of doughnut, and press Send. I don't need my sister's advice. I have a game plan. I will avoid George until he forgets about me.

I manage to avoid him all the next day, right up until 3:25 p.m., when (in my hurry to get to my first play practice) I accidentally turn down the hall where he has his locker and sure enough, he's right there, pretty much smack in front of me. I do an immediate (and obvious) U-turn. I see Catherine, and even though I'm in a total rush I go out of my way to say hello to her, but instead of saying hello back, she looks straight at me and kind of smirks as she walks away.

Excuse me? What was *that*? Although we weren't friends before my accident, we were definitely friendly. We have been in almost all of the same classes since freshman year.

But I don't have time to ponder my nonrelationship with Catherine. I glance over my shoulder and see that George is following me. Crap! I pick up my pace, practically running.

"Hey, Drew!" I burst into the classroom and slam the door shut with my foot.

"What's going on?" he asks, obviously startled by my grand entrance.

"Nothing," I say, as casually as I possibly can. I keep my back to the door as I unzip my backpack. Drew looks over my shoulder toward the window on the door and gives someone a nod.

"I think he's leaving," he says, his eyes shifting back to me.

"Who?" I ask innocently.

"Your boyfriend."

"He's not my boyfriend!" I practically shriek.

Drew raises his eyebrows.

"We're just . . . friends," I say carefully.

"Okay," he says as he looks back at his script.

Oh great. What a way to start my first play practice. This isn't exactly what I had in mind. What I had in mind was proving to him (and myself) that my looks were inconsequential. In other words, I was the best actress for this role. I turn back toward my backpack and pull out my script. George's voice floats through the room: *"Oh, it's time to start living, time to take a little from this world we're given!"*

"Pippin," Drew says quietly.

I turn around to face him. "What?"

"That song he's singing. It's from *Pippin*, the musical we did last year."

"I've never wondered if I was afraid when there was a challenge to take . . ."

"He's singing kind of loud," I say. "Do you think he's trying to impress you so you'll give him a good part in the musical?"

Drew rolls his eyes and laughs. "Man. He cornered me in the hall yesterday. He told me about this song he liked and he started singing it. He's like two feet in front of me and he's belting out this song. I could see right up his nose. I didn't know where to look." He's smiling, sort of to himself.

"I saw him singing to Michelle Berkowitz last year." I shrug, playing it cool. "At the time I thought it was really sweet, but . . ."

"She's a friend of mine. She was mortified when he did that. She didn't want to go with him but everyone was watching and she was too embarrassed to say no."

"I know the feeling," I reply.

Drew's lips curl upward as if . . . what? Is he relieved to find out that I'm not interested in George? Or am I just imagining that he looks relieved?

"He means well though," he says, glancing back at his script. The smile or whatever it was is gone and his face is once again unreadable. He looks like he did the first time I saw him: mysterious, emotionally distant, and totally smart.

And just like that, I forget all about George. I'm now thinking: *I am at play practice with Drew Reynolds! The door is closed and we have a script that calls for a lot of kissing!*

I swallow as my hands start to shake and my knees start to wobble.

"Take a seat anywhere." Drew is still focusing on the script. "I thought we'd begin by running the lines."

I settle into the chair nearest my rear end. My hands are shaking too badly to hold my script, so I place it on the desk and keep my hands in my lap where I clasp and unclasp them in rapid motion as I begin to read. I'm so nervous that I actually stutter, something I haven't done in years. Fortunately, the cool reserve Drew displayed only moments earlier evaporates as he adapts the patience and warmth of Mr. Rogers. After a while I start to relax. By the end, I'm even holding my script in my hands. It's easy to see why he was chosen to be the director of the spring musical. He's great. I wish I could say the same thing about me.

"Very good," Drew says when we're done. And then he smiles at me.

My heart must be having some sort of spasm because I can barely breath. I quickly set the script back on the desk.

Drew runs a hand through his hair. "I think you've got a good grip on your character."

He doesn't even know the half of it.

Suddenly, Drew unzips his backpack and starts gathering his things. This can all mean only one thing: Practice is over. Right now, I'm wishing I could fly around the earth like Superman and rewind time, just so I could stay with Drew a little longer.

Speaking of superheros, the theme from *Batman* emanates through the room. "My phone," Drew says, yanking it out of his backpack. "Hello?"

In a halfhearted effort to give him some privacy, I unzip my backpack and stuff my script inside, trying hard not to act like I'm listening to his every word, which, of course, I am.

"I'm finished now. All right," he says, checking his watch. "I'll be there as soon as I can. Give me an hour or so."

I turn back toward him as he flips his cell shut. I want to ask him who it was and where he's going to be in an hour but instead I say, "You like *Batman?*"

" 'Fraid so," he says bashfully.

"That's a techie thing." Drew looks a little confused so I explain. "Lots of techies are into *Batman.*"

"Really? I've got every *Batman* thing you can imagine. Everything but the Bat Alphabet Soup Container."

I laugh. "The what?"

"Nothing. Inside joke between us . . . *Batman* geeks."

Uh-oh. Does he think I was criticizing him for liking *Batman?* "You're not a geek."

Drew gives me sort of a sexy half smile and I almost lose consciousness.

"Are you okay?" he asks. "You're all flushed."

"I can draw Batman," I blurt as I try to steady myself.

"You can?"

I can't help but wince. Did I just brag about my *Batman* drawing skills?

"I took an illustration class and we studied some of the comic artists. My teacher said Breyfogle was the best Batman artist ever."

Drew's eyes open wide in surprise and his mouth falls open. "You know who Norm Breyfogle is? I love Breyfogle!" he practically shouts. I think it's the loudest I've ever heard him say anything. Then Drew checks his watch. "Crap, I gotta go. My stepdad is working late and my mom needs me to pick up some milk for the girls on my way home."

"The girls?"

"I have two little sisters. Cindy is two and Fergie is four. Believe me, I'd rather be here talking about Batman with you than at the grocery store."

"Me too," I say. And then I smile from ear to ear.

sixteen

physical theater (noun): a genre of
performance that relies on the body (as
opposed to the spoken word) as the
primary means of communication.

Tuesday. Normally, I don't consider a meal complete unless it
contains some hydrogenated oil, but as of 7:25 this morning
when my expensive jeans that Lucy said were ultracool and
looked great on me crossed the line from so-tight-they're-
uncomfortable to can't-zip-them-up, I've been on a diet. I'm op-
timistic that I will be fitting back into my jeans in no time, as the
diet I have chosen is pretty strict. I call it the Lucy diet. The
premise is simple: I eat whatever my sister eats and nothing else.
If Lucy chooses to have a half piece of her whole grain, no butter
on it at all toast, that's what I have, too. Whatever bits of lean
protein she packs in her lunch, that's what I pack, too. Whatever
few morsels she eats for dinner, that's my limit. Needless to say,

I've only been on the diet for four hours and I'm so famished I can barely stand up without feeling dizzy.

I told Simon I would wait for him (he was having problems with his contacts), so at lunch I take a seat by myself, facing the door. I grab my steno pad and pen and begin drawing my hundredth Batman of the day. It manages to distract me for a while at least, until my stomach growls so loudly it attracts the attention of the freshman techie sitting next to me, who begins to giggle.

I glance at my watch as I gnaw my thumb. (I have tossed in the towel and removed all the No More Nail Biting stuff since I was pretty sure that all the chemicals I was consuming were going to make me grow another head or something.) What in the world is taking Simon so long? I gather up my things and head toward the door to go find him.

"Hey, Megan," Jane Hitchens says as I grab the door. Jane is one of my sister's best friends. Like Lucy, she's a drama major and, like Lucy, is one of the most popular girls in school. "Are you done with lunch already?" she asks.

"No. I haven't even started yet. Simon got tied up."

"Have lunch with us," she says, nodding toward the table where my sister is sitting. None of Lucy's friends have ever invited me to sit with them before, and Jane's offer gives me a special thrill. I follow Jane to the table and plop down next to Marybeth, across from Lucy.

"Hi, guys," I say.

"What's up?" Lucy asks, obviously not happy to see me.

"Simon didn't show so I told her she should sit with us," Jane says.

"Where is he?" Lucy asks me.

I pull out my turkey rollup and apple and set them neatly on my napkin. "Contact problems," I reply.

"I almost didn't recognize him the other day," Marybeth says. "He has really pretty eyes."

We all look at her, startled by her confession. Does Simon have pretty eyes? They're brown, I know that.

"Hey," Marybeth says, pointing from my lunch to my sister's. "You guys have the same lunch. Cute."

Lucy looks from my rollup to hers. I can tell from the expression on her face she doesn't think it's so cute. "I have to go," she says.

"You just sat down a minute ago," Marybeth says.

"I have some things I need to take care of," Lucy says. "See you guys later."

"Adios!" I say, like *good riddance*. I feel like throwing my apple at the back of her dainty little head.

"What was that about?" Jane asks the rest of us as Lucy walks away.

Out of the corner of my eye I see Marybeth give a discreet nod in my direction. Lucy's departure has obviously thrown a wet blanket on the atmosphere. Even though Lucy's friends aren't exactly known for being quiet or pensive, the table is totally silent, the only sound coming from Marybeth munching on her carrots.

"So, Megan," Jane says finally. "How's everything been going for you lately?"

"Um, good."

More silence.

"You must be totally psyched," Jane says.

"Because of?"

She gives me a blank look. I can see we're about to play twenty questions so I begin with: "Because of Drew's play?"

Maria giggles. "No, silly. Because of your new face. Plus you got all skinny."

"It's got to be weird," Annie says to Maria before I can answer. "I mean, to go to sleep one day looking totally"—she makes a nasty face—"and to wake up all beautiful, it's got to be totally awesome."

"It wasn't quite like that—" I begin.

"I saw this movie once," Maria says, interrupting me. "It was about this girl who was all sweet and nice but so ugly she only has one friend, a guy who tries to protect her from this group of bullies who are always teasing her and making fun of her. One day she gets in an accident and becomes like, totally beautiful, and the gang of bullies all want to date her but she kills them all off one by one by chopping them up into little pieces and her friend has to kill her to stop her."

Gee. What a cute story. And so apropos.

Over Maria's shoulder, I see Simon sitting by himself, two

tables away. I'm not surprised to see that he's wearing his glasses again. His contacts have been nothing but trouble. Our eyes lock and he shoots me a pissed-off look before grabbing his tray and heading toward the cafeteria's industrial-sized garbage can.

What the hell?

"That's so funny," Marybeth says. "Because I was watching TV the other night and I saw this show . . ."

"I'll see you guys later." Angry or not, anything is better than this. I grab the rest of my lunch and hurry to catch up with him.

"Simon!" I call out. "When did you get here? I was waiting for you."

"Oh yeah," he says sarcastically. "I noticed."

"Hey, beeeeeautiful," I hear George say from behind me.

Simon looks over my shoulder at George and then at me again me, giving me a dirty look like (a) I just invited George over and (b) I did it just to make him even madder.

"I'll call you tonight," I say to Simon as he dumps the remainder of his lunch in the trash. He jams his hands in his pockets and walks away.

"I've been looking all over for you," George is saying. "You're harder to find than a needle in a haystack."

I really, really want to make a beeline out of there, and it takes every ounce of turkey-fortified energy to keep my feet planted exactly where they are. Lucy's right. I have no choice but to tell him the truth. And now's as good a time as any. The entire lunch period has stunk anyway. I might as well top it off with a bang.

"What are you doing next Tuesday night?" George asks.

On second thought, maybe I should stick to my original plan. "I'm . . . I'm busy."

"How about Thursday then? After practice."

I think about the line I have been practicing: *You're a really nice guy but I just don't see this working between us.*

"You're a . . . a great guy," I say stiffly. "It's just that, well, I can't see you anymore."

"Oh." George sounds surprised. "Are you, ah, seeing someone else?"

"No."

"I'm not asking you to be exclusive," he says. "I just want to spend some time with you. Get to know you."

It sounds reasonable enough. So how do I explain that I don't *want* to get to know him? "I'm sorry George. But I just . . . I can't handle this right now, okay?"

"Handle what?"

"Um . . . us . . . you and me . . . spending time together."

"Not now?"

"Not for a long, long, long time. Maybe never."

George's eyes drift down to his red tennis shoes. "I see."

"I'm really sorry," I sputter, as I turn and run toward the exit like the inexperienced coward I am. On the bright side, I haven't taken a hatchet to anyone. Yet, at least.

After school I head to the auditorium to meet Drew. This is our first practice onstage and I couldn't be more nervous if I was supposed to sing a capella on *American Idol.* I make my way through the backstage door out of habit since it's what we use when we're working on sets. But the minute I step inside I hear a cry so fierce and terrible, it makes my blood curdle. I stop still and listen while my flight-or-fight response kicks in. I hear it again, louder this time. Once again, the scream is followed by silence.

Holy crap. It's Lucy!

I race toward the sound of her voice, my body surging with adrenaline. *I'll save you, Lucy!* I'm almost relieved that after all this awfulness I have a chance to prove to her how much I love her. But as I hit the stage, I skid to a stop. Lucy's downstage center, looking perfectly cool and collected, making a notation in her script. When she's done, she tucks her pencil behind her ear, glances at sweet, gentle Harry Rice (the actor who's playing opposite her), screams: "Bastard!" and convulses into sobs.

All the senior productions deal with a breakup, and Lucy's character is a girl who is determined to fight for her man. But unlike my character (who pretty much throws in the towel with a minimum of drama), Lucy's goes bananas, actually attempting suicide. When I read the script I found it melodramatic and unbelievable, but I was wrong. Lucy seems so upset, so totally devastated, that if I didn't know any better, I'd think dopey, little Harry (who is rumored to have repeated fourth grade) just broke her heart. I hate to admit it, but Lucy is the star of the school for a reason. She deserves to be.

"There you are," Drew whispers, coming up behind me.

I learned a long time ago not to trust my instincts, which is good because otherwise I would tackle him to the ground and do whatever it takes to distract him from my sister's performance. Not that he doesn't already know how good an actress she is, but why remind him?

"I thought we were onstage today." I stand directly in front of him, effectively placing myself between him and the stage. Unfortunately, he's so tall that I don't even come close to blocking his view.

"My fault," he says. "I messed up the schedule. We have the stage tomorrow." Lucy sobs and Drew looks over my head at my sister.

His eyes kind of glisten and it's obvious he's totally, utterly transfixed. "She's good," he whispers.

My instincts are now telling me he's really wishing he had cast my sister instead of me and I'm tempted to believe them (just this once). "She's *amazing*," I admit.

"Come on." Drew nods toward the back door. "I brought something to show you."

I snap my head away from my sister, totally captivated by the excited tone in his voice. I follow him through the back door and out into the hall. I feel better as soon as I get away from the stage and can no longer hear my sister's voice. But then again, when I'm around Drew, I always feel as if I'm floating along on my tiptoes.

He leads me into the classroom where we met the day before, unzips his backpack, and pulls out a comic book wrapped in plastic. Hiding the cover from me, he opens the book and shows me a random page. "What do you think of the drawing?" he asks.

"I love it. It's Jim Lee, isn't it?"

"Yes!" he exclaims as he practically beams at me.

Until two seconds ago I never would've guessed how excited a comic book could make me. But now my hands are shaking and my heart is racing. It's hard to believe that only a few minutes ago I was so upset. It's almost as if Drew knew I needed some cheering up.

"How did you know?" he asks.

"I recognize Breyfogle's work, and I knew it wasn't him." I open my backpack and pull out the best of the one thousand Batmen I had drawn. "I have something to show you, too." I place it on the desk in front of him.

He places his comic book next to it so the two images are side by side.

"That's amazing," he says. "Did you copy this from something?"

"What?" Geesh. I wasn't *that* desperate. "No!"

"I'm sorry—I just . . . it's so good. Why aren't you a visual arts major?"

I swallow back a thick wad of pride. "I was just playing around. I thought about Batman and imagined a scene where he had to kick some butt, and that's what I came up with."

"I'll show you how I draw Batman," he says. As he reaches into his backpack, my heart skips a beat while the muscles in his arm flex and release. He grabs a pencil out of his back pocket and draws a stick figure complete with a triangular cape. He draws a bubble above the character that says, "Will you be my Catwoman?"

Is his Batman flirting with *me*? Is Catwoman code for girlfriend? I'm confused and excited at the same time, but I'm determined to play along. "Catwoman? I thought she was evil."

"Well, she's a villain, but they kinda, uh . . ."

"K-k-kinda what?" I stammer. It's really amazing that I'm still able to speak at all, because I feel as if something is wedged in my throat.

"Well . . . Batman gets all goofy around her."

He's getting red in the face so I stay quiet. Even though I find it hard to believe that Drew, who always seems so cool and collected, is actually capable of feeling such a simple mortal emotion like embarrassment, it's possible. After all, I hadn't pegged him as a Batman guy either.

"So, what do you think?" Drew motions toward his drawing. I know he's teasing me because of the twinkle in his eyes.

"It's not bad. I like the cape . . . you just need to fill out the legs a little. Maybe the arms, too. And the face."

"You're right. He's a little scrawny." Drew says, chuckling. "So where did you learn how to draw?"

I clear my throat in an attempt to calm myself. "I've taken a lot of art classes. Lucy was always taking drama and dance and I think my parents put me into art because I wasn't really into anything else. Or at least, I wasn't really good at anything else."

"What made you decide to study theater tech?"

How can I admit to Drew that the only reason I was a techie was because it was the only major that didn't require an audition? That if I had an ounce of my sister's talent I would have been a theater major? "I don't know. I didn't put that much thought into it."

"But you like it, right?"

"Yeah," I say, thinking about my dioramas and designing sets with Simon. "I guess I do." Oddly enough, I have never considered that before. It didn't seem to matter whether I liked it or not because I didn't have a choice.

"Well, I think you're really talented."

Drew smiles at me. I'm staring at his lips. They look so soft, and experienced. It seems like a heated moment where *something* could possibly happen and I'm hoping with every fiber of my being that it does. I'm looking into his eyes and he's looking into mine and I feel I'm about to melt when the unmistakable sound of George Longwell's soprano singing voice comes wafting into the room. *"What good is a field on a fine summer night if you sit alone in the weeds? Or a succulent pear if with each juicy bite you spit out your teeth with the seeds?"*

We both laugh and his hand gently rubs the back of my shoulder. It's a relief from the tension, if not the ending I hoped for.

seventeen

chewing the scenery (noun): a completely
hammy and over-the-top performance.

For some people a long, long, long time means months, maybe even years. For George Longwell it apparently means nineteen hours.

I'm walking to third period (stage production with Mr. Lucheki), trying to remember my discussion points on whether the light board operator is more important than the sound operator (which pretty much boils down to whether it is more important to see the play or hear it), when someone yells, "There she is!"

Just as I'm about to escape into the theater, George throws himself down on his knees in front of me.

"Megan, you are a rose
With a perfect nose
I know you are afraid

Of the love we could have made
But patient I will be
As I am sure you will eventually see
That I was meant for you
And you were meant for me."

George pats his heart twice (as per usual) and stands up. "Next Thursday." He kisses my hand for emphasis. "I won't take no for an answer."

I'm distracted by the appearance of Catherine's friend Laura, who has stopped in the hall to watch and is smiling at me from ear to ear, nodding encouragement. "I have to go to class," I say, stepping around him.

"Thursday night, Megan!" George calls out.

I want to tell him that I can't go, that in fact I don't want to go out with him at all, *ever*, but I can't bring myself to say the words.

"Okay," I say, hurrying into class. Simon is already there but he's not sitting in our seats. Once again, he's sitting across the aisle in the far corner of the auditorium, directly behind Laura and Catherine. The minute I see him leaning over their seats, chatting with them amiably as if there is nothing odd about his behavior or seat selection at all, I feel a little sick to my stomach. I'm getting extremely tired of this.

I pick up my stuff and walk over toward him. "What's going on? Why are you sitting back here?"

Out of the corner of my eye, I see Catherine shoot Laura a look as if to say, *Well, look who's here . . .* Miss *Attitude herself!*

"I didn't know we had assigned seats," Simon says with a shrug, giving Catherine and Laura a little grin.

What? What kind of smart-alecky response is that?

"Good morning, class," Mr. Lucheki says enthusiastically. I drop into the seat beside Simon as I attempt to focus my attention on Mr. Lucheki. Besides having been the stage manager for the Kennedy Center for fifteen years, Mr. Lucheki's other claim to fame is his shiny, not a hair on it, bald head. Normally his head is so shiny it reflects light all over the place. But not today, primarily because he's standing in complete and total darkness.

"Which is more important," Mr. Lucheki asks. "Sound? Or . . ." He claps his hands and suddenly he's bathed in an almost luminescent light. "Light?" he says silently, mouthing the words.

"I was waiting for you," I whisper to Simon. "Jane said I could sit—"

"I don't care about lunch," Simon whispers back.

"So why are you mad? Is this about George?"

"George?" Simon says. "I couldn't care less about George Longwell. I'm just tired of you making promises you don't keep."

Catherine glances back at me and sneers.

"What are you talking about?" I ask Simon, doing my best to ignore Catherine even though I'm really tempted to give the back of her chair a nice kick.

"What we're talking about, *Miss Fletcher*," Mr. Lucheki says, looking directly at me, "is the ability to attract attention. The ability to . . ." His voice fades away, replaced by static. He continues talking but all that is audible is a quiet mumble. He claps his hands again. "You see," he says clearly again, "without sound, there are no stars." He smiles, obviously extremely pleased with his demonstration. "I remember back in eighty-eight when *Gypsy* was in town. Tyne Daly was about to sing when . . ."

"You make plans, you cancel them," Simon whispers. "You tell me you're going to call, you don't. I'm getting sick of it, that's all."

And suddenly I remember that I was supposed to call Simon last night.

"I forgot," I whisper back. "I had practice after school and when I got home it was time for dinner and after dinner I had to study for the English test."

"Whatever," he says.

I'm silent for a few minutes as I turn my attention back to Mr. Lucheki. "Naturally her laryngitis made it difficult, if not impossible, to hear her," he is saying. "So I decided to increase the volume on the . . ."

"Of course," I say to Simon, "*you* could've called *me*."

"That's not the point," he says.

"Since when do we keep tabs on who's supposed to call who or who owes whom a phone call?"

"I knew you wouldn't get it," he says so loudly that Mr.

Lucheki stops talking. Catherine rolls her eyes toward me and whispers something to Laura, obviously mocking me.

"What is *your* problem?" I scream at Catherine.

"Miss Fletcher!" Mr. Lucheki says.

Simon is staring at me, openmouthed. So is the rest of the class, including Catherine who is looking at me like I just doused her with a freezing pail of water.

"Why don't you come sit down here?" Mr. Lucheki says sternly, pointing to a seat in the front row. I shoot Simon one last dirty look before grabbing my backpack and heading down the aisle.

Production class is right before lunch, and usually Simon and I walk each other to our lockers and go to lunch together, but not today. Even though I know Simon doesn't want to go to lunch with me any more than I want to go with him, I hurry out of class, dump my books into my locker, and slam the door for emphasis before heading to the lunchroom where I plop myself down at my sister's table as if I have been sitting there my entire life. As if I belong.

Maria and Jane look at me, but if they're surprised, they don't show it. The only person who seems surprised is Lucy, who greets me, once again, by asking me where Simon is.

"I don't know." Simon hightailed it out of class with his two little (in Catherine's case, not so little) minions and I'm not about to chase him down again. If he doesn't want to sit with me, then so be it.

The conversation stalls with my arrival, and I can feel Lucy's eyes on me as I put my lunch on the table.

"Why did you pack my yogurt?" Lucy asks, pointing toward the nonfat lemon yogurt that I have just taken out of my lunch bag.

Up until I began my official "Lucy" diet, Lucy is the only one in our family who ate yogurt. "I just grabbed it out of the fridge," I say nonchalantly.

"I only had two left."

I probably should apologize, but instead I just shrug.

"You don't even like yogurt," Lucy says.

"It's not bad," I say, peeling the top off the container and giving it a lick.

"I have to get going," Lucy says, disgustedly tossing her own half-eaten nonfat lemon yogurt into her bag.

She's leaving? *Again?* "You can have it," I shout, stopping her. I push my yogurt in her direction. "I'll go sit someplace else."

Lucy takes a look at my yogurt, sighs, and sits back down. "I guess I can wait a couple minutes," she says, sliding my yogurt back across the table toward me.

There are a few moments of uncomfortable silence. Marybeth, Jane, Maria, and Annie are looking at me, their eyes open wide. I think this is how sharks look when they see a sea lion swimming through the water. I don't know what Lucy's been telling them about me, but they seem a little anxious, as if they're expecting me to jump over the table and pummel my sister to the ground.

"So what were you talking to Drew about?" Jane says finally.

"When?" I ask, assuming she's talking to me.

But she's not. She's looking at my sister who says, "Figuring out the logistics for the Kennedy Center."

"What's going on at the Kennedy Center?" I ask.

"Drew and I are going to see a play," Lucy says casually.

I put down my spoon. I try to keep my reaction to a minimum as I begin to gnaw on my thumb.

"Just the two of you?" Jane asks, which coincidentally, is exactly what I'm wondering.

"She and Drew were talking to Mrs. Habersham and she told them she had seen this play last week by this new playwright," Annie says. "She mentioned they were doing a special weekday presentation. So Lucy asked Drew if he wanted to go see it with her."

Wait a minute.

Did Lucy ask out Drew or did Drew ask out Lucy?

"I don't remember who asked *who* first," Lucy says, correcting her. "But he offered to drive."

I glance longingly toward the vending machine at the opposite end of the room. When I walked past yesterday I had noticed that it now carried Oreos. I could really, really use an Oreo. But the question is: Are they on the Lucy diet?

"I hope it's a love story," Marybeth says. "One with a lot of make-out scenes."

"Yeah," agrees Jane, who laughs like the Wicked Witch of the West, surprisingly.

"Speaking of making out," Annie says, blinking her overly made-up eyes as she rests her giant boobs on the table, leaning toward me. "Do you have anything to share with us yet?"

"Like what?" I ask, as Lucy begins to dig through her wallet.

"Have you kissed Drew yet?" Jane asks. "On a scale of one to ten, how does he rate? And be honest."

"Lindsey gave him a ten," Annie says.

A ten. I can barely swallow my mouthful of yogurt. Although the news that Drew is a good kisser is hardly shocking, it doesn't exactly put me at ease, either. "I . . . we haven't gotten to that scene . . ."

"Not yet?" Jane gasps. "What have you guys been doing all this time anyway?"

Her question catches me by surprise and is enough to make me gag on my yogurt. I take a big sip of water.

"Leave her alone," Lucy says. I glance at her, stunned that she's actually standing up for me. "This is her first play, after all. It's probably taking her awhile to get used to blocking and everything."

"You have to be getting to it soon," Marybeth says.

In fact, we are on page five, which means that today (if we followed the same schedule as yesterday) we'll be blocking the kissing scene. Which is exactly why I took a double dose of my nose spray that morning. I have no intention of having snot on my face when I finally get to kiss the man of my dreams.

"Don't forget. We want a full report," Annie says.

"Won't it be weird when you see the play and have to watch your sister with the guy you like?" Jane asks Lucy.

But if Lucy's bothered by the visual, she doesn't show it. "I guess I'll find out. Russell is sick today and since Megan and Drew have the auditorium, I thought I'd watch."

I glance at Lucy, horrified. I do not want my sister to be in attendance on the day when I finally get to kiss Drew.

"Anyone else interested in coming?" Lucy asks, handing me a dollar for the vending machine.

Unfortunately for me, almost everyone is.

Great.

I've spent quite a bit of time imagining what it might be like to kiss a guy. Not just a quick peck, but a real, heavy-duty, make-out kiss. Never in my wildest dreams did I think it would be with Drew. Nor did I think it would be in front of an audience, especially one that consisted of my sister and her friends. Nor did I think I would be so nervous that I would spend the minutes leading up to it keeled over a toilet in the school's first-floor bathroom. But that's where I've been for the past half hour.

I didn't throw up, which was fortunate, considering I'm pretty sure my breath is stinky enough as it is. I purposely laid out my toothbrush and toothpaste this morning but I forgot it on the kitchen counter. I tried to touch my tongue to my nose to smell my breath and I'm pretty sure it smells like peanut butter. (The vending machine was out of Oreos, and the only other thing that looked good was the Nutter Butters.)

When I was in the bathroom I kept reassuring myself I'd feel much better once I actually got onstage. Lucy has always said that the minute she gets onstage she feels as though she's been transported to another world and is never aware of the audience. But as I stand in the middle of the stage, gagging on my own peanut butter breath while holding my script and waiting for Drew to give me my blocking, I couldn't be more aware of the audience if they were still giving me dirty looks across the lunch table. And it certainly does not help that (unlike in Mr. Lucheki's demonstration) the auditorium lights are on. They're all right there in front of me, sitting in the third row: Annie Carmichael, Jane Hitchins, Maria Merton, Marybeth Wilkens, and last but not least, Lucy Fletcher.

"Okay," Drew is saying. "Let's start at the bottom of page four. I remember . . ."

I glance at the script, but my hands are shaking so badly I'm having trouble reading it. I think about how great Lucy was yesterday and how she had moved me to tears even though she was just receiving her blocking and was still reading from her script.

Oh crap.

I attempt to steady the script by balancing it on the edge of my belt as I clear my throat. "I remember the first time we got together. You told me I was special . . . that you had never felt like this about anyone before. Remember?"

"I remember," Drew says, reading the part of Guy.

"Was it a lie?" I glance into the audience. Lucy's arms are crossed and she's giving me a smug *you stink* sort of look. I wipe away a bead of sweat from my forehead. I had a feeling I shouldn't wear my hoodie but I just felt safer in it. But here I was, onstage for two seconds, and already dripping with sweat.

"Of course not."

"When you first broke up with me I was so devastated, I couldn't sleep." I'm speaking in a monotone voice, with no inflection, no emotion, no nothing.

"I couldn't eat . . . I couldn't do anything. And then I thought . . . I'll be okay as long as he doesn't date anyone else. As long as I know his heart still belongs to me."

Drew gives me a little smile that is definitely not in the script. It's as if he knows I'm nervous and he's sending me a message, like, *don't worry, I'll be gentle.* I gag on a lump of saliva and clear my throat again.

"When I heard that you and Wendy were hanging out," I say, "I told myself that you guys were just friends. And last night, when you saw me talking to that guy, I could see the pain in your eyes and I knew you were jealous. I knew you still cared about me." I pause and look directly at Lucy. She narrows her eyes and shifts uncomfortably in her seat. I look back at my script, but I've lost my place.

"And then you touched my arm," Drew says, feeding me my line.

"And then you touched my arm," I say, reading my line.

"Okay," Drew says. "As you say that line I want you to walk over to me and stand in front of me, slightly downstage."

"And then you touched my arm," I repeat yet again, walking toward him. Four steps to go. Four steps and I'll be touching his lips to mine. My breath catches in my throat as I take another step. Three, two . . . my heart is banging against my chest. "Remember 'I miss you,' you said."

"Okay," Drew says, stopping me. "I want you to run your finger down my arm as you say the next line."

"You still love me," I say, pointing my finger and running it down the length of his arm. I know it's supposed to be a sexy sort of move, but mine is anything but. It's more like, hey you have a bug on your arm and I'll just squash it and smear right on down.

"But that doesn't change how I feel about us," Drew says, reading his line. "Now I'm going to turn away from you," he says, as he proceeds to explain the blocking. "I want you to walk stage right."

I know (of course) that stage directions are the opposite of what they seem. Yet I still move to the wrong side.

"Stage right," Drew repeats. "Over here."

Out of the corner of my eye I see Lucy grin and look at Marybeth, as if to say: *My sister is such an idiot she doesn't even understand stage directions!*

"Then Guy says: I can't . . . I don't want a relationship right now. I want you to come up from behind me and stand as close as you can without touching me and say your line."

I stand behind him, as close as I possibly can. OHMYGOD. *Just breathe*, I command myself. *Just breathe*. I stare up at the back of Drew's head as I take a big whiff of his musky-smelling hair.

"So we won't call it a relationship," I say. "It's just about what feels good. And this feels good."

"Okay," Drew says, out of character once again. "I want you to be the aggressor, so as soon as you say your line, put your hands on my shoulders and spin me around and let me have it." And then he gives me that smile once again, the smile that makes me go weak in the knees, the smile that makes it feel as if someone is squeezing my heart like a bottle of ketchup.

I can do this, I can do this, I can do this . . . I purse my lips as I put my hands on his shoulders. As he spins toward me, I step forward, stand on my tiptoes, and pucker up. I give him a smooch right on the lips that ends with the unmistakable sound of a plunger unclogging a toilet.

My sister and her friends begin to snicker. I step backward in horror as I raise my hands to my lips. What the hell was that? This was not the kiss of my dreams. No, no, *NO!*

"Very funny," he says. "One more time."

I don't want to kiss Drew anymore. I want to get off this stage and find a quiet place to cry and blow a lung through my nose.

Lucy straightens in her chair and crosses her arms. She's smiling and I can tell she's enjoying this. I glance offstage, as if I'm hoping to see Simon waiting in the wings, cheering me on. I really wish he were here. I'm totally outnumbered.

Drew gives me a little nod as if encouraging me to continue.

I have no choice. I take a deep breath and lick my lips. Just as I'm going in for the kill, I hear my sister give a little snort that is masquerading as a giggle. I hit Drew smack on the kisser. With my eyes and mouth wide open and my arms straight down beside me, I slowly and robotically swipe my lips across his: up, down, right, left. There's more snickering in the auditorium. "Okay," Drew says afterward, silencing the audience. He looks like he's just been attacked by a slobbering mastiff. "From the kiss I want you to move stage left . . ."

Afterward, Drew thanks everyone for coming and then takes me by the arm.

"Don't worry," he says, as he leads me offstage. "This was your first time onstage, right?"

First time on stage, obviously code for first kiss. Ugh. Just shoot me. Shoot me and put me out of my misery. I nod.

"By the time you get back onstage you'll have this scene down pat. I promise."

I feel a tiny bit of relief. This may have been the most humiliating experience of my life, but I take a small shred of comfort in the fact that Drew is not giving up on me.

At least not yet.

eighteen

mime (noun): the art or technique of
portraying a character, mood, idea, or
narration by gestures and bodily
movements.

When I arrive at school the next morning, there's a note from
Drew taped on my locker. My hands start to shake as I open it. I
was so terrible at practice the day before that in spite of his reas-
surance to the contrary, I'm pretty sure I'm getting canned. But
the note doesn't say that, at least not exactly. He wants me to
meet him in the production studio at four-thirty. I read it over
again just to make sure I've got it right. Yep. The production studio. Why would he want to meet me there? And why at four-
thirty? Why not immediately after school? Whatever the reason
is, I don't think it's good.

I'm so nervous that at three-thirty I walk to the Inner Harbor
and back just to kill time before our meeting. I arrive a couple of
minutes before we're scheduled to meet. The production studio

is empty with the exception of Drew, who's sitting on a stool beside the table saw, reading his dictionary. In his faded Levis and a snug-fitting black T-shirt, he looks more like a teacher than a student. As I glance behind him at the paint cans and the background scenes stacked neatly against the wall, I feel an immediate sense of relief. We're on my turf now, my territory. Whatever I look like, I can work a miter saw better than Bob the Builder. Whatever Drew's about to tell me, I can handle.

"Hey, Drew," I say cheerfully, as though there is nothing on my mind.

All he does is grin.

Weird.

"So," I say, swallowing and forcing myself to plaster on a smile. I glance at the floor beside the table saw where someone has left a big pile of sawdust. Freshmen! This incoming class are a bunch of knuckleheads. Besides being incompetent, they're slobs. "What's the word?"

"Mea culpa," Drew says. "An acknowledgment of error or guilt. As in I never should have had you block such a difficult scene in front of all those people, mea culpa. I'm sorry."

"It's not your fault." I walk over to the corner where the cleaning supplies are kept and grab the broom and dustbin.

"I put you in an awkward position." Drew looks at me curiously as I begin to sweep around his feet. Then he jumps off the stool and grabs the dustbin, holding it on the floor for me. "I know it can be pretty intimidating to be on the stage. Especially having to perform a . . . well, difficult scene in front of your sister

216

and her friends. I could see you were nervous. I should've called it quits."

"That's nice of you to say, but I was the one doing the stinky acting." And now he's helping me clean up. It's almost too much sweetness for a girl to take.

"I just want to reassure you that by the time we get back onstage, kissing me will be as comfortable for you as shaking my hand, okay?" Drew hands the empty bin back to me.

"Thanks," I reply, although I didn't hear a word of what he just said.

"Are you okay?" he asks.

"Yes, fine." I turn away and pretend to cough just so that I can catch my breath. "So why did you want to meet here?" I put away the broom and dustbin and turn back around to face him.

"Because the other day I could tell how comfortable you were in here. You seemed so relaxed. I thought it might be a good place to block a tough scene. I asked Lucheki if he would mind if I borrowed it this afternoon and he gave me permission."

"Really?" We're blocking the kissing scene in the production studio? Right next to the turpentine?

"Acting is acting," Drew says with an authority that's self-assured instead of arrogant. "It doesn't matter where you are. Onstage or in the production studio. It's all the same."

He gives me a smile of encouragement.

"Whew," I say, jiggling the top of my hoodie. "It's usually freezing in here, but today it's smoking. Aren't you hot?"

"Not really. But then again, I don't have a coat and a hoodie over my T-shirt." I can tell by his grin that he thinks he's pretty funny. But then, I do, too.

I take off my peacoat, followed by my hoodie. Although I hated to part with it, I was not about to have another sweating fit like I did yesterday.

"What does your T-shirt say?" Drew squints at my boobs. "Mmm . . . mmm . . . good!" he reads out loud.

I'm gaping at my B cups bulging out from underneath my sister's undersized T-shirt as if I've never seen them before in my life. Why did I take off my hoodie? And why didn't I pay more attention to what I wore? "Campbell's soup," I say quickly. "Gotta love it."

"Yeah." He grins. "I do."

I shake my head. I can imagine Lucy snickering to herself. I take a quick look around to make sure no one is hiding behind the garbage cans.

Drew stands in the rectangular open space in between the old set screens stacked against the wall and the table saws. "This is our stage," he begins.

Since I'm an adult (not really) and a professional (not really), I stop staring at my boobs and put the Campbell soup incident behind me (not really) as I walk over to him.

Drew is suddenly all business and we begin running our lines, doing the blocking as if there's nothing unusual about our location at all. I have to admit that Drew might be onto something about this whole rehearsing in the production studio thing. I *am* better than I was onstage. I'm even better than I was in the classroom. I interrupt him once to ask if we can do the actual performance in here, but he just smiles at me and keeps going. Even here, though, I'm still nervous, and by the time we get to the first kiss at the bottom of page five, my knees are so wobbly I have to keep a hand on the table saw just to steady myself.

Drew stops and sets down his script. He crosses his arms and leans against a stool. "I have an idea. I'd like to try this exercise with you that I saw a teacher use once to help an actress get through a love scene in a play. It's a little like hypnosis. Are you game?"

"You're not going to make me act like a chicken, are you?"

Drew just smiles and I'm prepared to squawk. "I want you to remember the last time you felt really, really attracted to someone. Close your eyes and think about him . . . try to picture him in your mind."

Not a hard assignment, considering my one eye is still open.

"Keep your eyes closed," Drew advises. "And we're going to switch gears. I want you to picture a hot fudge sundae."

I close my eyes tight, attempting to visualize my sundae. It's in a big parfait glass, loaded with whipped cream, no nuts, and no cherry. Four scoops of creamy chocolate-chip cookie dough loaded with thick hot fudge.

"Take a bite," he says. "Think about how good it tastes, how good it feels on your tongue . . . sliding down your throat. As it melts, I want you to commit every sensation to memory as if this is the last hot fudge sundae you're ever going to have and you want to remember every single second, every single detail."

In my mind, I see Drew that first day of school, sitting on the window ledge, reading a dictionary. His hair is tousled, his backpack swung over his shoulder.

"Now, I want you to think about your crush. I want you to imagine touching your lips to his. I want you to savor his lips just like you did that sundae, enjoying the touch, the feel, the sensation . . . and then, when you're ready, I want you to become the character of the Girl. I want you to kiss me."

I open one eye. Drew is standing across the room from me, his arms slightly behind him while he leans against the table saw as casually as if he is going to play ball with a friend, as in, I've kissed so many girls, what's one more?

I close my eyes again as my heart continues to clang at warp speed.

Focus.

I open my eyes and stand up straight. I take a deep breath and begin to march toward Drew like a soldier entering a battlefield.

"Okay, stop," he says. "You look terrified."

I tuck my shaking hands behind me as I flash him what I have the feeling is an idiotic grin. He bites his lower lip as he looks into the distance, thinking *if it looks like a doofus, talks like a doofus and acts like a doofus, it's a doofus.*

"Just forget about the whole sundae thing," he says finally.

"It was dumb anyway. I want you to tell me how to work the miter saw."

"The miter saw?"

"That one," he says, pointing to the saw beside me. "The one you used to make the star."

I breathe a huge sigh of relief. Kissing scene postponed! "Well, first you . . ." I begin, as I head toward it.

"Don't show me," he says. "Just stand still and tell me."

Huh?

He nods, encouraging me to continue.

"All right." This is going to be a little tough, but I'm not about to complain. Anything is easier than a stage kiss. "First, you need to turn it on."

"Okay," he says, walking toward me.

"What are we making?"

"Let's do a star again."

"Well, you're going to need a board. Not too thick. Maybe . . . oh, an eighth of . . ."

He takes my hand.

Whoa. I'm staring at our hands locked together.

"How thick?" he asks.

His other hand is on my cheek. HIS OTHER HAND IS ON MY CHEEK.

"Like an inch, two inches?" he asks.

I close my eyes. Think miter saw. "Since you've never done this before, I wouldn't go more than an eighth of an inch."

"Why?" His face is about two inches from mine.

I can feel his breath on my face. Oh God. Oh God. Houston, we have a problem.

"Why?" he repeats.

Miter Saw, miter saw, miter saw . . .

"If it's too thick . . . ," I begin. Houston? Are you there?

He's getting closer. Five, four, three . . .

"Too thick and you won't be able to rotate the . . ." Houston, if you can hear me, abort! Abort, abort . . .

But it's too late. The *Eagle* has landed.

His lips are soft and warm and taste a little like peppermint. The kiss is nice and dry, gentle and sweet. Not nearly as passionate as my make-out sessions with my pillow, but not at all platonic, either. Either way, my toes are literally curling.

Drew steps back and looks at me, giving me a sly grin. "See? Nothing to it."

I smile and then I lean against the table saw so I don't collapse and die of happiness.

I'm at the top of Federal Hill Park, skipping toward home gleefully, when I see Simon. He's sitting on the front steps of our row house, reading *Moby-Dick*. Once again he's retired his shorts and sneakers and is wearing jeans and loafers with a crisp-looking button-down shirt under his corduroy jacket.

I blink twice, convinced that I'm experiencing some sort of apparition, because it can't possibly be Simon sitting there in front of my house since he has gone out of his way to avoid me since the whole Catherine incident.

"Hi," Simon says, standing and giving me a little wave as I walk down the hill toward him. We meet halfway, across the street from my house.

"Can we talk for a minute?" he asks.

Even though he sounds pretty serious and I'd really like to enjoy my kissing high a few more minutes, I nod and follow him back toward the park and up the hill. I'm pretty sure I don't have a choice. Listening to your best friend even if you don't want to hear what he/she has to say is like the number one BFF rule.

We sit side by side on a bench overlooking Key Highway, the Inner Harbor, and his apartment building. "I just wanted to tell you that, well, I'm sorry," Simon says. "I have been acting like a jerk lately. I just—I've been going through kind of a tough time. I'm . . . I'm trying to deal with a couple of things."

I know I could really go off on a tangent with all this stuff that just came out of his mouth, *like what kind of tough time* and *what things are you dealing with*, but even though I kind of have to listen to Simon, I don't think the best friend manual requires that you totally trash your good mood by getting into a serious tête-à-tête. I'll have to check, but I'm willing to swear that I just have to listen.

And so I say cheerfully, "I'm sorry, too. I didn't mean to lose my temper like that."

"Catherine deserved it. She was being a bitch. She can be

like that. I've talked to her about the ways she was treating you and she agreed it wasn't anything you'd actually done to her. She's just jealous. Ignore her."

The news that Simon spoke to Catherine on my behalf, that he actually stood up for me, is actually a little surprising since he's been such a jerk lately. But why bring up that unpleasantness now. What's past is past, right?

"It's not all Catherine's fault," I say, doing my best to be gracious. "I'm still trying to feel my way, you know? Everything is different this year."

"It's hard to be beautiful? Harder than it looks, at least?"

I hate it when Simon uses his sarcastic voice. (Well, that's not exactly true. I hate it when he uses it on *me*.)

I'm just about ready to start swinging the nasty retorts when he says, "So how was practice today?"

All right. I was willing to forget about the nasty retorts (they weren't that good anyway), but there is no way in hell I'm going to regal him with the truth, specifically the truth about Drew. "Good, I guess."

"You . . . you haven't talked too much about Drew lately."

"I haven't talked to *you* too much lately."

"I know," Simon mumbles. "I miss you."

Poof. Just like that all my anger fades away. Unfortunately, so does any remnant of Drew-inspired happiness. I stare back at the water and we're both quiet for a minute.

A fly lands on his jacket and I attempt to change the direction of our conversation by playfully brushing it off. "Hey, by the way, I saw the set you're working on for Drew's play. It's looking great."

Even though the scenery for the senior productions was usually pretty simplistic, Simon's was head and shoulders above the rest. He had designed a night backdrop that was covered in wildflowers. He was even making a battery-operated lamppost.

"If you want I can stop by and give you a hand," I offer. "Maybe when I'm done with practice one day."

"Sure," he says. "That would be nice. Oh, by the way, my mom loved your new design for the living room. She said she should pay you instead of her interior decorator."

"Ha, ha! Okay, great!" It comes out really forced. Like it's obvious that I'm not sincere. "Oh, and I've got a compliment for you as well. Guess who was talking about you at lunch the other day? Marybeth. She was saying how great she thinks you look with contacts. She said she never noticed until now what cute eyes you have."

"Really?" he asks with a sad smile. "That's nice, I guess."

When I get home, Lucy isn't there. On the kitchen table is a handwritten note explaining that she is going out to dinner with Marybeth and will see me later. I tell myself I really shouldn't care. After all, in spite of Lucy I've had a pretty good day. I kissed Drew, left my mom a very long-winded, ecstatic message, and had a nice talk with Simon. So what if my sister can't stand the sight of me?

I make myself a tuna fish sandwich with lite mayo as I try to ignore the Lucy-inspired pit in my stomach. I think about what Lucy said about being charming and nice and then I think about George. I grab my sandwich and head to the computer, determined to deal with him once and for all.

After several drafts, I type an e-mail that I'm pretty sure is good:

```
Dear George,
I'm really sorry but I can't go out
with you on Thursday night. In fact, I
can't go out with you at all. I think
you are a GREAT guy and wish you all
the best.
Sincerely, Megan
```

I'm just about to press Send when I hear the front door open. "Mom?" I call out.

"Just me," Lucy replies.

I check my watch. It's nearly eight o'clock and I haven't heard from Mom since I left her that message. I can't help but feel disappointed. So much for her sharing my excitement over my first (stage) kiss. Still, I'm happy that at least Lucy is home.

"What did you get?" I ask cheerfully as she walks in the bedroom carrying a Bebe's bag.

"Pants," she says. "They were on sale. We stopped there before dinner."

"Where did you go to dinner?" I ask.

"Cheesecake Factory," she says.

As Lucy is well aware, I absolutely love the Cheesecake Factory. In the old days she probably would've said something like *I was thinking about you the whole time* or *I brought you back some cheesecake.* But it's as if she's forgotten that I've ever even been there, not to mention that it's one of my favorite places on earth.

"Hey," she says, motioning toward the shirt under my hoodie. "Is that my shirt?"

"It was in our share pile."

Lucy doesn't say anything more, but I can tell she's not too happy by the way she turns away from me. I curse myself for wearing the shirt. I knew it was hers but since she lets me wear some of her other shirts, I didn't think she'd care. Still, it was a dumb thing to do, especially considering the sorry state of our relationship.

"Will you read this?" I ask, motioning toward the computer screen. "It's to George."

Lucy leans over my shoulder and reads it. "That's not a letter. That's a bitchy note. Have you not been listening to a word I've been saying to you? You have to be bend over backward to be nice now or people are going to hate you."

"I know, I know," I say defensively. "I really do understand what you're saying. Honest. But what's nasty about this?" I glance at the note again as I begin to chew on my thumbnail. "I say he's a great guy."

"I don't understand why you don't want to go out with him," Lucy snaps. "He's cute and popular . . . he's funny . . ."

"He's kind of annoying. And also . . . he has girl hair." I'm stunned that I remember what Simon had said last year.

"Girl hair?" Lucy asks, wrinkling up her nose and raising her eyebrows like I had just spoken in tongues. "You don't like him because of his *hair*?"

I never should have brought up the girl-hair thing. I know it sounds superficial, I should've just stopped at annoying. But I'm not about to back down. "I would think you, of all people, would understand. Remember Andy?" I say, mentioning the guy who asked her to the fall festival the previous year. "You said you didn't like him because of his hands."

"This isn't the same thing. Not even close."

"Why?"

"Because a year ago you would've been counting your blessings to be fortunate enough to be asked out by someone like George!"

"I see," I say calmly, yanking my thumb away from my mouth. "So, as far as you're concerned, Miss Pathetic BuckTeeth Fatso on the inside is lucky that I even caught George's eye. I'm so sorry to disappoint you, Lucy, but he's . . . he's not my type."

"How would you know what your type is when you've never gone out with anyone? When, up until yesterday, you'd never even kissed anyone?" she adds.

It's a low blow, but Lucy doesn't seem to realize it. She is just standing there giving me her cool-as-a-cucumber icy glare.

I forget all about my vow to be nice. As far as I'm concerned, the gloves are off. "Well," I say, "you'll be glad to know that my kissing ability has improved significantly. Drew and I worked on our kiss all afternoon and according to him, I'm a natural."

"Good for you," she snaps.

But I don't gloat. I send the e-mail to George as Lucy gathers her pajamas, her pillow, and her comforter and leaves the room, shutting the door behind her. As I look at the bulletin board crammed with all her theater pictures, I can't help but feel overwhelmed by a sense of nostalgia and longing for simpler times, when my dream of looking like Lucy hadn't come true yet.

nineteen

rehearsal (noun): a practice session,
usually private, in preparation for a
public performance.

Dear Megan,
I know you're a novice in love and
life and I fear I have frightened you
by my exuberance. All I can say is
that your smile continues to haunt
my sleep. Go with me to the fall
festival. It is the only way to soothe
my restless soul.
G

"That's pathetic," Simon says, as he finishes reading George's note. "Oooh. I am haunting your dreams, wooooo."

"Woooo," I say, but it's a halfhearted, sick to my stomach, wooo.

A week has passed since I sent George that e-mail and I haven't spoken or communicated with him at all. I was just beginning to relax and not run in the opposite direction when I saw him. But his note put me back on high alert. As a result, even though it's been raining off and on all day, Simon and I are eating our lunch on the steps of a deserted church a block away from school. "What's it going to take for old Wayne Newton to get the message?" Simon asks.

"Wayne Newton?"

"Tony Roberts."

"Tony Roberts? The giant you-can-do-it guy?"

"That's Tony Robbins. I was trying to think of some big Broadway singer."

"Kristin Chenoweth," I say.

"What's it going to take for old Kristin to get the message?" Simon asks.

"I wish I knew."

I take back the note and stick it into my purse. I rub my half-frozen hands together. Baltimore has been suffering through a totally schizoid fall with hot, sunny days sandwiched in between unusually cold and damp weather. Today it's freezing cold, and even though I'm wearing two hoodies underneath my giant raincoat from last year, I'm still shivering.

I pick up my turkey sandwich (that was made as designated by my Lucy diet: whole wheat bread, mustard—no mayo) and a glob of mustard slides off the sandwich onto the step. As I wipe it off with my napkin, I'm happy that no one (besides Simon) is there to witness my messy eating. "I have to say I'm surprised. I thought this whole dating thing was a dead issue."

"What does Lucy say?"

"She's not really talking to me these days," I say, choking down a bite. I really hate mustard. "We've gotten into fights before but nothing ever like this. She's really ticked about the way I've handled this whole George thing."

"I guarantee you, Lucy couldn't care less about George. She's just jealous," he says matter-of-factly as he leans back and tucks his hands into the pocket of his brown corduroy jacket. Simon is an incredibly fast eater, and as per usual, he's already finished with his lunch.

"Because I got the part in Drew's play?"

"She's used to being the star of the show. And now you're the pretty one."

"Don't say that," I say quickly.

"Why not? It's true," Simon says. "In fact, I think you're the most beautiful girl I've ever seen."

Amazingly enough, I'm no longer cold. In fact, I'm so warm I've begun to sweat. I fiddle with the napkin in my lap. "So what should I do about George?"

"Maybe you should accept a date to the fall festival with someone else. He'll get the message."

"That's an idea," I say. I stick the lite fruit cocktail back in my bag, untouched.

"What about Drew?"

I have thought about this, of course. I have thought about

this a lot. But although practice has been coming along really well and we always have a great time together (at least, I think so) and my kissing had improved dramatically (at least, I think so), I still can't tell if he's really into me or not.

"I'm not sure how much Drew likes me. A little bit at least, but then he and Lucy are going to see that play at the Kennedy Center tomorrow, so I don't really know." I have discovered they're going to a matinee, not an evening performance, which makes me feel a tiny bit better since it doesn't seem so date-ish. But still, just thinking about it is enough to make my angina flare up.

"So maybe you should go to the dance with me," Simon says casually.

My heart begins thwacking. "Oh, Simon," I say, with a little forced laugh as I clutch my chest. "I made you take me last year. You should ask someone you really like."

"I just did: you."

I laugh a little louder, as if by sheer force of will I can turn this whole thing into a harmless joke at no one's expense. "No," I say. "You know what I mean. Someone you *like*-like."

He's not laughing. In fact, he's not even smiling anymore. "I just did," he says softly. "You."

In addition to my worsening case of angina, I now have emphysema. *No, no, no . . .*

Simon sighs and says, "Last week, when I told you I needed to work some stuff out? Well, I wasn't exactly honest when I said it didn't have anything to do with you. It didn't have anything to do with anything you've done or said . . . it's just that, well, my feelings for you have changed—developed."

But you're my friend, I want to say, *my best friend.*

"I've tried to ignore it, but I, well, I can't. I want to be more than friends."

For the second time in five minutes I'm unable to speak.

"I know how you feel about Drew, but, I mean, you don't really know him. And, well, like you said, Lucy likes him. Maybe if you gave us a chance . . . you might be able to forget about him."

I swallow the lump in my throat as I stare at my lap.

"Do you . . . do you think you could see me as more than just a friend?"

Simon. My Simon. "I want things to be like they were before the accident," I somehow manage to spit out. "I want you to be my best friend."

"I can't keep doing this, Megan," he says. "I don't want to be just friends anymore." He picks up his lunch bag and crumples it into a ball. "I just want you to give me a chance. That's all I'm asking. Come to the fall festival with me. As my date."

"I . . . I . . ." What can I say that will make this all better? "I can't."

Simon's eyes fill with tears. "I have to go," he says quickly. "My contacts are bugging me."

I sit still, watching him walk away from me, heading back toward school. Only then do I realize that my nose is running.

I'm so miserable that I'm tempted to blow off play practice. It's not that I don't want to see Drew, it's just that I'm so upset I doubt I'll be able to concentrate. And I'm right. Within the first few minutes of practice, it's obvious that I made a mistake in coming. Even though I'm supposed to be off script, I'm not even remembering the most basic of words, like "yes" and "no." After only the second page of dialogue, Drew says, "Are you okay?"

"Sure," I say with a subdued laugh.

"You seem a little distracted."

"I, well . . ." I desperately blink back tears as I wipe my nose with the back of my hand. I can't allow myself to cry. Not in front of Drew. "It's Simon."

And suddenly I feel guilty for even mentioning Simon's name in front of Drew. How can I tell Drew what happened at lunch without breaking some unspoken trust between Simon and me?

"It's not just Simon . . . it's, well, everything. This year has just been weird, that's all."

He's silent for a minute, just looking at me. "Maybe we should call it quits for today."

"I don't want to go home," I say, my voice cracking. "I'm *not* going to go home."

"I have to run an errand," he says. "Do you want to come with me?"

"With you?" I ask.

He nods.

"Okay," I say, grabbing my coat. I don't even ask where he's going. It seems irrelevant, somehow. We're both silent as we leave the school, walking side by side to the parking structure. Even though I'm fulfilling a fantasy by spending some one-on-one time with him away from the school, and should therefore be totally, absolutely over the moon, I'm not. I'm too numb to be excited. The whole Simon thing has left me feeling like a wet noodle.

We walk up the stairs to the second floor of the lot, where he stops beside a brand-spanking-new and shiny BMW.

"Nice wheels," I say, after I climb inside. Then I cringe. Who says wheels? Whenever I try to be cool, the words come out all wrong. But fortunately, Drew doesn't seem to notice.

"Thanks," he says. "It's my stepfather's but he lets me use it. He's a lawyer for some big law firm. Actually, his office isn't too far from here. He works in the Legg Mason building."

"My mom's a lawyer, too. She works in a renovated town house down the street from the Legg Mason building. It's totally trashed but . . . she loves her job, which I guess is good because she works twenty-four seven."

Drew's quiet as he drives out of the structure. I notice he's suddenly got a little crinkle in his brow, like he's forgotten how to get where he's going or he's suddenly regretting asking such a clinically depressed person to join him.

"So where are we going?" I ask, trying my best to sound cheerful.

Drew grins as if he's happy to know something I don't. "You'll see."

As we drive through the Inner Harbor and head up to Route 83, we sit in nervous silence until Drew clears his throat.

"So," he says finally. "Do you, ah, want to talk about whatever got you so upset today?"

"It wasn't that big a deal," I say quickly, not sure if I want to burden him with the details. Plus the last thing I need is to find out that underneath it all Drew is alien, like everyone else I know.

But then he raises his eyebrows and gives me a sweet smile. It's all the encouragement I need.

"It's Simon. He's been my best friend since my first day of school here. Until my accident, we did everything together. But lately, well, he's been . . . going through a hard time. But it's not all his fault. I mean, I have, too."

Drew keeps his magnificent eyes on the road. "With good reason. Look at what you've been through."

He's right. *I* have been though a lot. If anyone deserves to be miserable right now, it's me. "Well, I always thought life would be easier, you know, if I looked like Lucy and lived in the spotlight. But now that it's all real, a lot of it isn't the way I imagined."

Drew turns down the volume of the car radio. It's as though he wants to be listening only to me. "What do you mean?"

"Before my accident, I thought if people just got to know me that they'd like me, but they never got past my face or body. Or that's what I told myself. I believed things would be different this year. I thought I'd have a ton of friends and everybody would like me . . ." Oh, man. Wa-wa-wa. What a cry baby. If Simon were here, he'd be having a field day. *"Poor baby . . . it's so hard to be beautiful . . ."* "I know it sounds conceited," I say, just in case Drew's having the same thought.

"It actually sounds a little sad."

I blink away the extra water in my eyes as I wipe my nose with the back of my hand. Must be my nonexistent allergies.

"Look, Megan, I'm no expert, but it seems to me that anyone in your shoes would be out of sorts right now."

Drew has a point. After all, less than a year ago Simon and I were arguing over who got to be Luke Skywalker.

"And as far as what the other people think or don't think of you . . . ," he continues, "so what? You can't worry about other people. You just have to be who you are."

"What if I don't know who I am anymore?"

"Luckily I know who you are." Drew takes one hand off the steering wheel and places it on my knee. "You're fun, you're smart, you're interesting to talk to. And I want to know more."

The words came out of him just like that, as if they were indisputably true. I'm not used to cute guys saying nice things to me—or touching me!—and although I have the feeling I'm supposed to say something really sweet back to him, I'm not sure what that might be.

"Thank you." The words squeak out of me in a quiet little voice. I'm not even sure Drew hears me.

But when I feel his hand squeeze my knee, I can tell he did.

Drew takes an exit off 83 and soon we stop on a slightly war–torn looking street, just like a million other streets around Baltimore. "We're here," he says, nodding toward the building beside us.

"Green Alien Comics?" I say, reading the sign above the beat-up glass storefront.

"The owner is one of my best friends. I showed him your Batman and he was really impressed."

"Really?" I can't believe Drew was talking about me to one of his best friends.

Drew grabs the door for me and holds it open. He smiles at me as I walk inside.

The store is divided into three big and shabby-looking rooms. Neat rows of comics line the dirty pale yellow walls, intermixed with stands displaying comic dolls and assorted comic-related accessories, such as a Wonder Woman hairbrush and a giant Xena doll.

"Hey, Fred," Drew says.

A scrawny, studious-looking man in his twenties with small wire-rimmed glasses (and wearing a T-shirt heralding the last *Superman* movie) jumps off his stool behind the cash register and bounds over to us. "Drew!" he says, and gives Drew a high-five. "Good to see you, dude."

"Likewise. Fred, this is Megan," Drew says, nodding in my direction. "She's the one I was telling you about."

"The Batman girl," Fred says with a wink. "You're awesome."

I can't believe this. I'm actually blushing because the comic book guy called me awesome.

"Big news, guy," Fred says to Drew. "Look what I got." He holds up a comic book wrapped in what appears to be layers of plastic.

Drew takes a step back and gasps. "Is that what I think it is?"

Fred stands perfectly still, a slight smile creeping up his lips. "A *D* copy," he whispers.

"How much?" Drew says feverishly.

"Two-six-five," Fred replies. Once he sees the confused expression on my face, he is kind enough to translate. "That's two hundred and sixty-five dollars."

"For a comic book?" I ask.

"Not just any comic book," Fred says solemnly. "Part of the D collection."

"The D collection because they belonged to a collector who handwrote the letter D on his comic books," Drew explains. "He started collecting in the thirties, and when he died, his family put his entire collection up for auction. This one is from the nineteen fifties."

"You want to see it up close?" Fred asks, once again as excited as if he's offering us a chance to see a treasure from Tutankhamen's tomb. "I'll let you view it in the back where there's more room."

Drew takes my hand in his. "Lead the way."

I follow along behind him, thinking about how amazing his

skin feels against mine. But soon I remember that tomorrow Drew and Lucy will be at the Kennedy Center together. I get a sick feeling in my stomach that spreads everywhere in a matter of seconds. I just know Lucy will use on him that weird power she has over men and he'll have no choice but to hold her hand, too.

twenty

typecast (verb): to cast a performer in
a role that requires characteristics of
physique, manner, personality, etc., similar
to those possessed by the performer.

"Were you up here all night?"

It's seven-thirty in the morning and I'm on the roof, wearing my coat over my pajamas, covered in sawdust.

Lucy is standing in the doorway. She looks exactly like the Valentine's Day Barbie I got from Aunt Shelley in third grade. She's wearing the outfit she and Marybeth picked out for her date with Drew: red velvet jeans (that she has dry-cleaned) and a tight pink turtleneck, topped with a fuzzy white shrug and long, dangly rhinestone earrings.

"I couldn't sleep." In fact, I have been up since four. I tossed and turned for a half hour before grabbing a large shoe box from the back of the closet, taking out the chinchilla-trimmed boots that Lucy bought on eBay last year for a hundred and fifty dollars, and heading up to the roof. Since we don't have a basement, my dad built a little shed for my equipment and that's where my mom prefers me to work on my projects, especially the big messy ones.

Lucy goes to the edge of the balcony and glances toward the harbor. "I don't know how you can stand to be up here at night by yourself. It would creep me out."

"It's kind of nice," I say.

"What are you working on?" she asks, motioning toward my diorama.

I hesitate. I'm not sure if Lucy knows about Drew's Batman obsession or not. One thing is certain. If she does, she's going to know in a second what I'm up to. "A . . . cave. You know, for Batman."

"For Batman? As in the comic books?"

The knowledge that I know something about Drew that she obviously doesn't gives me a little thrill.

"Graphic novels," I say authoritatively. "They're not just for kids anymore. Some go for as much as, well, two hundred and sixty-five dollars."

Lucy just shrugs and heads toward the door.

"So what time are you guys leaving?" I ask, before she can escape. I don't really want to know, of course. But I just can't help myself.

"At lunch."

I hear a horn beep. Marybeth just got a new car and I overheard Lucy and her making plans for her to swing by and pick her up early so they could get some coffee and discuss her "strategy" for her date with Drew.

As Lucy leaves, I think about her and Drew sitting in his stepfather's fancy car, just the two of them. I think about the romantic walk through the glitzy lobby of the Kennedy Center. I think about them sitting side by side in the dark theater. I think about the ride home, the big dramatic moment when the music reaches a crescendo and Drew turns toward Lucy and realizes she's the girl of his dreams, his real-life Valentine's Day Barbie.

I wipe my nose on my coat sleeve and turn my diorama back around. It really wasn't that elaborate, at least, not yet. I had painted the inside of the box black and was in the process of building a computer console and elevator. The diorama wasn't nearly finished but I suddenly wondered if it was even worth the effort. Although I thought it a great idea a couple of hours ago, it now seems a little sad (in a really pathetic sort of way). What was I thinking? That a little extra credit might win Drew's affection? A *Batman* diorama was not going to make up for me not having my sister's innate sensuality, or her ability to morph into whatever person someone might want her to be.

Somehow I know that a diorama will not win Drew's affection. I gather up all the pieces and head back inside. I walk to the kitchen, yank out a black Hefty bag, and stuff it in. I tie it up, walk it out the back door, and toss it into the trash. And then I go upstairs to get cleaned up for school. I forget all about my promise to be true to my old self. Intent on looking good today, I'm determined to give Valentine's Day Barbie a run for her money.

In production class I barely hear a word of Mr. Lucheki's discussion on the importance of properly miking the actors. I'm too busy thinking about how Drew had taken my hand in his at the comic book store, and how he'd used the word *we*, intimating that he and I were actually a real couple. Sitting all by myself in the front row, I couldn't feel more lonely if I was stranded in the middle of the Sahara.

After class, I wait until everybody has left before I exit the auditorium. It's almost twelve o'clock, time for Drew and Lucy to leave on their big date. Even though I had gotten all dressed up just so I could purposely run into Drew before he left and attempt to distract him from my sister, I don't go to the cafeteria. (It just seems too pathetic.) Instead I head toward the Cross Street Market to stake out a table for myself. But on the way there, I start to feel worse. I keep thinking about Lucy being alone with Drew and wondering what's going on between them at that very minute. I'm so upset that I stop walking and call my mom. But once again, she doesn't pick up. Her not being there so annoys me that I slam the phone shut before leaving a message. I gnaw on my finger for a minute before doing something so desperate it surprises even me. I call my dad.

He picks up on the third ring. "Hi, Megan." I can hear the

clanging of pots and loud voices in the background and I know immediately that he's in the kitchen of some Lucky Lou's. "Is everything okay?"

"No, not really." My voice is cracking as I step away from the busy sidewalk, taking refuge in the doorway of an abandoned building.

"@#$%!" he screams, causing me to jump straight up in the air. "Check the temperature on those next time! Ugh! @#$%!" I catch my breath as I listen to my dad yelling out instructions to the unlucky kitchen staff. "Sorry 'bout that princess," he says finally, once again talking in a normal voice. "Dealing with idiots over here. Anyway . . . let me go somewhere more private." I can hear the background din grow still. "All right, so tell me. What's wrong?"

I hate to admit it, but the few minutes it has taken to get my dad's attention have helped to calm me down somewhat. But when I realize that I'm going to tell Dad about my feelings for Drew, I can feel my heart cave in on itself. "I just . . . I just . . ."

"Megan?" he says.

"I don't feel good," I say, turning back toward the street as I wipe my runny nose with the back of my hand.

"You don't?" he says, surprisingly sympathetic. "What's the matter?"

"It's just . . . my . . . my heart."

"Your head?" my dad says. "Does it ache or something?"

Close enough. "Uh-huh."

"I want you to go home right now and take it easy, you hear

me? You want me to call the school? Because I'll call them right now and tell them."

Just hearing the protective tone in my dad's voice makes me feel better. At least there's *someone* who still cares about me.

Even though I have my dad's permission to get out of school for the rest of the day, I somehow manage to tough it out through the final bell. When I get home I throw my hair in a ponytail, put on my sweatpants, and zip up the hoodie I've been wearing all day. I'm pouring myself my third bowl of Cap'n Crunch when I hear a knock on the door. I open it while chewing on a mouthful of cereal.

Oh my God. It's Drew.

"Hey," he says, holding Lucy's white fuzzy sweater up in the air. "Your sister forgot this."

I'm so incredibly relieved and happy to see him that I'm tempted to fling my arms around his neck and smother him with kisses. After I swallow my Crunchberries, of course.

"Is she here?" he asks, glancing over my shoulder.

Huh? What is he talking about? "I thought she was with you."

Drew scratches the back of his arm nervously. "I dropped her off an hour or so ago."

Okay, this is really odd. "She must've gone back to school or to Marybeth's or something."

Suddenly, we're gazing at each other and my legs almost give out. Damn those mesmerizing eyes of his.

"Um, I'll give her the sweater when she gets back," I say, taking it from him.

"Great, thanks." Drew starts walking back down the steps. As I watch him go, I think of all the things I could say to keep him here, like, "Could you open up this jar for me?" Or, "I think there's a burglar in the house!" But instead I wipe my nose with the sleeve of my hoodie and step backward so I can shut the door.

"Megan!"

I whip the door back open.

"I've got an hour to kill before I have to pick my stepdad," Drew says. "Do you mind if I hang out here for a while? Maybe we can run lines or something."

Drew wants to hang out? With *me*? "Okay," I say, as my heart turns into rubble.

He walks inside and I lead him into the living room and then stop so suddenly he almost crashes into me. My emphysema has returned and now I'm practically gasping for air. Drew is *here*, in my house, alone with me. What will we do? What will we talk about? And why am I wearing my old fat girl sweatpants with a hoodie that has a ketchup stain above my right boob?

"What's this?" Drew points at the diorama in the middle of the coffee table.

"It's a diorama I'm working on."

"Cool. Of what?"

I adore how Drew seems interested and curious—about everything. "It's Captain Ahab's cabin, from *Moby-Dick*. I was hoping Mrs. Bordeaux might give me some extra credit." I do a mental head slap. Why did I admit that I needed extra credit? It sounded so . . . loserish. "Pretty pathetic, I know."

"That's not pathetic!" he says. "I wish I had your talent. I could barely get through *Moby-Dick*."

"Same here."

"So . . . how do you do this? Get a shoe box from . . ." Drew picks it up and checks the bottom of the box. "Manolo Blahnik."

"I stole it from my sister." I look for a reaction from him at the mention of Lucy. As happy as I am that he's here, it still feels weird, considering he was just on a date with her.

"Step one, steal a shoe box," Drew says, running his fingers on the inside. "Hey, what's this lined with?"

Hmmm. Not much of a reaction there.

"Oh, the wood? It's really thin Baltic Birch. You can get it in sheets that are an eighth of an inch," I announce, as if that news will really make his day.

"Eighth of an inch? So that makes it easier to cut."

How cute. He's trying to speak geek with me. "Yes, it does."

"Is this Ahab's ivory stool?" he asks, picking up a tiny stool from my dollhouse stash.

"You have a great memory," I blurt out.

Ugh. I sound like one of my teachers.

"And what's this going to be?" he asks, picking up a piece of wood that has a square peg attached to the bottom.

"That's going to be his bed, but I haven't finished yet."

"What kind of tools do we need to finish it?" he asks, motioning toward all the equipment that I have scattered about the coffee table. I was not allowed to do this kind of thing in the living room since it was too easy to nick up furniture with all my saws and knives. But I don't care. In an act of defiance against my mom and the lack of her parental support, I purposely defied the rules. Not that I'm worried, since Mom will never know. I'm too careful and skilled to nick furniture anymore.

"This looks like this could do some serious damage in the wrong hands." Drew gingerly picks up my miter saw, which looks like a long, thin razor blade with a handle.

"That's good for cutting little pieces of wood. And this," I add, picking up the saw next to it, "is a jeweler's saw. See this?" I point to the V-Block bench extension that I've hooked onto the coffee table. "I can put the wood on top and hold it in place so that I can cut shapes and designs into it." I pick up the headboard for Ahab's bed that I had cut in the shape of a whale and show it to him.

"Wow." Drew's hands touch mine as he traces his fingers around the tiny headboard in my hand.

The hair on the back of my neck stands up. I feel totally lightheaded and giddy, like the sugar rush I got from eating five glazed Krispy Kremes in a row (with custard filling).

"Can you teach me how to do this?" he asks, taking the circular saw.

"Make a diorama?"

"Sure," he replies.

I feel like doing my George Longwell imitation and bursting into song, but mine would come with high leg kicks.

I put a piece of wood on the V block and wrap Drew's fingers around the saw, showing him how to hold it. Even though he assures me he understands what he's supposed to do, I can't help but wince, since I'm pretty sure he's going to cut off a finger or something. Amazingly enough, he doesn't. It takes him a while, but he's determined. And finally, he's sawing through two pieces of wood. After he finishes, Drew holds them up for my approval.

"Well done, Drew," I say.

Maybe I should just ask him to call me Miss Fletcher.

Drew puts down the wood and smiles at me while I imagine us in the production room, kissing. "Thanks, Megan. You're pretty cool. There aren't many beautiful girls who can handle a . . . what's this called again?"

Beautiful? Drew just called me beautiful! I need to say something, but what? Should I thank him? Or does that seem too presumptuous? "Miter saw" is the only thing I can get out.

Obviously, Drew doesn't interpret this as seductive come-on. Instead of grabbing me and throwing me on a bed of roses, he grabs Captain Ahab's bed and places it in the diorama cabin. It immediately falls over. "Hmm," he says. "I think we have a leg problem."

I feel like whacking myself on the head for blowing a potential romantic moment. What is wrong with me? "It needs to be cut down a little."

Drew sticks the bed on the butcher's block. "Can I do it?"

"Yeah, just let me help you for a sec." I lean back into him, purposely resting my arm against his as I show him how to work the saw.

"I think I've got it," he says finally, taking the saw from me.

Another missed opportunity. Sheesh. "Be careful. That leg is kind of thick. It'll be a little harder to cut than the boards."

Drew slowly begins sawing off a little piece of the leg with the miter saw.

"Ouch!" he yelps as the saw knicks his finger.

Oh crap. I've killed him.

"Are you okay?" I shriek as I see red trickling down the palm of his hand.

"It's nothing," he says, wincing. "Just a little cut."

I instinctively reach for his finger and put pressure on the wound, just like I've done for every single one of the freshman class. Even still, I'm borderline hysterical. "Maybe we should get you to a hospital!"

Drew laughs and leans his forehead against mine. This excites me in a way I never thought possible. "It's no big deal, Megan. You're pressing on my hand so hard you've definitely cut off my blood supply."

I giggle, but the tone of it is anxious and worried.

Then Drew does something incredible. He kisses me softly on the forehead and says, "You're so sweet."

It's funny. Even though I've shared my first kiss with Drew, and fantasized about having another one with him a million times afterward, this moment is far more intimate and thrilling than what we've already shared and what I've imagined might happen in the future. The reason why is because it's unscripted. There are no stage directions telling us what to do. There is just him and me, standing close to each other, looking into each others eyes, waiting for someone else to make a bold move.

And then someone does.

Drew clears his throat and takes a step back, but I'm still clinging to his hand for dear life. "I guess I should probably get going."

"We should really clean this cut, though," I hear myself say.

Why do I even bother talking?

"I have a first-aid kit in the car," Drew says quickly and looks at his watch. His voice sounds warbly, like he's frightened of someone coming home and finding us there. "See you tomorrow," he adds, before walking out the door.

When it closes behind him, I'm not so sure that I will.

Lucy arrives home nearly a half hour later and finds me in the backyard jumping rope. I have no idea why I'm doing this, considering that:

I haven't jumped rope in about a million years.

Our yard is pretty much just a cement slab the size of a postage stamp.

I can probably count the number of times I've actually been *in* our "backyard."

As anyone who's ever jumped rope knows, after about two seconds you're ready to keel over from exhaustion.

Nevertheless, here I am, jumping rope with all the energy and enthusiasm of a fourth-grader. But I don't feel energized or enthused. The truth of the matter is that I have been suffering from severe anxiety ever since Drew left, and although I've felt anxious many times before, my usual solution (eating) just didn't appeal to me at the moment. Besides, we were out of Oreos. I checked.

"What are you doing?" Lucy looks surprised and horrified, as if she just found me drinking directly out of the milk container.

I continue to jump even though I'm so winded I'm having trouble exhaling. "Interpretive dance."

Lucy shakes her head, not finding my joke the least bit funny. She glances from the backyard of one neighbor to the other, apparently concerned that someone might witness my insanity. And then she goes back inside.

I stop jumping rope and go after her. "Drew brought back your sweater," I say nonchalantly while following Lucy into the kitchen.

At the mention of Drew, my sister's whole demeanor changes. Her sour expression morphs into one of sweetness and joy causing several of my internal organs to fail.

"Where is it?" she asks.

I point to the coffee table in the living room.

I'm kind of expecting Lucy to say something nasty about me having all my diorama crap on the table when I wasn't supposed to, but instead she picks up her sweater and hugs it to her chest. "I can't believe he dropped it off. How incredibly sweet. It's like he was looking for an excuse to see me again."

I stop still as my worst fear comes to life.

"So you guys had fun?" I force myself to ask, trailing behind Lucy as she practically skips up the stairs like Tinker Bell tiptoeing through a field of fairy dust. I spent an hour with Drew, but I didn't ask him a single thing about the play. The slight was intentional. I didn't want to ruin our time together.

"Fabulous," Lucy says with a big sigh. "It was so romantic."

"Romantic? Are you talking about Drew or the play?" I think about how he kissed me on the forehead and wonder if I'd imagined it.

Lucy laughs as she opens our closet, expertly holding her dollhouse in place with her high-heeled boot. I haven't seen her this happy since she was ten and the mall Santa told her she was the prettiest girl he had seen all day. "I was talking about the play," she says. "But I have to say it was romantic being with Drew, too. He's so different than I imagined. He's sweet and funny . . . so easy to talk to. I had so much fun I didn't want to leave. At least I have Friday to look forward to."

"Friday?" I say quietly, my heart suddenly cramped in my throat.

"Drew and I are going to Marybeth's party."

WHAT? He asked my sister out *again*?

"You don't look so good," Lucy says, uncharacteristically (at least for the past month) demonstrating some concern for my well-being. "You better lie down."

My brain simply does not possess the capability to digest the information my sister had so excitedly presented. Drew, the guy who hates parties unless he has someone special to talk to, asked my sister to go to a party with him on Friday night. That tender forehead kiss was nothing but my overactive imagination looking for proof that Drew might actually like me.

I'm such a fool.

I take Lucy's advice and lie on the bed, throwing my arm over my eyes.

"What do you think of this top?"

I open one eye. Lucy is dancing around the room holding her bright purple cashmere sweater to her chest. "This and my new jeans."

After I say what I used to tell Lucy all the time before the accident—"You'll look beautiful"—I put a pillow over my face so she won't see me cry through my nose.

twenty-one

climax (noun): the significant moment in
the plot of a play, when things change
or reach a crisis.

I haven't been to school in two days. My official reason for stay-ing home is that I'm sick with the flu, and since both of my par-ents are out of town on business trips and my sister is not about to shove a thermometer in my mouth, it's an excuse I've gotten away with simply by not showering, neglecting to take my nasal spray (causing my nose to run like a faucet), and staying in bed. The real reason I'm staying home has nothing to do with my physical well-being and everything to do with my emotional state. Simply put: I can't deal.

"Too bad you're still sick," Lucy says, walking into our room. "Marybeth said you were invited, too."

The aroma of Lucy's sweet-smelling perfume fills the air as she sits on the edge of my bed and puts her hand on my forehead, her bracelets jingling as she moves. Lucy has spent the past forty-five minutes getting ready for school and looks as if she just stepped out of a fashion shoot. She is wearing a bright-red low-cut, skintight top; black jeans; and the same high-heeled boots she wore on her date to the play. "You don't have a temperature."

"I still feel sick, though." I pull out two tissues and wipe the snot off my face for emphasis. There is no way I'm going to Marybeth's. The whole reason I'm staying home from school is so I don't have to see Drew.

"Do you need anything?" she asks.

On my first day of claiming to be sick, my sister practically ignored me. On the second day, she began to pay me a little bit of attention, grudgingly bringing me soup and ginger ale in bed. Even though I feel a little guilty about having her wait on me when I'm not really sick, a part of me is enjoying it. It is a restoration of the natural order of the world, the way things are supposed to be. I'm Lucy's little sister. It's her job to look out for my best interests and take care of me.

"More ginger ale," I say, as I crumple the tissues into a ball and shoot it toward the trash. I miss the basket by a solid foot but my sister pretends not to notice.

"You finished it off last night," Lucy says, standing. "I'll pick some up on my way home from school. I don't have practice today because Russell is going to New York this weekend and he's leaving early." She stops in the doorway. "If you want me to stay home with you tonight, I will."

Lucy is willing to miss her date with Drew for me? After weeks of acting like she couldn't stand to be around me, the generosity of her offer is surprising and astounding, not to mention tempting. "No," I say finally. "You should go."

"Are you sure?" she asks.

I rub my forehead in an attempt to stop the sudden pounding inside my head. I'm doing the right thing, right? I can't ask her to stay home just because I don't want her getting her grubby paws on the guy I thought for a split second might be . . . mine. Or can I?

"Yes, of course," I manage. Once again I have an urge to tell Lucy the truth, that I'm so in love with Drew that the thought of her alone with him makes me feel physically sick, but instead I say, "What time is he picking you up?"

"I don't know," she says. "I think we're meeting there."

I'm relieved. I had actually planned on locking the bedroom door, putting on my iPod, and hiding under the covers if Drew came by to get Lucy.

After my sister leaves for school, I check my e-mail. I have been hoping that Simon might contact me just to ask how I'm feeling, or maybe just to tell me that he's reconsidered his ultimatum. But there's nothing. In the past few days I've pretty much alternated from feeling furious (why did he even give me an ultimatum and how come he didn't feel this way about me before my accident) to sad (what am I going to do without my best friend?). The truth of the matter is that I really *need* Simon right now. And I do not appreciate him bagging out on me in the middle of my crisis.

For the umpteenth time I attempt to write him an e-mail.

Dear Simon,
I think this is really unfair.

Scratch that. After all, it's not like he dumped me out of the blue because he couldn't stand the sight of me anymore. He dumped me because he cared about me more than I cared about him. Well, maybe not more, but in a different way. Perhaps I needed to show him some compassion. Especially since I of all people understand what it's like to care about someone who doesn't feel the same way about you.

Dear Simon,
I really do love you. But I just don't
think we're meant for

I stop. How can I tell my best friend that I'm not attracted to him? And why did he have to go and get attracted to me in the first place?

Dear Simon,
I find it very interesting that you
were never ever interested in me
romantically before my accident and
now, a little more than a month after
you first saw me with my new face, you
have given me an ultimatum, i.e.: If I
don't go out with you, you will have

nothing more to do with me. Well, let
me tell you that . . .

Suddenly, my computer dings and I see I have a message—
from Drew. My hands begin to shake. I click on his name and his
message fills the screen.

Lucy says you're still sick. What's
wrong?

I don't answer him. I can't. Just him inquiring about my
health is enough to make my heart ache all over again. No matter how hard I try, I can't figure out how he could have asked my
sister out on a date and then come over here and act as if nothing
had transpired between him and Lucy at all.

I'm in bed (still wearing my pajamas) when Lucy gets home
at four. I finished my Captain Ahab diorama yesterday and although I've had more than enough time to catch up on my
schoolwork this afternoon, I haven't done anything expect try
on my once too-snug jeans to see if my Lucy diet is working (it is)
and watch TV.

"You don't look so good," she says. "Maybe you should go to
the doctor."

"I'm fine," I say, blowing my nose again.

"Are you sure you don't want me to stay home with you?"

"I'm sure."

Lucy fluffs my pillows and sits on the bed with me and

watches MTV. In spite of everything, it feels good to be with her. We used to hang out all the time, and it's nice to experience something familiar after all these weeks of strangeness.

My sister seems to feel the same way and even kisses my forehead before she goes into the bathroom to get ready for her party. She comes out with her hair sleek and silky and wearing a cream-colored off-the-shoulders shirt and her dry-clean-only jeans. Lucy always looks good, but tonight she looks especially drop-dead gorgeous.

"Well?" she asks, giving me a little spin. "Do you think this will be enough to get me an invitation to the fall festival?"

Instead of responding, I blow my nose and nod.

I'm watching *Trauma: Life in the ER* and a doctor is just about to pull a live insect out of a woman's scalp when the doorbell rings. Because it's nearly eight o'clock and has been dark for over an hour, I grab the baseball bat my dad keeps behind his bedroom door just in case he has to whack any intruders. I remember what he has always said when Lucy and I have had to stay home alone: NEVER EVER OPEN THE DOOR FOR SOMEONE YOU DON'T KNOW.

But it's not a stranger waiting outside the door. It's Drew. Once again my heart feels as though it's about to explode.

I put down the bat and open the door. Drew's wearing his leather bomber jacket with a black T-shirt and jeans that are fraying around the pockets. His thick black hair looks as if he combed it with his fingers, and he's holding a bouquet of daises in his hand. "In the mood for some baseball?" he jokes, nodding toward the bat.

I glance at the flowers and swallow hard when I realize that these are for my sister. I have spent a lot of time over the past few days imagining what I'd say to Drew when I finally saw him again. Right now I'm torn between "What's your deal, anyway?" and "What kind of games are you playing?" But it comes out:

"Lucy's already at the party."

Drew's grin is the same as the one he flashed in the car on the way to the comic book store—he knows something I don't again. "I stopped by to see you," Drew says, holding up the flowers.

I look at the bouquet and then back at him. "Those are for *me*?"

He nods. "Can I come in? I won't stay long."

"Okay," I squeak, pushing the door open. I suddenly realize I'm wearing the same hoodie I've had on for the past few days and I'm still in my gross pajamas, the ones I got for Christmas two years ago that have little monkeys eating bananas all over them and a hole in the butt. I haven't showered or brushed my hair or teeth in three days, either.

"I'll be right back." Holding on to the butt of my pajamas, I turn and race upstairs. I throw on jeans and a T-shirt and pull my hair back in a ponytail. I flick on some mascara and brush my teeth until they're sparkling.

When I get back downstairs, Drew is sitting on the couch, holding my daisies and watching me walk toward him. Although neither of us say anything, I can feel this electricity charging the air. I know I'm not imagining it, because Drew stands up and looks at me with such intensity that I can almost predict what he's going to do next.

"Do you have a vase?" he asks.

Okay. Didn't predict that.

"Sure," I say as I turn and walk into the kitchen. Drew follows close behind. I reach under the sink and pull out one of Mom's big crystal vases. I'm about to take the daisies from him when I notice that he's staring at my nose.

"Do you have the flu or something?"

I instinctively lick the top of my lip and realize that it's wet. Damn. "No," I say quickly, grabbing a tissue off the table. "I just didn't take my nose spray." I rush upstairs and give myself a double dose. Fortunately, it works almost immediately and lasts for almost twelve hours.

By the time I get back to the kitchen, Drew has already filled the vase with water and put the flowers inside.

"All better," I say, pointing to my now wiped-so-clean-it's-red nose. We stare at each other and the electricity finds us once again. I glance from his eyes to his lips and feel my body trembling. "Thanks for the flowers. I love yellow. It's my favorite color."

Drew takes a couple steps toward me, reaches out, and runs his hand down my arm lightly. "You're welcome."

I grab on to the back of the chair to hold myself up.

He must misread this reaction of mine because he backs off and shifts gears on me. "So . . . how's that diorama coming?"

I don't answer him. I'm too busy thinking about what a miracle it is that he's here *and* that he brought me yellow flowers. What happened to his big plans with my sister?

"The one you were working on the other day. Remember? I almost cut off my finger," he teases, holding up his hand and pointing to a Big Bird Band-Aid.

"How could I forget," I say, instinctually reaching out to touch it. The minute our fingers make contact a charge rips through me. But there's this worried look in his eyes and I'm scared that I'm not misreading it. "Aren't you supposed to be at a party with Lucy?" I ask, stepping away from him.

"No. I mean, I told her I might stop by, but that's it." Wait, he didn't ask my sister out on a date? Why did Lucy tell me he did? Then something awful dawns on me. Perhaps she intentionally lied about Drew asking her out so she could keep me away from him. As terrible as that sounds, at the moment, none of it really seems to matter. I feel as if a major load has been taken off my shoulders. *Drew didn't ask Lucy out! Drew is here with ME!*

"Anyway, when Bill told me you were sick, I decided to come over and check up on you."

"Bill? Bill who?"

"Bill Williams. He's a sophomore."

"I've never even met him. How would he know I was sick?"

"When the prettiest girl in school is sick," Drew says, "people notice."

"That's what he said?" I ask as my face grows warm.

"No. I did."

My face burst into flames as I give him a little grin and stare at my feet.

"So are you hungry?" he asks. "I can make you dinner if you'd like."

"*You* cook?" I can't exactly envision Drew in an apron, stirring a steaming kettle on a hot stove.

"Well, I can make ratatouille," Drew says, taking my hand.

My breath catches in my throat. Even though I kind of feel like I did when I was in the finals of the fifth-grade spelling bee and was asked to spell myrrh, I'm determined not to let my fear get the best of me, like I did before.

"Do you like ratatouille?"

I am looking at my hand in his and about to melt onto the linoleum. "I hate it," I whisper almost seductively.

Drew laughs. "I'll just have to make something else. Anything you want."

As if holding on to my hand wasn't enough to make me faint, he pulls me in closer so I'm standing only inches away from him. I'm so startled by this that I blurt out the word *spaghetti*.

Ugh. Every toddler's favorite food.

But Drew doesn't care. "Spaghetti it is," he says, and then he kisses my hand.

My heart stops beating and my head is spinning. Drew puts my hand to his cheek and his skin is incredibly warm. He leans in and I'm totally paralyzed, but with sheer joy, not fear. It's as though everything up until this moment in time has been scripted to a fault, and with one improvised action, the story will need a different ending.

Megan Fletcher, ugly duckling techie turned beautiful swan actress, will ride off into the sunset with the hero.

Drew gently presses his lips to mine, kissing me softly and slowly. My pulse is racing when he sticks his tongue in my mouth just a little bit. Before now, I would've thought that touching someone else's tongue with mine was right up there with scraping the gum off from underneath my desk and sticking it in my mouth, but it's not that at all. It feels . . . unbelievable. In fact, I want to swallow him whole. Drew's kiss is getting hungrier, too. My chest is pressed up against his and his hands are going up the back of my T-shirt. Then they travel south toward my rear when I hear it.

Click.

Through the fog it hits me: It's a key in a lock. Which can only mean one thing: someone's home. With all the strength of a superhero, I push Drew off me. He topples over into the stove, stunned and surprised.

I hear footsteps storming through the living room and within seconds, Lucy is standing in the kitchen. "Drew? What are you doing here?"

"He just stopped by to see how I was feeling," I say in a high-pitch voice.

It makes me sound guilty of something, I'm just not sure what anymore.

"Oh?" Lucy says, narrowing her eyes at him.

"What are you doing home?" I say to Lucy. Surprisingly, this question almost comes out as an accusation.

"I was worried about you," she replies sternly, looking as though she'd like to strangle me and dump my body in the Chesapeake. "I'm surprised to see you out of bed."

Now that I see the rage in her eyes, I feel like the wind has been sucked right out of my lungs. "Right, I should, well, get back in it." I turn toward Drew. "Thanks for stopping by."

"Oh," he says, clearly surprised by his sudden dismissal. "Um, sure."

Lucy crosses her arms but doesn't move. She's just standing there, glaring at me.

"Well, good night," I say as I run back up the stairs, leaving Drew and Lucy alone. I turn off the bedroom light and crawl back into bed, still wearing my clothes. I can hear Lucy saying "so long" to Drew, then padding up the stairs.

"He brought you flowers?" she asks, flipping on the overhead light.

Half of me wants to defend myself and rip into Lucy for misleading me about her "date" with Drew. The other half wants to apologize. But for what? Getting what I *want*? Being *happy* for the first time in my life? For being (according to Drew at least) the prettiest girl in school?

But instead I say nothing.

Lucy just shakes her head in disgust and walks into the bathroom, slamming the door behind her.

The shower turns on and I hear a muffled noise. I get out of bed and creep out of the room, pausing at the closed bathroom door. I stand still, listening to Lucy cry in the shower. It's clear from the level of her devastation that maybe she really did like Drew. And she had come home to find him with someone she never thought she'd have to fight with for any boy.

Her sister. Her *beautiful* sister.

I've never made Lucy so upset before and I'm not sure what I'm supposed to do next. It's totally unnerving, especially since Lucy has always seemed so strong, so capable of not only taking care of herself, but me as well. She has saved my neck so many times. Ten years ago, when we were playing dolls in our backyard and Warren Gumbar, a neighborhood bully at least four years older than me, started calling me werewolf girl, barking and howling at me through the fence. Even though he was twice Lucy's size and all the kids at school were terrified of him, Lucy grabbed a branch and jammed it right at him, right through the fence.

And what about freshman year, when Angie Rembleaux wrote *Megan Fletcher is the ugliest dog EVER* inside all the bathroom stalls on the second floor and the very next day Lucy made her apologize and then wipe it all off by hand? It seems like there were a million instances just like that, and even though I really don't want to be thinking about them right now because they only make me feel worse, they're all fast-forwarding through my mind at the speed of light.

When Lucy comes out of the bathroom, I've relived sixteen years of her saving my ass and am sitting on the hallway floor, wiping my nose with the back of my hand. I open my mouth to say something, I'm still not sure what, but Lucy snaps before I can speak.

"How could you do this to me?!"

And with that, all of my sympathy and guilt morph into an anger that rivals my sister's.

"For once, Lucy, this isn't about *you!*" I shout.

I'm not even sure what I mean by that. But I know it's enough to drive Lucy away.

She storms into our room and grabs her pillow. "I was so excited for this year, Megan. I thought it was going to be great for *both of us*. But I never would have guessed that you'd *turn on me.*"

After that dramatic statement, Lucy makes her grand exit and seeks shelter in our parents' bedroom.

As for me, I go into the bathroom, stare at my undoubtedly pretty face in the mirror, and think about what would have happened with Drew if my sister hadn't come home.

twenty-two

vomitory (noun): an auditorium entrance or
exit that emerges through banked seating
from below.

I'm awake half the night, thinking about Drew and Lucy and my parents and Simon and George and Catherine and people at school I barely know. My mind has never been this cluttered and I can't help but believe that my new face is to blame.

I must have fallen asleep at some point, though, because when I sit up in bed, light is spilling through the curtains. I'm not surprised to see that the door to my parents' room is wide open and the bed already made. I hear a noise in the kitchen and I take a deep breath as I steady myself against the railing, mentally preparing myself for the fireworks. But as I walk downstairs the smell of coffee hits me right between the eyes. There's only person who drinks coffee in this house: my mom.

I burst into the kitchen and fly into her arms, almost tackling her to the ground. "When did you get home?"

"A couple hours ago."

Maybe I'm just overly sensitive, but the sight of me doesn't seem to be making her delirious with happiness. And she has been gone for three days, definitely long enough for some delirium. This can only mean one thing: "I take it you saw Lucy?"

She nods. "She was sleeping in my bed."

"Look, Mom, I know what Lucy thinks, but I didn't invite Drew over here last night. In fact, he had sent me an e-mail earlier in the day and I didn't even respond."

My mom looks perplexed. "What are you talking about?"

Hold everything. "Didn't she tell you?"

"She just said that she's been having trouble sleeping and so she stayed up and fell asleep in front of the TV."

It hits me that Lucy may have been trying to protect me, like she used to when we were little, and my eyes fill with tears. Suddenly, I'm spilling my guts to my mom, starting with the most recent events and working my way backward.

At the end of my story, my mother sighs. "So Lucy thinks you purposefully came in between her and this boy Drew?"

I nod, miserable.

My mom gives me a sympathetic smile. "You look tired," she says. "Do you want some tea?"

I hug my knees to my chest and nod again. My mom fills a mug with water and pops it in the microwave.

"So are you?"

"Am I what?"

"Interested in Drew?"

Even though I know Mom's not the type to point an accusatory finger, I still feel defensive. "Well, I liked him first," I say quickly. "In fact, from the moment I saw him. Lucy never even paid any attention to him until she found out he was directing the spring musical."

"Come on, now," Mom says.

"It's true!" I say emphatically, like I'm trying to convince my mother that Drew belongs with me. "I know him a lot better than Lucy does. I know that he likes Batman and has two little sisters and carries a dictionary around."

My mom's eyebrows twitch. "That's a little weird."

And I know that, "Well, I know that I *love* him."

I can't believe I said that out loud. And in front of my mother. She smiles a little bit but doesn't say a word.

"And I think . . . I'm pretty sure he likes me, too."

"Oh yeah?"

"Well, he cast me in the play when I know for a fact there were better actresses. And last night he brought me flowers . . . and he told me I was the prettiest girl in the school."

"The prettiest girl in the school? Well . . . that is nice," my mom says simply.

Excusez-moi? Nice? It's obvious my mom thinks Drew is full of crap. I'm silent for a minute. "Why would he say that if he didn't like me?"

My mom sighs and gives me one of her "kindly" smiles. "You don't really know this boy yet."

"He's not the type of guy to give out compliments he doesn't mean."

"I'm sure he does think you're the prettiest girl in school. But he doesn't really know you. Not yet, at least."

Oh, I get it. "So once he gets to know me, he'll run screaming for the hills. Is that it? Because I may not look like an ugly duckling but inside I'm still the same old nasty—"

"Whoa, whoa, whoa." My mom puts her hand on top of mine. "Where is this coming from?"

"I'm just tired of this! First Lucy, then Simon, now you. The only person around here who seems excited about me and my new life is Dad!"

"That's not true, Megan. I am excited for you. Your new face . . . well, you've been given a wonderful opportunity. But I just don't want to see you get hurt or—"

"Or what?"

"Or lose sight of who you are and what's important."

"What's important is that the guy who I've loved forever seems to feel the same way about me, too." I grab a tissue and blow my nose. I'd really like to prove to my mom that she's totally, completely wrong about Drew, that what we have is the real deal, that he loves me sincerely and totally and couldn't care less what I look like—but I can't. And I can't because at least twenty-eight percent of me thinks she might have a point. "And

I'm sorry. But if that makes Lucy and Simon hate my guts, so be it."

"Simon? Why should he care?"

"Because of my new face and this wonderful opportunity, he's decided he wants to be my boyfriend now. He gave me the ultimatum: all or nothing."

My mom winces.

"How do I tell my best friend that the thought of being his girlfriend grosses me out?"

"Maybe you can be honest with him without mentioning the grosses-you-out part."

"And what about Lucy? She hates me."

"Lucy may be mad at you, but she certainly doesn't *hate* you."

"You're wrong, Mom. She not only hates me, she can't stand the sight of me."

"Come on, now. I know you're upset, but you don't really believe that, do you?" My mother takes a sip of her coffee while she pauses a moment to gather her thoughts. "You know, Lucy told me about what happened at the dance last year, and all the hurtful things she'd said."

My mom and I have never spoken about the moments leading up to the accident. At first I was too injured to talk, and by the time I could, it didn't seem to matter anymore. After all, Lucy was so upset and obviously trying very hard to make it all up to me. There didn't seem to be any point in dredging it up again.

"Lucy relieved that moment over and over again. The whole time you were in the hospital, she slept on the floor of our room. She woke up screaming in the middle of the night, she couldn't eat, her grades suffered, she completely dropped out of the theater program . . . all because . . ." My mom takes a deep breath. "She didn't want to leave your side. She was haunted by the thought that she could have lost you." Mom's eyes get all teary. "We all were."

I take a tissue and blow my nose. I have never heard about Lucy's nightmares, and although I remember thinking that she looked really skinny, I didn't know that she stopped eating and slept on the floor of my parents' room. And I have to say, the news makes me feel horrible and wonderful at the same time. I'm totally relieved to hear how much she loves me, but I feel awful that my sister has suffered because of me.

My mom sighs long and deep. She stands up and gives me a hug. Even though I'm normally not the huggy-feely type, I rest my head on her shoulder as my nose drips on her shirt.

"Oh, Megan. What you're experiencing now . . . all this attention . . . anyone would be having a difficult time. I know you're doing the best you can. All I'm saying is that you need to be careful. I have the feeling a lot of boys are going to be proclaiming their love. Some will be sincere and some won't. You'll have to decide which one is which. And it's not going to be easy."

And then she tucks a strand of hair behind my ear and gives me the same kind smile she always gives me when she's trying to convince me that things will be all right. "I know things seem complicated right now, but everything will work out in the long run. You'll see."

As I look at my mom, I do my best to smile even though I have a feeling she's dead wrong.

twenty-three

morality play (noun): a type of theatrical
allegory in which the protagonist is met by
personifications of various moral attributes
who try to prompt him to choose a godly
life over one of evil.

On Monday I arrive at Lucheki's class before Simon. I optimistically sit in my regular seat but Simon gets there late and sits about ten rows behind me. He looks like crap. He has dark circles under his eyes and his hair is abnormally messy. He's wearing his glasses but he's still dressed like a prep student, albeit one who has slept in his clothes. His wrinkled blue shirt is only half tucked in and his pants look a size too big.

I'm not one to make judgments, however, since I'm not faring much better. In fact, I'm pretty much a total wreck. Lucy has been avoiding me, staying away from the house as much as possible and sleeping on the couch. The couple of times I've tried to talk to her she's been polite yet distant. It's not like she's mad. It's much, much worse. It's like she doesn't even care about me enough to be angry. That, in addition to Simon's behavior, not to mention the whole "does Drew just like me because I'm pretty" talk I had with my mom has turned me into a crazy, anxious shell of myself. I haven't slept, and even though I've been taking my nose spray, my nose is running like a sieve.

And now, sitting in the same room as Simon and not being able to talk to him or laugh with him or just be with him—it makes everything ten times worse. Even though I turn around and look at him more than once, he never even glances in my direction. When class is over I solemnly file out, convinced Simon is never going to talk to me again. The minute I get into the hall, though, I feel a hand on my arm.

"Can I talk to you for a minute?" Simon asks.

I feel a rush of relief. I'm so happy and grateful that someone I care about is actually talking to me that I want to say, yes, of course, I'll talk wherever and whenever you want, but before I get an opportunity, I see George heading in my direction. Why does George always seem to appear when I'm with Simon? And suddenly I realize that I have been so distracted by my other problems that I never responded to George's invitation to the fall festival.

"Did you get the invite?" George calls out cheerfully.

Simon winces, but makes no effort to leave.

"Yeah," I say to George. "But ah, well, can we talk later?"

"It's a simple question, beautiful," he says, stopping in front of me. I wince at his use of the word "beautiful." "Yes or no?" he asks.

I take a breath. "I'm sorry," I say quickly. "I can't go because, well . . ." I look at Simon. I think about him and Lucy and Drew and how terrible and complicated everything has become. "I'm going with Simon."

Simon's eyes open wide as his mouth falls open.

I stop breathing. What? Did I just say I was going with Simon?

"Oh," George says. "Okay. That's cool."

Neither Simon nor I say anything as George walks away. We just stand there, staring at each other. I feel like I'm having some sort of weird, awful dream. What about Drew? *What about Drew?*

The bell rings and the halls clear out, leaving us alone.

"I need to take it slow," I say finally. "Really slow."

"Okay," he says.

"Like working our way up to holding hands slow."

"Okay," he says again.

I think I'm going to throw up. Right here. Right outside the theater, right in the middle of the window-lined hall. The janitor will have to come clean it up, but he won't be able to get rid of the smell, and all day long, any time anyone even walks near it, they're going to wrinkle their nose and ask: Who puked?

"What made you change your mind?" Simon asks.

"Because you like me for who I am on the inside," I hear

myself say. Which is true. Unfortunately, it doesn't help my nausea at all.

I don't go to lunch. Instead I tell Simon I have a doctor's appointment and leave school. I don't get permission. I just open the front door and start walking with no particular destination in mind. I spend the entire afternoon walking and walking and wondering how in hell I could've told Simon that I would go to the dance with him.

To be honest, I had considered it. After all, I had spent the entire weekend thinking about him, Drew, and Lucy and trying to figure out what to do. And when George asked me in front of Simon and I saw the pain on his face—I cracked. I just couldn't take it anymore.

But what's done is done, right? All I can do now is reassure myself that what's done is/was the right thing. After all, could I really have given up both Lucy and Simon for Drew, a guy who probably would never have been interested in me if I was still ugly? I should be commending myself, not walking around feeling as if I just stepped into a pool of quicksand.

But I haven't stepped in quicksand. I've walked right back to school and into the classroom where I'm meeting Drew.

"Hey," he says, jumping off a desk to greet me as I walk into the room.

I really, really wanted to blow off play practice, but due to my imaginary illness, I missed almost all of last week. But even if

I hadn't, I doubted I would've been able to blow it off. I'm just too much of a masochist.

"I've been trying to reach you," Drew says.

He had called twice over the weekend and once today but I hadn't had the heart to answer or call him back. "I'm sorry. I had . . . well, some things to take care of."

The smile fades from his face. "What's wrong?"

I turn away. I can't tell him what I have done. I know I can't keep it a secret forever but I just can't handle it right now.

"Nothing." I set down my backpack and take out my script. "I'm almost done memorizing my lines," I say, in a voice I'm hoping he'll interpret as enthusiastic.

He takes my hand and says, "I was a little worried about you the other night. You kind of disappeared when Lucy got home. And then when I couldn't reach you, well, I didn't know what had happened."

Once again I get a visual of Lucy's face when she came out of the shower after she'd been crying. I pull away and take a couple of steps back. "My head was hurting."

"I'm sorry," he says. "Are you feeling better?"

"I'm all right," I manage.

"I never got a chance to do what I had intended to do the other night. I came over because I wanted to ask you if you wanted to go to the fall festival with me."

I can't breathe.

"What do you think?"

I think . . . I think . . . I think I need a tissue. My hands are shaking so wildly I can barely unzip the side pocket of my backpack to pull out the little package I always carry with me. "I can't," I spit out before blowing my nose into a Kleenex.

It's totally, unnaturally, quiet.

I clear my throat and turn back to face him. I might as well get this over with now. "I told Simon I would go with him."

"Simon?"

I pick up my script and stare at it.

Drew starts walking to the front of the room and stops. "So . . . you and Simon . . . are you guys just friends, or is it . . . something else?"

"Something else?" I want to tell him that it's not just about Simon. It's about my sister, too. And it's about being true to my old self.

"Are you and Simon dating?"

I swallow hard. "We've been best friends forever."

"So you're just friends?"

"Not exactly," I whisper.

I can see a flash of pain in Drew's eyes as he pauses a second.

"He just . . . he really knows me. He cares about me for who I am." There. That should do it. Relationship over.

"Okay," he says finally, and motions for me to take my place.

But as we begin to recite our lines, I notice that Drew's demeanor has changed. Usually he's patient and encouraging when I forget a line, but today he seems annoyed, almost angry. All I can I think about is how tender he was to me the other night and how he offered to make me spaghetti and how it felt when he kissed me and now it's all gone.

When Drew decides to call it quits a half hour early, I'm relieved and upset at the same time. It's torture to be with him and look into his eyes and know that when I walk out the door, I'll be leaving a part of myself behind.

But it's the sacrifice I have to make.

twenty-four

catharsis (noun): a moment of high
tragedy at the emotional climax of a play,
followed by an emotional cleansing for the
characters and the audience.

When I get home, Lucy is in our parents' room with the door
shut. I knock but she doesn't answer. I turn the knob and peek
inside. She is wearing a bright yellow sweat suit, listening to music on her iPod as she writes in a spiral notebook.

"Hey," I say.

She doesn't bother to glance up.

"I just wanted to tell you that I'm going to the fall festival
with Simon."

Lucy pauses a split second before glancing at me.

I've been around Lucy enough to recognize a nice dramatic
moment when I see it, so I seize the opportunity, turning on my
heel and shutting the door behind me.

I'm halfway down the stairs when I hear the bedroom door

open. "What do you mean you're going with Simon?" Lucy calls out.

"He asked me and I said yes," I reply.

"What about Drew?" she asks, following me.

I shrug. "What about him?"

"I thought . . ."

Even though I'm kind of happy Lucy is speaking to me again, I can't have a conversation about Drew with her right now. I turn away from her and hurry into the kitchen. I begin rummaging through the cupboards with all the nervous energy of an addict. I find a half-eaten bag of Oreos and rip it open.

"When did all this happen with Simon?"

I twist an Oreo apart and pop the slightly soggy and stale creme-covered side in my mouth. I chew a couple of times and then say, "Well, things have been weird since the beginning of the year. He told me last week that his feelings for me have changed and he wanted to go to the fall festival with me."

"Wow," she says, dropping into a chair.

I sit down across from her and pop another Oreo into my mouth without bothering to twist it apart. I swallow the huge glob in one gulp.

"So do you like him?"

"Of course I do. He's my best friend."

"That's not what I meant."

"I, well, I guess I'll find out. He just called a few minutes ago and asked me out on an official date this weekend."

My sister's brow is furrowed and I can tell she's feeling something unpleasant. But what? Guilt? Remorse?

"Look," she says. "I'm sorry about the other night. I just, well, things are weird this year, you know?"

It's good to hear Lucy apologize, but when she doesn't tell me that I don't have to give up Drew, my heart feels almost hollow.

"So what are you and Simon doing this weekend?" she asks.

"We're going to go see the new movie about the space invaders on Saturday. Maybe get some coffee afterward."

"You should wear my yellow BCBG top," Lucy says with a smile. "It looks so awesome on you. Or maybe my pink Michael Kors instead. Let's go try them on and see which one looks better."

My sister stands and extends her hand to me. I accept her hand and tuck the package of Oreos under my arm, hoping that somehow Lucy will do something unscripted.

On Saturday night, Simon picks me up for our official date looking like he's going to his mother's country club. He's wearing ironed khakis and a starched button-down shirt topped by a blue blazer with gold buttons. I know he dressed up for me, and although on some level I'm sure a little part of me appreciates the effort, the majority of me just finds it annoying. I have not dressed up for him. In spite of my sister's protests, I'm not wearing any makeup and my slightly dirty hair is pulled back in a ponytail. I'm wearing my loose-fitting jeans and one of my old hoodies. Why bother dressing up? I'm more comfortable this way, and since Simon likes me for who I am on the inside, I figure he couldn't care less what I looked like. Right? Obviously, I'm still a little frustrated that he and I are in this situation in the first place. I really wish he never gave me an ultimatum. I know that Simon knows me a lot better than Drew, but if he really loved me, would he/could he have walked away from more than two years of best friendship?

But, as I kept reminding myself all week, he hadn't actually *done* anything. He had just *threatened* it. I have to believe that if push came to shove, he would've been happy with whatever level of friendship I offered.

At least, that's what I keep telling myself.

Due to the fact that I fell off the Lucy diet this past week and consumed more calories than I would've thought humanly possible, I have pledged to drink only Diet Pepsi for the next two days. But as we walk into the movies Simon asks me if I want anything to eat and I order a box of Dots and a small popcorn with butter. (Simon insists on paying even though he bought our tickets.)

As we take our seats I glance at his hand perched on our communal armrest and wonder if he will try to hold my hand. I hold the Dots in one hand while using the other to shovel popcorn in my mouth just in case. After the movie, we climb back into his Honda Civic and he drives us back to Federal Hill. We stop at Spoons and Simon orders a black tea and I order an iced mocha cappuccino and a chocolate chip cookie. And even though I manage to whip out a ten-dollar bill, Simon beats me to the punch, handing the cashier a crisp twenty. We take seats across from each other and I keep my hands in my lap as I bend over and suck my drink out of the straw.

"It's nice," he says, finally. "Being out with you like this."

I think about how weird it is that only a week ago I was with Drew and he was kissing me. "Me too," I say, reaching into my purse for a tissue. And then I realize what I just said doesn't make any sense. I don't bother to correct myself. Instead, I blow my nose and take another sip of my drink.

"You look great," he says.

I catch sight of my reflection in the café window. I definitely look a lot better than I did last year at this time, but I couldn't look much worse if I tried. Which, of course, I had. "Thanks," I reply stiffly.

We stare at each other in silence.

"Do you want something else to eat?" Simon is trying to be a gentleman here but I keep imagining myself with Drew.

This just isn't fair. To either of us.

I wipe my nose again. "I don't think so. I've been eating nonstop all day." Then I finish off my cookie and order a brownie with icing.

When I'm done making a pig of myself, Simon takes me home. As he drives, I study his profile, paying close attention to his aquiline nose, his curly brown hair, and his lopsided grin. He isn't bad-looking. And he's sweet, funny, and smart. So why can't I stop thinking about Drew?

Simon parks in front of our house and hurries to get my door for me. "I had a great time tonight," he says, as he walks me up the steps of our row house.

I can see him hesitate and I know he's working up the nerve to do something. As tempted as I am to escape inside and lock the door behind me, I keep my feet firmly planted. I can do this. This is Simon. And I adore him.

Simon sweeps his hand around me, pulling me in to him and giving me a big, long, and passionate kiss.

Wow. I knew Simon had learned a little more than how to play the clarinet at band camp, but I didn't know he could do *that*. But despite the expertise of his kiss, the electricity I felt with Drew isn't here. Not even close.

Simon slowly backs away. When I open my eyes, I see him grinning. "I'll call you tomorrow," he says happily before shuffling down the sidewalk.

As I creep into the house, I hear a noise coming from the kitchen. I know it's Mom, because Lucy is at a party tonight. But when I enter the kitchen, I see that I'm wrong.

"Have you seen the Oreos?" my dad asks.

twenty-five

cheat (verb): to make an action onstage
look realistic without actually performing it;
e.g., an actor looking toward the audience
in the general direction of the person
he is talking to is cheating.

"I ate them all," I tell my father as he rummages through our cupboards.

"The whole bag?"

"They were stale anyway," I reply. Like that makes it all okay.

"What about the pretzels?"

"I finished those off, too." I brace myself for the lecture I'm pretty sure I'm going to get by chewing on my thumb cuticles. All my dad likes to talk about now is how good-looking I am. I'm pretty sure he won't be happy to hear that I've reverted back to my old eating habits.

Instead, he turns around holding a container of peanut butter and says, "You look nice."

What? This wasn't the response I was expecting. I guess when you have a pretty face no one notices little things like unwashed hair and dirty jeans. "Thanks," I say.

"Where were you?"

I pull my thumb away from my mouth. "I went out with Simon."

"Oh, that's right," he says, setting the peanut butter down on the counter and turning back toward the cupboards again. He pulls out a grody-looking open bag of marshmallows that I'm pretty sure we bought for sleepover camp in fifth grade. "Your mom said you were going out with Simon tonight." He unrolls the bag of marshmallows, unscrews the top of the peanut butter, dips a marshmallow in, and pops one in his mouth.

I'm not hungry in the slightest and the marshmallow–peanut butter combo looks about as appetizing as a cold bowl of spinach, but I still reach into the bag and follow suit, taking out a marshmallow, dipping it in the peanut butter, and eating it.

My dad grabs a couple more marshmallows out of the bag. We both sit there looking at each other. "These are terrible," he says finally, opening up his hand and studying the marshmallows cupped inside it.

"Awful," I agree, taking another one.

"And I'm not even hungry," he admits.

"I'm stuffed," I say.

"Like father, like daughter."

Even though my dad isn't exactly paying me a compliment, I

don't mind. I'm just happy to be sharing something with some-one I love. And if it can't be an oversized nose and puffy cheeks, it might as well be a bag of stale marshmallows.

"My mom was the same way. She always ate when she was stressed."

"I wish I had met her," I say quietly. My dad's mom died right after Mom and Dad got married. According to my mom she was smart, funny, and quite round.

"She would've just loved you. You got your love of art from her. She was always dragging me and my sister to museums every chance she got." He smiles. "And she would've been so proud of how you've handled everything the past year."

"I'm not sure there's so much to be proud of," I say, thinking of the turmoil in my life. "It's been a little tough since I went back to school."

"I bet it has. But you're obviously dealing with everything. It's nothing like how things used to be. Christ, every time I turned around Lucy was going out to one party or another and you were sitting home all by yourself."

Ouch. I put down the marshmallow.

My dad's eyes shift from my discarded marshmallow back to me. "Sorry," he says. "All I'm trying to say is that I used to worry about you. It didn't seem healthy. Who wants to be . . ." He looks around and laughs. "Alone in the kitchen at ten o'clock on a Saturday night stuffing your face with marshmallows and peanut butter."

"I don't know, Dad. Sometimes I kind of miss my old life."

"Oh, come on," he laughs, as if he's sure I'm joking.

I shrug as I glance away. Even though I'm definitely enjoying hanging out with my dad, I'm not sure I'm ready to bare my soul to him.

"You're serious?" he says, putting down the marshmallows. "What's going on?"

I sigh. Where to begin? And how much did I really want to share? "For starters, I just had my first date with Simon."

"Tonight was a *date?*"

I nod.

He leans back, surprised. "Your mom told me you were going out with Simon, but I didn't realize it was an official date. How about that? It's kind of like me and Mom, huh?"

"That's right!" I say enthusiastically. "You guys were friends at first, too."

"Not really friends. More like a one-sided love affair. It took me a long time to win over your mom. She used to come in every day and order the exact same thing: coffee, no sugar, a hardboiled egg, and whole wheat toast with the butter on the side. I thought things between us were progressing pretty well. At least, until I asked her out." He chuckles.

"And what did she say?" I had heard this story at least a hundred times before, but I thought it might do me some good to hear it once more.

"She thanked me and told me how flattered she was, but that she was in a relationship. And then she stopped coming in. About a year later, I saw her at a bar in town. I had lost about thirty pounds and cut off my mustache and started working out . . . I don't think she recognized me, even though to this day she insists she did. Anyway, turns out that she had broken up with the guy she was dating. And I had moved on, too. I had graduated from school and taken a job with Cisco. Just that day I had bought two concert tickets and I thought, what the hell. So I asked her."

My dad's BlackBerry goes off and we're both silent as he checks his messages. He shakes his head after he puts it away. "As for Simon . . . sometimes these things take time," he says. "Time and patience. It's like anything else."

Lucy wakes me up at twelve-thirty that night to ask me how things went with Simon. Before my accident, she used to do this so she could tell me about *her* night out, and it's yet another reminder of how different things are between us.

"Fine," I tell her as I rub my eyes.

"Did he kiss you?"

I nod.

"And?"

I'm really surprised at what I say. "Actually, he's a really good kisser."

"Get out!" she practically yells. "I can't wait to tell Marybeth. She said she could just tell he'd be a good kisser."

I can't help but wonder what there is about Simon that would make Marybeth think that.

"Guess what? I got asked to the fall festival!" Lucy shouts.

A chill runs down my spine.

"When I went to Jane's tonight, I walked in the door and the first person I saw was Drew."

I think I might pass out.

"Anyway, he kept following me around all night. No matter where I went or what I did, Drew was right there. Finally I was like, what's going on? And then he basically asked me to go with him."

I'm in a state of shock. I can't do anything but stare at my sister, dumbfounded. My mom had been right about Drew after all.

Lucy stands up and walks over to her dresser. She takes a purple silk nightgown out of her bottom drawer. I curl up in the fetal position as my mind frantically tries to absorb everything my sister has told me. Maybe I was delusional when I told Mom I knew Drew better than Lucy did. Maybe I didn't know him at all.

When Lucy gets into bed, she doesn't say good night. Instead she says, "I'm glad everything worked out for us in the end. Aren't you?"

I feel a burning sensation deep in my esophagus as I picture Simon in his tux and pray that the mere sight of him makes me want to kiss him and forget all about Drew. I keep praying until I fall asleep, when the sun comes up.

twenty-six

dry (verb): to fail to memorize lines.

On Friday I get to play practice twenty minutes late. Drew is sitting on a desk, his arms crossed in front of him. He looks like he's about to blow a gasket.

"Hey," I say casually.

I know why Drew is so angry. I've been late to play practice every day this week, each day a little bit later than the one previous. Although I normally hate being late, I would rather rip off my fingernails with my teeth one by one than endure another full day of play practice. As far as I'm concerned, I'm entitled to be mad at Drew for asking Lucy to the fall festival after I said no. If I had any nerve, I'd quit this play right now and he'd be left high and dry and without an actress for his stupid one-act. In fact, if I wasn't pretty sure he'd just replace me with Lucy, I'd quit this minute.

"Why are you so late?" His eyes are practically smoking with rage.

"I had . . . some . . . some things to do."

"Some things to do?" he repeats sarcastically. He stands up, his arms still crossed.

I try to give him my special I'm-not-afraid-of-you stare, but it's been a long time since I've used it.

"What *things?"*

Yep, it's not working. Surprise, surprise.

"Personal things," I say simply.

The muscles in Drew's jaw clench, and for a minute I wonder if I've gone just a tad too far. He looks as if he's about to erupt into one of my dad's furious tirades. But he just runs a hand through his thick black hair and says, "Megan, this is our last practice before the dress rehearsal. Let's just . . . let's just try to focus."

Over the past week, every now and then Drew says or does something that makes me forget how upset I am that he went after Lucy and wish that we were back in my house kissing. This is one of those times. There's something about the way he ran his fingers through his hair that makes me want to throw my arms around him and hold on forever.

God help me.

How can I still feel like this? I'd have to be crazy to still like Drew after he asked my sister to the dance.

Drew and I assume our positions at the front of the classroom. I start saying my lines but I'm having trouble concentrating. Still, I persevere and only sneak a peek at the script twice. Although that's an all-time record for me, Drew looks annoyed, like he really can't believe I'm not completely offscript yet. As we get closer to the kiss, my anxiety starts getting the best of me. I begin my mantra: *I'm an actress—I'm an actress—I'm an actress.*

"So . . ." So what? What is my line, anyway? I nervously glance toward the open script that is lying on top of a desk on the front row. Unfortunately, it's upside down and more than five feet away. Although my eyesight's good, it's not *that* good.

"So we won't call it a relationship," Drew says quickly, feeding me my line.

"We won't call it a relationship," I mumble. "It's just about what feels good. And this . . . this feels good."

The script calls for us to kiss now, so I press my lips against his for a second and step away quickly as if he has a contagious disease.

"What the hell was that?" Drew asks, breaking character.

"What?"

"Your character is supposed to be totally head over heels in love with my character and determined to do whatever it takes to keep him."

"I know but . . ."

"I'm not going to get the wrong idea again, if that's what you're worried about."

Again? "What? I'm not . . ."

"No excuses. I don't know what your deal is or why you've suddenly started playing games, but I'm sick of it. If you don't think you can do this, walk out the door right now. I'd rather cancel the play than have to get on stage with an actress who doesn't give a shit."

Drew's verbal attack has rendered me speechless. He takes a step toward me. "So what it's going to be?"

I'm breathing fast and my fists are clenched at my side. I'm so furious I'm tempted to either slug him or just walk out of here and never come back.

"We won't call it a relationship." My voice is loud and clear. If he wants a kiss, he's going to get a kiss. He's going to get a kiss he will remember for the rest of his life. "It's just about what feels good. And this . . . this feels good." I grab him by the neck, pull him close, and kiss him.

The minute our lips connect, however, something happens. It's like I'm being hit by that car in the rain all over again, but instead of being hurt, I feel more alive than I ever have before. His hands are clutching at my hips and his mouth starts to trail down my neck. I lose track of seconds and then minutes.

By the time he whispers "Megan" in my ear, I'm out of breath and on a totally different planet.

But then I crash back to earth, so hard it sends a jolt through my body and I leap away from Drew. When I see the longing in his eyes, I can't trust that it's real. So I snatch my backpack and hightail it out of there as fast as I can.

twenty-seven

dénouement (noun): the moment in a
drama when the essential plot point
is revealed or explained.

Any enthusiasm I've managed to conjure up for the fall festival
disappears the minute Simon and I arrive.

"This looks nice," Simon says, as he glances around the gym.
"They did a pretty good job with the decorations."

Simon is full of crap. Becky Silva, a fellow junior and drama
major, was in charge of the decorations this year and chose her
favorite book, *The Secret Garden*, as the theme. Becky, although
a talented actress, is no beauty nor does she possess an ounce of
my sister's "charm," which meant the techies weren't nearly as
anxious to help as they were for my sister. Becky and a few of her
friends ended up doing most of the work themselves, which
(from the looks of it) amounted to tossing pots and vases filled
with horrible-looking, fake plastic flowers around the room. The

only thing Becky appears to have succeeded in is getting the janitor to unscrew the lightbulbs again.

"Allergy sufferers will be happy," I say, motioning toward the fake flowers as I make a weak attempt at humor.

I had Simon pick me up early so I wouldn't have to have an awkward encounter with Drew. I have managed to avoid Drew for twenty-nine hours and hoped to keep it up until dress rehearsal tomorrow morning, where we will be safely surrounded by techies. In the meantime, I am determined to stop thinking about him. Otherwise, I will lose my mind.

"Do you want to dance?" Simon asks, as he puts his arm around my waist. This uncharacteristic public display of affection only adds to my bad mood, a state of mind made worse by the fact that I have decided that I absolutely hate my black dress. It looks like I'm going to a costume party dressed like Morticia Addams. I should never have gone shopping alone, but the other choice was to go with Lucy, and there was no way I could have handled that.

I follow Simon to the dance floor and the two of us stake out a spot toward the side. As the DJ blasts Justin Timberlake I do my best to wiggle my torso to the beat but I feel stiff and unnatural, as if I'm playing the part of a girl who is happy to be at a dance with her boyfriend. And Simon doesn't appear to be doing much better. Unlike the previous year when he imitated a chicken just to get me to laugh, this year he has taken on the serious air of a prince looking for someone to bear his children. He sucks in his cheeks and dances by shifting his weight from foot to foot as he snaps his fingers.

Simon and I are on our third dance when I see Drew. He's not with my sister and is instead standing alone on the edge of the dance floor, watching me. The minute I lay eyes on him I feel the same magnetic pull, as if he could yank me toward him with a simple nod of his head. He looks totally drop-dead gorgeous, too. His longish hair curls up on the collar of his starched white shirt and his dark blue-green eyes stand out against the black material of his tux. Just the sight of him is enough to take my breath away.

"Maybe we should go get some punch or something," I say to Simon.

"Actually, I'm having a problem with my contacts," Simon says, cupping his left eye and blinking. "I'll be right back."

This is not a good time for Simon to be fiddling with his contacts. But I don't say that. Instead, unable to look away from Drew and rendered helpless by his power over me, I nod and say, "I'll wait here."

As Simon walks away, Drew heads straight toward me. I know I should get off the dance floor and run as far and fast as I can in the opposite direction, but I still can't move.

"Megan," he says quietly, stopping in front of me.

We stand still, just looking at each other, while couples continue to dance around us. My heart is clanging against my chest and my breathing is ragged and irregular. "You look beautiful," he says finally.

"Hah!" I say sarcastically.

He takes a step back. "What's that supposed to mean?"

"I think you know what I mean."

"No, I don't."

"Well . . ." I need to say something that will really put him in his place. "Well . . . you *should*!" Not exactly what I was hoping for.

"I should what?"

I shake my head in disgust and raise my hands, as if surrendering. "Why are you talking to me, anyway? Go be with your *date*." I spin on my heel, walking away from him.

"*What* date?" he calls out. "I don't have a date."

Everything stops. "Isn't Lucy here with you?"

"With *me*? She was supposed to come with Marybeth. There's a whole bunch of us meeting here as a group."

I feel a rush of relief, but after that passes, I close my eyes and for a moment I think I'm going to bawl like a baby.

"You thought I brought Lucy to the festival?" he asks, like this is the dumbest thing he's ever heard.

I really think I'm going to die right here and now, just fall flat on my face in the middle of the fall festival and croak.

"We need to talk." Drew gently takes my arm and steers me off the dance floor. He lets go of my arm and I keep my eyes firmly on him as I follow him through the crowd and out of the gym. We walk down the hall, toward the auditorium. We walk past the front door and all the excited, dressed-up couples who are still arriving and head directly down toward the opposite end of the hall, where the auditorium and production studio are located. I keep my eyes on the floor, not making eye contact with anyone. I can't talk. Nor can I think or even feel. I'm totally, absolutely numb.

Drew reaches the end of the hall and turns into the dark, unlit window-lined hall that leads to the auditorium. He stops outside the auditorium door and turns to face me. "Is that why you're here with Simon? Because you thought I liked Lucy?"

"No. Yes. It's complicated."

"Try me."

Even though it's dark and the only light is coming from the main hall, his eyes still sparkle. I glance away and take a step backward, so that I'm standing up against the wall. "*Lucy* likes *you*."

Drew breathes in deep. He takes a minute to collect his thoughts. "I . . . I have never been interested in Lucy. And I never will be."

"She told me you asked her to the fall festival."

"What?" Drew's eyes open wide. He shakes his head in disbelief. "If I said or did anything to give her that impression, well, then I'm very, very sorry."

I think about my sister and how she misled me on purpose. It hurts so bad, but at the same time, I'm so relieved that Drew isn't interested in her, I feel so light, like I'm floating.

He steps toward me and touches my chin with his index finger, lifting it up toward him. "I like *you*, Megan. In fact, all I can think about is you."

I touch my hand to his cheek. He likes me. *Me*.

Drew takes my hand and kisses it. And then he leans toward me, lightly pressing his lips against mine. We kiss long and slow, as if there is no one else in the world but us.

And then I hear it. A little gasp from whoever is now at the end of the hall, spying on us. I jump away from Drew and turn toward the main hall, half expecting to see my sister. But it's not Lucy. It's Annie Carmichael, the biggest mouth in the school. Before I can say anything (not that I would have anyway) she turns and hurries away.

"Oh, great," I say under my breath. "The whole school's going to know in the next fifteen minutes." By the time it finished making the rounds, I have no doubt Annie will have (supposedly) discovered us completely naked and doing the mambo jambo.

This was not good. Not good at all. True, my sister had lied to me; true, she deserved to be tossed into a dungeon and hung by her fingernails, but I still couldn't help but feel a tiny bit protective of her. She needed to be told the truth, but by me.

I hurry toward the main hallway and arrive just in time to see Annie push past Simon.

"Megan?" Simon calls out to me. He's standing at the other end of the hall, two glasses of punch in his hands. I feel as though someone has kicked me in the stomach the minute I see him.

Simon looks from me to Drew.

"Do you want me to stay?" Drew asks, half under his breath.

"No," I say, still looking at Simon. He's walking toward me now, trying not to spill the punch.

"I'm sorry," Drew whispers, as if he was to blame for my present situation. Even though Drew nods in Simon's direction as they pass each other, Simon doesn't acknowledge him.

"What's the deal with Annie?" Simon asks, handing me a glass of punch as he watches Drew go back into the auditorium. "She went tearing into the gym like she was being chased by Bigfoot."

"We need to talk," I say quietly to Simon.

Simon's breathing a little harder than normal and there is nervousness in his eyes, the same look he had the first day of freshman year when I met him in the office during lunch. We walk back in the direction I had just come. Only this time, when I get to the end of the hall I turn toward the production studio.

"So what do you want to talk about?" Simon asks as he follows me inside the studio.

I turn on the lights and pause, taking a moment to gather my thoughts. I look at the table saw and the circular saw and the cupboards lined with turpentine and neatly stacked cans of paint. I have spent so many hours in this room, all of them happy and almost all of them working alongside Simon.

"Oh, Simon," I say, sinking back against the wall as my nose starts to run. I wipe my nose with the back of my hand. "The past few weeks have been so awful. I wanted to talk to you about everything but I . . . I didn't know how."

Simon's frozen still, staring into his glass of punch.

"I really do love you, I do, just not in the way . . ."

"Don't!" he says, holding up his hands as if to ward me off. "What were you and Drew doing back there in the dark anyway? Did Annie catch you making out or something?"

"This isn't all my fault," I plead.

"I don't believe this!" Simon yells.

"You were the one who threatened to walk away from our friendship," I say. "You were the one who . . . who gave me an ultimatum."

"*Ultimatum?* I told you how I felt. I was honest."

"Honest? Then answer me this. Why were you content to be just friends when I was ugly?"

Simon's mouth drops open, as if he's flabbergasted by my accusation.

"I would never have done this to you," I say. "I would never have given you an ultimatum. I would've been there for you. I would've wanted you to be happy."

"You think I *want* to feel this way?"

I don't respond.

"You think I *chose* this?" He drops his head. A tear falls, splattering against the blue concrete floor. "Every time I see you talking to Drew, or to any other guy for that matter, I feel like my heart is being ripped to shreds. Every time I'm with you I want to touch you. I want to kiss you. I want to show you how much I care about you." He shakes his head as he gives me a sad smile. "Don't you get it, you idiot? I'm in love with you."

He puts his hand on the door and stops. He swipes away a tear with the back of his hand, still holding on to the punch. "Let me ask you something, Megan. What about Drew? I mean, at least I was your friend before the accident."

I want to tell him how wrong he is, how wrong *I* was, too. And I want to give him a tip for future reference: When you tell a girl you love her don't call her an idiot. But instead I stand there silent, my nose running like crazy, unable to speak. But it doesn't matter. The door is shut and Simon is already gone.

twenty-eight

break a leg (interjection): a traditional good-
luck greeting between cast and crew
before a performance.

The minute I step into the house I'm confronted with silence. Absolute, total silence.

"Lucy?" I call out. No answer. "Mom?" Still no answer.

I'm really hoping Lucy is here. By the time I got to the gym, big-mouthed Annie had already spilled the beans and word on the street was that my sister had left in a huff.

"Lucy?" My parents' door is shut. I turn the knob but the door is locked.

"Lucy," I say loudly and firmly. "We need to talk."

Silence.

"This isn't fair, Lucy. You didn't even like Drew before this year. You couldn't have cared less about him until you found out he was directing the spring musical."

Silence.

"I've liked him for a long, long time. Since the first time I ever saw him."

The door flies open. My sister is standing in front of me. I've never seen her like this. Her carefully coiffed updo is half down. Her eyes are red and puffy and her mascara is smeared. "You are such a liar," she spits.

Her uncontrolled venom takes my breath away. I have never seen her so angry. "It's true," I say calmly. "I liked him from the first time I saw him . . ."

"You never *ever* mentioned a word about liking Drew . . ."

"What difference does it make? You knew how I felt about him. You had to know."

She pauses just long enough for me to know I'm right.

"So what is this all about?" I ask. "You think you deserve him because you were the first to call dibs?"

"Are you kidding me?"

"I'm trying to understand you," I say. Due to Lucy's obvious state of hysteria, it's more important than ever that I stay calm, cool, and collected. "You outright lied to me. First you tell me that he asked you to Marybeth's party, which was a lie, then you tell me he asked you to the fall festival, which was a lie . . . what the *hell* is your problem?" A reasonable question, worthy of a reasonable answer.

"I didn't lie! Everyone kept telling me how much he liked me and he is the one who asked me if I had a date . . . and even though I suggested that we all go together he seemed really happy and excited and I assumed he wanted to be with me and was just too shy . . ."

"Assumed?" I cross my arms, just to hammer the point home. *"Assumed?"*

"Stop it! Stop it! *Stop it!"* Lucy screams, holding her hands to her ears. "Stop being so terrible to me. It's like you're out to get me! It's like you're obsessed with me. You want to be an actress, wear my clothes, eat what I eat, date the guy I like, take over my friends . . . you're trying to steal my life."

Steal her life? Just because I eat whatever she does, just because I sit with her friends at lunch, just because I sometimes wear her clothes, just because I tried out for the part she wanted . . .

"I don't want your life. I just want Drew." I take a step back and take a deep breath. "And the truth of the matter is, he wants me, too. He asked me to the fall festival, Lucy. *Me.* Not you."

"So why didn't you accept? Why did you go with Simon instead?"

"Because . . . because you liked him and also . . . I thought Drew only liked me because I was pretty."

"You're pathetic!" Lucy yells. "You've become such a . . . such a conceited, selfish bitch."

Lucy never swears. The sheer force of her words sends me reeling backward, clutching my chest. She bursts into tears, hysterically sobbing, and sits back down on the edge of our parents' bed. "I just want things to be the way they were."

"The way they were?" Suddenly I'm strong again. "You mean with you always being the one in the spotlight and me always stuck in the shadows, cheering you on? With you always being the strong one, the confident one, the one who always has to take care of her poor, lonely, ugly little sister? Is that what you want? Is that what you miss?"

Lucy doesn't answer.

"You know why you're so mad at me?" I'm yelling, but I don't care. "Because I finally got something that you wanted. And you can't stand it." I'm breathing hard. "I thought I wanted things to be like they were between us before, too. But I'm realizing I don't. I want to be able to win sometimes, too. I want to be able to get what I want, too."

She clenches her fists, and for a moment I think she's going to slug me. Instead she pushes past me and stomps down the stairs.

"Where are you going?" I shout, as Lucy unlocks the front door.

"I'm going back to the dance and you can sit here by yourself. Eat a bag of Oreos while you're at it."

It is a low blow, made even worse by the fact that we don't have any Oreos. I already ate them.

Fortunately, I have not eaten the Doritos. Still in my dress, I grab the Doritos and head back upstairs to the hall bathroom. I turn on the light and stop, staring at my reflection. As I look at the high cheekbones; the small, almost perfectly shaped nose;

the straight white even teeth, there is no sense of recognition or familiarity. I'm looking at the face of a stranger.

I turn on the water and grab a bar of soap, scrubbing all the makeup off my face. I let down my hair and yank it back in a ponytail. I take off my dress and put on my pajamas. I leave my dress in a pile on my floor and head back downstairs. I sit on the couch facing the door, waiting for Mom to come home, my ire at her absence increasing by the minute. By the time she arrives (two hours later), I have not only finished off an entire one-pound bag of Doritos, I'm working my way through an old, stale bag of chocolate chips that I found in the freezer.

"Hello?" Mom calls out, opening the door.

"Hello," I say calmly from the kitchen.

"Megan?" she says, walking into the kitchen and turning on the overhead light. She takes one look at me and stops still. "What's wrong?"

"Where have you been?" I ask.

"I dropped your dad off at the airport and then I met Francis for dinner in Little Italy. What's going on?" she asks, concerned. "Why are you home so early?"

"You missed it," I say quietly. "You missed it all per usual."

"Missed what?"

"Lucy and me . . . it was terrible."

"Did you guys have a fight?" Mom says gently, sitting next to me.

"Drew and I kind of got together at the dance and Lucy's

big-mouthed friend Annie saw us." I say this like the whole thing is Annie's fault.

"Oh," Mom says. I half expect her to jump away from me in horror, but instead she puts an arm around me and hugs me.

"I didn't mean for it to happen," I say, slobbering on her shoulder. "It's just . . . after our talk, I started to think that you were right, that Drew only liked me because of the way I look. And I thought, at least Simon loves me for who I am. And if I went to the dance with Simon, then he would be happy, Lucy would be happy . . ."

"But what about you?" Mom asks.

"Exactly! And you know what else? Drew didn't even ask Lucy to the dance, Mom. She made it all up. She knew I liked him and still . . ."

"I don't know if you can blame this on Lucy. You were already going with Simon, right?"

My mom has a point. Not that it makes me feel any better.

"Yes, but you know how I feel about Drew. And she knows, too. She knew all along. She was trying to hurt me."

"I'm not saying what she did was right, but I'm not so sure she was just trying to hurt you. Lucy's been struggling lately, too, just like you. Sometimes people find themselves in a situation that's new and unfamiliar and they get swept up in the emotion of it all. As a result, they say and do surprising things."

I hate it when Mom does her Dr. Phil imitation. I start crying again. I grab the last tissue and blow my nose. "I've made such a mess of everything. I kept trying to make everybody happy and it just made things a million times worse."

"Don't be so hard on yourself," Mom says and sighs. "Anyone would be having a tough time right now. To have everything coming at you at once, all this attention and on this magnitude, well, it has to be overwhelming."

I take another tissue and blow my nose.

"I want you to know that what happened to you—your new face—was never anything I would have chosen for you. I thought you were perfect before. But after the accident, well, we didn't really have any choice. I told myself that maybe it would all work out for the best, that perhaps your new face would give you more choices. And it has. Unfortunately, you've also inherited all the complications of being beautiful without having the skills to deal with it all."

"I've been trying but I keep screwing up. Everybody hates me."

"That's ridiculous!"

"What about you? You used to love spending time with me. And now . . ."

"I've been busy with work. You know that."

"You haven't been working Saturday nights. You've been going out with your friends."

"Oh, Megan," she says sadly as her eyes well with tears. "You know why I keep making plans on Saturday nights? I was afraid if I didn't have plans you would feel too guilty to go out. I wanted you to have some fun and develop your own social life and I didn't think you would if you felt obligated to me."

My mom has been making plans to go out every Saturday night for me? "But I loved our Saturday nights."

"I know, but that was before you had other choices . . . better offers, so to speak."

"Oh, Mom," I say as I begin to cry again. "I don't even know who I am anymore."

"I do," my mom says, grabbing another tissue box out from under the sink. "And I think deep down, you do, too."

"So who am I?"

She pulls out a tissue and wipes my nose for me. "You're who you've always been and who you'll always be. And it has nothing to do with the way you look."

I appreciate where my mom is going with all this, but she's wrong. As much as I hate to admit it, Lucy's right. I *have* changed.

And it has everything to do with the way I look.

twenty-nine

feedback (noun): a loud whistle or rumble
emanating from a sound system in an
auditorium, caused by a sound's being
amplified many times.

The morning after the fall festival, the school is quiet, the halls empty. I walk toward the auditorium with a pit in my stomach. I enter through the back door and wander toward the center of the stage. I arrived early so that I could practice my lines onstage before our last rehearsal, but as I take my place and look out at the empty auditorium, I realize I don't want to be here by myself.

I turn to leave and stop as I notice a stack of freshly painted screens leaning against the back of the stage. I walk over to the screens and thumb through them, silently evaluating each one until I reach the end. There, up against the wall, is an old background scene that Simon and I painted our freshman year for a senior production of *The Wizard of Oz*. It was our first project together and Simon and I worked hard on the design, creating a stylized farmhouse that was designed in three pieces so that when the tornado hit it could fly up and off to the sides simultaneously while splitting up. Instead of making the farmhouse all drab and gray like it was in the film, we took the opposite approach. We researched the era and decided that Aunty Em would have too much pride to let her house get all trashed. After all, why would Dorothy keep saying "There's no place like home" if her house was a pit? And so Simon and I had created the farmhouse of our dreams, using the brightest, most cheerful colors we could find.

I feel like whistling the theme to "Moon River" (an old song I have always found inherently sad). Everything seemed so simple back in the days when all Simon and I would argue about was the color of the paint we should use. I let the background screens fall back into place and turn away from the stage, heading toward the production studio. I walk to the door and stop, staring through the glass window at all the hubbub inside. Besides Simon and me (and Laura, who ended up attending the dance with George), no techies were at the dance and therefore were no more bleary-eyed than usual. The sound of laughter ricochets off the walls as everyone rushes to take care of the last-minute details, putting the final touches on the various sets for the senior productions. They're so busy that no one notices me as I open the door. I pause for a minute, taking time to listen to the comforting whir of the circular saw while breathing in the familiar smell of wet paint and turpentine. I suddenly wish that I was at school this morning not to act, but to design the sets; that tomorrow I would be at the performance not standing onstage, but in the audience, watching with paint-stained fingernails.

The saw stops and I open my eyes. Simon is in the corner of the production studio, standing on a ladder, finishing up the purple and gold wildflowers for the backdrop of Drew's set. He's wearing his glasses again, along with his black T-shirt, Bermuda shorts, and trademark silver sneakers. He seems to sense my presence. He stops painting and turns to face me.

Catherine and Laura are standing beside the table saw, just staring at me. I'm a little bothered to see that even normally cheerful Laura is now giving me the same evil eye as Catherine. Simon has obviously told them what happened at the dance. Or Annie.

"Simon, can I talk to you for a minute? Please?" I beg.

Finally, with what appears to be considerable thought, Simon puts down his brush and climbs down the ladder. We walk out of the production studio and down the hall and up the marble staircase, to the deserted second floor. When we reach the top of the stairs, I notice his shoe is untied. I attempt to point it out to him by tapping it with my foot but he moves away from me as if he can't stand to have me touch him, even with my foot.

I swallow back the lump in my throat. What can I possibly say to make things better? "So you gave up on your contacts, huh?"

He sighs as if he's not sure whether to answer me or not. "I hated them," he said. "I was just wearing them to try to look a little better for you."

"Oh, Simon," I breathe. "I'm so sorry."

He raises his hand as if to silence me. "It's not all your fault. I knew how you felt about Drew. I was just . . . stupid."

I chew on my bottom lip while he tucks his hands in his pockets and looks at the floor. "What's going to happen to us?" I ask.

"I don't know," he says. "I wish we could go back to how things were between us before your accident, but . . . I don't think I can."

"What are you saying?" I wipe my nose on the back of my sleeve as I blink back my tears. "That you need some time apart? Some time to think things through?"

"No." Simon closes his eyes for a minute and breathes in deep. "What I'm saying is that . . . I can't be *just* your friend, Megan. I wish I could, but I can't."

"But . . . I love you."

He gives me a little grin. "I know. Just not the way I want you to."

After my talk with Simon I go back to the auditorium and stare blindly at my script until Drew arrives with Mrs. Habersham, who is there to give us our final critique. I nod at Drew as we take our places onstage. I'm glad that when the play opens I'm supposed to be sitting down because knowing that Mrs. Habersham is there evaluating me is making my knees so wobbly I don't think I could stand if I had to. I do my best to remember my lines, but I keep getting distracted by Mrs. Habersham, who is in the front row, watching me intently as she takes copious notes on the spiral pad in her lap. I feel totally, utterly sick to my stomach. As I forget yet another line, I can't help but feel bad for Drew. He has put so much time and energy into this whole thing and I am going to blow it for him. We finally finish and I brace myself for a lecture as I walk to the edge of the stage to receive Mrs. Habersham's critique.

"That was terrible," she says simply.

Drew inhales deeply as he crosses his arms.

"Miss Fletcher," she continues, as she pushes her glasses up her nose and leans forward. "I know you saw the script at the audition because I was there, but have you even looked at it since?"

I stare down at my feet. There's nothing to say. She's right. I'm terrible.

"Why haven't you memorized your lines yet?" she asks.

"I, ah, well, I'm trying."

"With less than thirty-six hours until your performance, I would suggest you try a little harder," she says crisply.

"She's had a lot of stuff going on," Drew says, courageously rising to my defense.

"Let me remind you that this is *your* play Drew," she says, almost angrily. "And casting Megan was your decision. As the director, writer, and star, you're the person who will be held accountable. Your entire grade is riding on the performance—the *entire* performance." And with that threat, she turns and spins away, walking up the aisle with her notebook tucked under her arm.

"I'm sorry," I say to Drew as soon as Mrs. Habersham is out of earshot.

"No," he says. "I'm sorry. About last night . . . I had no idea that Lucy . . . I wasn't thinking."

"It's not your fault," I say. "It's mine."

He takes a breath and glances toward the back of the theater. "I tried to call you."

"I know. I just, well, I had a lot of things to think about."

He walks toward the edge of the stage. He sits down and motions for me to join him. "How did everything go?"

"Not so good," I say, sitting next to him. "Lucy's furious. And Simon, well, I told him I could never see him as anything more than a friend. Needless to say, he doesn't want anything to do with me anymore."

"I'm sorry," he says quietly. "Megan, what I said last night, about how I feel about you . . . if it helps at all—"

"It does," I say quickly.

"I just want you to know that I've never felt like this about anyone before."

I look into Drew's eyes. A year ago it would've been inconceivable to me, almost laughable that I might question whether or not someone might want to be with me because of the way I look. As of last year, people liked me *in spite of* the way I looked, not *because*. "The way you feel about me . . . does it . . . would it matter . . ." I swallow. "What if I looked like I used to?"

"What do you mean?"

"Would this—us—have happened if I had never been in that accident? If I was still ugly?"

And then I wait. I look into his eyes and wait for him to tell me that of course he would, that he would love me no matter what I looked like, no matter how ugly I was. That he didn't care about high cheekbones, small noses, or straight white teeth. I wait for him to reassure me that Simon and my mom were wrong, that even if I was the most horrible-looking person in the world he would still be sitting next to me telling me how he's never felt this way about anyone before.

"I don't know." He takes my hand and squeezes it. "All I know is how I feel about you now. And I can tell you this: I love you."

thirty

deus ex machina (noun): an event or
character that appears out of nowhere
to resolve the dramatic conflict.

When I get home, Lucy is in our bedroom, packing her suitcase.
She spent the night at Marybeth's and I haven't seen her since
our argument. It's obvious from the look of surprise on her face
that she didn't plan on seeing me now, either.

"Hi," I say nervously. I take a breath as I ready myself for another confrontation.

But Lucy doesn't even answer me. She just continues packing, as if I'm not even there.

"Are you going someplace?" I ask, finally. (Even though the
suitcase is a fairly big clue.)

"I'm going to New York for a few days."

"When will you be back?"

"Don't know," she says, zipping up her suitcase.

"Look," I begin. "About last night . . ."

"Let's just forget it."

I know Lucy doesn't really mean that she intends to forget it. What she's really saying is: I'm convinced I'm in the right and you totally screwed me over and I will never ever forgive you as long as I live. I swallow and clear my throat. "This thing with Drew . . ."

"Over it," she says, raising her hands.

"I know you're mad," I interrupt. "But . . ."

"I'm not mad," she says.

Truth be told, she doesn't sound mad. She sounds a little tired, and maybe a little rushed, but not mad. "Then why the silent treatment?"

"Marybeth and I have a train to catch." She wheels her suitcase out of the room and bangs it down the steps. I hear the front door open and close and I know she's gone.

I glance back toward the closet. I see my reflection in the mirror, complete with runny nose and thumb cuticle in mouth. I take my thumb out of my mouth and stare at the face looking back at me. I feel like I'm looking into the eyes of the enemy. But like Lucy, I don't want to fight anymore. I just want it all to go away. I'm ready to admit defeat.

I lunge at the door, slamming it shut. I run downstairs and grab the Hefty bags out of the kitchen cupboard. I hurry back up to my bedroom, determined to rid myself of every stitch of clothing, every stick of makeup, everything and anything that was bought to showcase the new me. I fling open the closet door. As Lucy's dollhouse crashes to the floor, I ignore my reflection while

I take my pile of cute tight little shirts my sister had picked out for me and throw them in the Hefty bag. Then I yank all my skinny jeans off the hangers and toss them in, too. In between blowing my nose I fill two oversized Hefty bags full of clothes before heading to the bathroom. I open the makeup drawer that I share with Lucy and begin to quickly sort through it, putting my stuff in the trash and leaving Lucy's scattered across the floor.

After I'm done with the makeup I open the medicine cabinet. I pull my stent out of its protective case and whip it into the Hefty bag. As it disappears into the trove of lip glosses and snot-filled tissues, I'm suddenly so disgusted that I feel nauseous. I wrap my arms around my belly as I bend over the toilet and begin to dry heave. When I'm done, I wipe my face with my hands and turn back toward the medicine cabinet. I shut it closed, inadvertently glimpsing my reflection in the mirror. I pause to look at my mascara-streaked and snot-filled face and wonder how awful-looking I'll be when my nose closes up. Will it just collapse or will it shrink in place? Before I can stop myself, I'm rifling through the Hefty bag, desperately picking through snot-filled tissues and tubes of lip gloss looking for my stent.

"Megan?" My dad is standing in the doorway. "What are you doing?"

"I threw out my stent," I sob.

He hesitates and for a minute, I'm pretty certain he's going to blow his top. As in: YOU THREW OUT YOUR STENT? ARE YOU @#$%! CRAZY??

But he doesn't say a word. He steps over the makeup

scattered across the bathroom floor and kneels beside me as he starts digging through the bag.

"Here it is," he says, handing it back to me.

I take the stent and drop backward, leaning up against the bathroom wall. He pauses, just looking at me. We sit there for a while, neither of us speaking.

"Come on," he says finally, offering me his hand. "I just found a bag of Fig Newtons your mom hid from me."

"Fig Newtons?" I say, wrinkling up my nose.

"She's on a health kick." He shrugs. "I figure they're better than nothing."

He has a point. I take his hand and follow him downstairs. I take a seat at the table and he hands me a box of Kleenex. I wipe my nose as he pours us two humongous glasses of milk and sticks a brand-new bag of Fig Newtons on the table.

"I heard about the fall festival," he says.

"So you know Lucy hates me," I say, using three tissues to wipe my nose.

"She doesn't hate you."

I rip open the bag of Fig Newtons and pop one in my mouth. I don't want to talk about Lucy with my dad. I have already gone down this road with Mom and I know Dad will pretty much tell me the exact same thing she already did. Besides, I just don't have the energy right now.

"Can I ask you a question?" I say, as soon as I swallow the cookie. "Do you think Mom would've liked you if you had never shaved off your mustache and lost all that weight?"

"What? Why do you ask that?"

"Drew . . . the guy I like."

"I know who he is," he says.

"He practically admitted that he never would have cast me in his play if I wasn't pretty. He never would have liked me."

"But you *are* pretty."

"Yes but . . ."

"Let me ask you something, Megan," Dad says quietly. "Would you like him if *he* was fat and ugly?"

"Yes," I announce.

"Uh-huh," he says sarcastically, rolling his eyes. "It's human nature, Megan. Look at your mother. She's the least superficial person I know. She couldn't care less what people look like. But, when she first saw me, she didn't have any interest in me. It was only after I lost all that weight and my silly mustache and white apron that she agreed to go out with me."

"But she loves you."

"I know. She loves me even though I've lost my hair and gained almost all that weight back. She doesn't care anymore because she loves me for who I am. But would she have ever agreed to go out with me if I came up to her looking like I do now? Maybe not."

"I think she would. I mean, you still look like *you*. It's not like you got a completely new face."

He looks at me. I can tell he's at a loss for words. He takes a bite of a Fig Newton and makes a face as he chews. "It needs something," he says, holding the remaining portion up to the light.

"Like some chocolate and a creme filling?"

"Exactly," he says, popping the rest in his mouth and winking at me. He takes another one.

I push back my chair. I don't want to upset my dad with all my *poor me* talk. "I better get back upstairs and start memorizing my lines or tomorrow's going to be a disaster."

"Megan," he says, stopping me. "This guy of yours . . . this Drew. Would you like him if he was a jerk?"

"What? No."

"What I'm trying to say is that a pretty face may increase your chances of getting inside the house, but it's not going to keep you from getting kicked out on your ass. That's up to you." He smiles as he offers me the bag of Fig Newtons.

I think I understand what he's saying. A beautiful face might win me the attention of the guy I loved, but it wasn't going to win his affection. After all, lots of pretty girls were interested in Drew (besides Lucy). But I was the one he liked. I was the one he loved.

I take a couple Fig Newtons for the road and head back upstairs, determined to study my lines. I pick up the script as I sit on my sister's bed. I look at the yellow-colored walls and the matching comforter covers and think about how happy I was when Lucy told me how much she loved the color. Her approval meant so much to me—and unfortunately, it still does.

I glance at the dog-eared script on my bed and I think about how in thirty-one hours I will be up onstage, performing in front of a crowd of people who have actually paid money to witness my disaster. I have no choice but to refocus and settle in for a long night of memorization. I brush the cookie crumbs off my blue hoodie and pick at the crusty stuff on the pocket. Gross. I force myself off the bed and go toward the clothes-strewn closet to grab a clean hoodie. But before I get a chance, I trip over Lucy's dollhouse.

I land on my knees and wince in pain as my eyes fill with tears and my nose begins to run. I stop crying and just stare at the house. I remember before the flood, when the dollhouse was in perfect condition. Lucy and I each had a little doll that we pretended were sisters. We spent hours playing with the house, making the dolls imitate the mundane grown-up rituals of life—cooking, cleaning, and sleeping.

I run my finger over the broken balcony and across the warped wood floors. It wouldn't be that hard to fix. The floors would need to be replaced, but that wouldn't be difficult. I could cut out some new wood, hammer it back into place, stain, and shellac it. The walls could be repainted and I could even stencil in the design of the wallpaper. The stairway could be rebuilt.

Why had it never occurred to me to fix it up for Lucy before? Was it because the dollhouse was just one more thing she had that I didn't?

I turn back toward the closet and glance at my reflection in the mirror, me kneeling beside a broken dollhouse. I crawl on my knees so that I'm directly in front of the mirror. I touch the cool glass, tracing my face with my finger. As I stare into my own eyes I suddenly realize what I have to do. And unfortunately for Drew, it has nothing to do with his play. As much as I hate to disappoint him, I don't have much choice. I know who I am. And I'm not an actress. I'm Megan Fletcher. I'm a techie.

thirty-one

finale (noun): the conclusion of
a performance.

"Oh my God," my mom says as she pokes her head outside. I'm on the roof, covered in sawdust and paint.

"Ron," she says, calling back inside to my dad. "Come up here and see what Megan did last night."

My dad comes out on the roof and stands beside my mom, his mouth open in surprise as he stares not at me, but at the dollhouse beside me.

"You did all that last night?" my dad says, pointing to the house.

"Yeah." I've not only fixed the sagging walls and restored the floors to their polished glory, I've repainted it from top to bottom. It looks brand new, as I imagined it did when my grandfather first presented it to Lucy.

My dad kneels down in front of it and peers inside. "How did you know to do the railing like that?" he says, pointing to the staircase railing that twists up the steps.

"I don't know," I say, suppressing a yawn. I have never pulled an all-nighter before. But I was a girl possessed, one with a mission. "I just built it."

"Funny. I asked your grandpa the same question and he told me the same thing." My dad is practically beaming at me. "It's nice that someone in this family has his talent!"

"You must be exhausted," my mom says. "Are you okay to go to school?"

I check my watch. I have less than an hour to get ready, which, considering my sawdust-spattered hair and paint-stained fingernails, is not a lot of time. "Sure," I say. "Have you heard from Lucy?" I add, as if it is just an afterthought.

"I talked to her last night," my mom says. "She sounded . . . good."

My dad walks over and puts his arm around me. "Everything is going to be okay, kiddo. I promise."

I somehow make it through the entire day at school. Even though it's clear everyone heard what happened at the dance and I'm now going to be ostracized by both the techies and the drama majors. But for some reason I don't really care. Maybe I'm still numb, but for today at least, I'm content to be alone.

When I get home my parents insist I lay down for a while. I take their advice even though weirdly I'm not tired in the least.

Much to my surprise I fall asleep and when my mom wakes me up, I barely have time for a quick shower and a Diet Pepsi before returning to school for the performance. But unfortunately, as I step back inside the familiar brick building the sense of peace and calm that has enveloped me all day is quickly replaced by an anxiety so intense I think I might have to bend over and breathe into a paper bag.

The first person I see is Drew, who's backstage reading his dictionary. When he sees me, he puts down his dictionary and stands.

"How are you doing?" he asks, taking my hand.

"Okay," I manage. I haven't seen him all day and just the sight of him provides me with a certain sense of relief.

"You're going to do great. Just remember, I'm going to be right there with you the whole time."

I force myself to take a deep breath. I know he's going to be right up there with me, but it still feels good to have him say it.

Drew and I walk across the stage and toward the dressing room. Unlike the day before, everything is quiet. Since the sets are finished and it's a small production, there are only a handful of production techs milling about. And since there is only one senior production each night, there are no other actors (besides Drew) to commiserate with.

Drew says good-bye at the door and I step into my dressing room. I sit down in front of the makeup mirror. And once again, I'm staring at my reflection.

I have waited so long for this moment, for my turn in front of the mirror. But now that I'm finally here, it seems sort of anticlimactic. I'm not sure what I expected to feel, but I didn't expect this. The only thing I feel right now is lonely. And a little bit sad.

Which is weird, because before my accident, if someone would have told me that one day I'd be sitting in this chair, looking at this face, I would have been ecstatic. Even if they would have told me about all the surgeries and what I would have to endure to get here, I would've assumed it would all be worth it, just to be pretty. It never would have occurred to me that when the bandages came off and the swelling went down, the earth would tilt. That even now, months later, I still wouldn't have regained my balance. Because the same pretty face that had won me a coveted spot in front of the mirror, was also the reason why I'm sitting here all alone.

I take another sip of my (now slightly warm) Diet Pepsi and apply my makeup the way I've watched my sister do it so many times. With less than a half hour left to showtime, my all-nighter catches up to me with a fury and I'm suddenly so tired that I'm tempted to curl up on the grody couch in the dressing room and go to sleep. Instead, I change into my costume and resolutely head backstage, determined to get this thing over with as soon as possible so I can go home and get some sleep. I spend the next ten minutes in my place on the bench, listening to people talk and laugh as they take their seats on the other side of the curtain.

I feel a hand on my shoulder. It's Drew. "Megan . . . ," he begins, and I can tell he's about to tell me something, something important. Something earth-shattering.

"Ten seconds!" the rodent announces from his perch stage right.

"Break a leg," Drew whispers.

And just like that, I'm awake.

I turn back toward the curtain, keeping my eyes trained on the rodent. The rodent says something into his headset and gives us a nod, indicating that it's showtime.

I feel like I licked my finger and stuck it into an electrical outlet. Every single muscle is wound tight and ready to spring into action.

Just breathe.

Just breathe.

Just breathe.

The curtains open and I'm suddenly flooded in light. I'm supposed to look over the audience at the moon in the corner of the theater that Laura made out of cardboard and painted a fluorescent, glow-in-the-dark yellow, but instead I make my first mistake, staring directly into the packed audience. At first I can't see anything, but I keep staring until my eyes adjust to the darkness. I squint, trying to make out the shapes and forms in front of me. Slowly, recognizable figures form in front of me: my parents front row center; off to the left, on the side of the theater, Simon. Toward the back of the auditorium is George, sitting next to Laura and Catherine. A couple of rows in front of them are Lucy's friends Annie, Maria, and Jane. A couple rows over from them are Mr. Lucheki, Mrs. Bordeaux, Mrs. Habersham . . . in fact, everywhere I look I see someone I recognize. Everyone, apparently, has come to see Drew's play. Everyone except Lucy.

"Hey," Drew says, as he walks toward me.

The entire audience is looking at me. I swallow, readying myself for my first line. "What . . . what . . . ," I begin. What am I doing here? Someone help me!

"You're probably wondering what I'm doing here," Drew says, covering for me. My first line. I screwed up my first line. How in the world am I going to make it through the rest of the play?

"I've been looking for you," Drew continues. "We need to talk." He sits down next to me. He pauses, glancing toward my hand, which is visibly shaking. MY HAND. That's right. I'm supposed to take his hand. I put my quivering hand on his and he withdraws it, just like he's supposed to. Just like we've done a million times before.

"Don't you want to know why I was afraid?" I blurt out. Oh God—that's the wrong line. I skipped a line.

"I know why," Drew calmly improvises. "Because you heard that bad things happen on a full moon. That all the vampire lore, the werewolf stuff—that it's based on documented truth."

I'm breathing *really* hard now and even though I took a double dose of my nasal spray I can still taste something dripping into my mouth. I wipe my nose with my other hand as I glance at Drew as if to say I'm sorry.

"That's why I gave you the necklace," Drew says. I know he's trying to feed me my line but it doesn't help. I'm drawing a complete and total blank.

"Do you still have it?" he asks calmly, trying to feed me my line again.

But I can't think. Instead, I stare into the audience. I can see people begin to look at one another, like, what the hell is going on? Why is she dripping snot all over the place? Why doesn't she wipe her nose? Why doesn't she KNOW HER LINES? Simon has taken a seat in the third row and is covering his eyes as if he can't bear to watch.

Oh God. I can't do this. I'm sinking. I'm dying a slow, painful death . . .

"You told me that the Rune is the key to eternal life, that it would protect me . . ." I hear someone whispering offstage.

I glance over Drew's shoulder, to where the rodent is standing. But he's no longer there. In his place is Lucy, standing with Drew's script in hand. She nods at me to continue as she mouths my line once again.

"You told me that the Rune is the key to eternal life, that it would protect me . . . ," I say. My eyes fill with tears. She came.

"Even when you weren't around to do it yourself . . . ," Lucy whispers.

"Even when you weren't around to do it yourself," I say loud and strong, blinking back the tears and wiping my nose again. "I never take it off."

"Look, about last night . . . I—we—it was a mistake," Drew says, visibly relieved.

I glance at Lucy, waiting for my next line.

"Personally, I think there's something to it . . . ," she whispers.

"Personally, I think there's something to it. The werewolves and vampires theory, I mean," I say. And then, even though my character is supposed to be totally upset, I smile. I can't help my-self. I'm so happy that my sister is here, that it's impossible to pre-tend otherwise. I'm not that good of an actress.

I make it through the rest of the play with Lucy in the wings, feeding me an occasional line. Finally, the lights go down as the curtain closes. It opens again almost immediately and I take my bow as the audience claps. I think a lot of people are happy and relieved that I made it through without having a heart attack or gushing anymore cerebrospinal fluid in front of everyone. But I'm pretty sure the applause has little to do with me and almost everything to do with Drew. But even though I may not have knocked it out of the park and wowed the crowd with my performance, it wasn't horrible. I mean, *I* wasn't horrible.

When the curtain closes again, Drew takes my hand and sweeps me into his arms. "You did it!"

But there's no time for tender moments. Almost immedi-ately, Drew is surrounded by well-wishers and I finally have an opportunity to do what I've wanted to do all night. I hurry over to the side of the theater where Lucy was just standing. But she's not there.

"Have you seen Lucy?" I ask the rodent.

"I think she left," he says casually.

Lucy left? Without saying good-bye?

I run to the side door and peer out into the hall, but there's only a few techs milling about.

"There she is!" I hear my dad yell.

I turn around as he makes his way up the side stage steps, followed by my mom. He's holding a big bouquet of red roses in his hand.

"You were great!" he says, handing me the roses and kissing me on the forehead.

"We're so proud of you," my mom adds, giving me a hug.

"Thanks," I say, accepting the roses. "They're beautiful." I had watched my sister receive more bouquets than I could count, and it feels good to finally be getting my own. "Did you guys see Lucy?" My dad glances at my mom as though he doesn't quite know how to respond. "She didn't say good-bye."

"She said to tell you that she thought you did great and that she would see you at home later," Mom says.

"Oh . . . okay," I mumble, trying hard not to look as upset as I feel.

"She said this is your moment. She thought she'd just be in the way," Dad says.

This was your moment . . .

I press my nose to the petals as I clutch the bouquet to my chest.

"But she did come home early just to be here for you tonight, Megan," Mom reminds me.

I flash my parents a smile. "I know," I say.

The rodent has opened the curtains again. I look at the people still filing out of the auditorium and catch sight of Simon toward the back. He gives me a little smile and for one terrific moment, I think he's going to come and see me. But instead, he turns his back to me and walks in the opposite direction. As he exits the theater, I give him a little wave good-bye.

"Should we go get something to eat?" my dad asks enthusiastically.

"Thanks, Dad," I say. "But I'm not all that hungry."

"Are you sure?" Mom says, glancing after Simon.

I look around. Although the stage is still crowded, Drew is no longer in sight. "I'm sure."

I say good-bye to my parents and head back to my dressing room, once again, alone. I step inside and turn on the light.

That's when I see it: a shoe box. But it's no ordinary shoe box. The inside has been made to resemble the production studio, complete with ugly blue floor, little bookshelves stacked with miniature paint cans, a miniature table saw, and a miniature circular saw. There's even sawdust scattered across the floor. And in the middle of it all, is Catwoman.

"Thank God for eBay, huh?" I hear Drew say.

I turn around to face him. He looks like he's just stepped out of the shower, his face free of stage makeup and his longish hair damp and combed back off his face.

I swallow and say, "You did this?"

"You seem to be so happy when you're there. I thought, this way, you can take it home with you."

I glance from Drew back to the gift he has made for me with

his own hands. I feel like I'm going to melt right into the casting couch.

"I wanted to give you something and, well, flowers just didn't seem right. Too corny or impersonal or something."

I pick it up to get a better look. I can still see the insignia on the side of the box. "Aerosoles?"

"I wasn't sure if they were expensive or not. But I do know my mom's boots are happy to be out of the box and free in the back of her closet."

If this was a year or two ago, and I had just done something momentous, Lucy and Simon would have been here with me. Instead, I have Drew. It would have been nice to have all three, but I'm learning the world doesn't work like that. Not for me anyway.

"I wasn't sure about Catwoman," he says.

"I think she fits in perfectly." I gently set the diorama back on the table.

Drew moves closer. He looks at me with a singular attention and adoration, the colors in his irises changing and crackling, like tiny fireworks exploding just for me. It's enough to make me feel like I'm in the spotlight again (but in a good way).

I reach out for him and put my hand in his, as much to steady myself as for his touch. For the first time I feel like I'm alone with Drew, just the two of us, the rest of the world having faded into the background.

"So you like it?" he asks softly, brushing a wayward strand of hair away from my eyes.

If ever there was a moment when it would be appropriate to burst into song, this is it. But fortunately for Drew, George Longwell has ruined impromptu singing for me forever.

"Yeah," I say. "I like it." And then I give him my open-mouthed smile.

THE END
By Drew Reynolds

CHARACTERS

GIRL: A girl in her late teens.
GUY: A guy in his late teens.

PLACE
A public park.

TIME
A summer night.

(Lights up on PARK. GIRL is sitting on park bench, staring up at FULL MOON. GUY ENTERS.)

GUY   Hey.

GIRL   *(Looks up and smiles, surprised and happy.)*

                 What are you doing here?

GUY   I've been looking for you.

(GUY sits down next to her. GIRL takes his hand. GUY looks at their hands entwined together and pauses a beat, before pulling his hand away. GIRL looks back up at the moon.)

                 We need to talk.

GIRL *(Sadly.)* When I was little I used to be afraid of full moons.

GUY   I've been thinking about . . . about what happened last night . . .

GIRL   Don't you want to know why I was afraid?

GUY *(Frustrated.)* I know why. Because you heard that bad things happen on a full moon. That all

the vampire lore, the werewolf stuff—
that it's based on documented truth.

GIRL

That's right. There could be monsters in
this park right now. Just because we don't
see them doesn't mean they're not here.
At least, that's what they say. Good thing
you gave me that necklace, remember?

GUY (*Annoyed*)

Of course.

GIRL

You told me that the Rune is the key to
eternal life, that it would protect me even
when you weren't around to do it
yourself. I never take it off.

(*SHE pulls out necklace and shows it to him.*)

GUY

Look, about last night . . . I—we—it was
a mistake.

GIRL

Personally, I think there's something to it.
The werewolves and vampire theory, I
mean.

GUY

Are you listening to me?

(SHE doesn't answer but continues looking at the necklace.)

> It never should have happened. And it can never happen again.

(Stands up and begins walking away.)

GIRL *(Tearfully.)*   I remember the first time I saw you. You walked into class and I just felt something . . . I can't describe it. I'd never felt like that before.

(HE stops.)

> I had such a crush on you.

GUY   Look, we both need to move on . . .

GIRL   You didn't notice me at first. I was always trying to think of reasons to talk to you. And then one day you dropped your pencil and I remember, I remember I said . . .

GUY   You're a nice girl, okay? It's just that, well, I think we're better off as friends.

GIRL (*GIRL stands up and crosses her arms, angry.*)

                        Are you breaking up with me again?

GUY   It's not like we were ever back together.
We just hooked up, that's all.

GIRL   There's someone else, isn't there?

GUY (*Stumbling*)   No . . . no.

GIRL (*GIRL sits back on the bench, as if defeated. She hugs her
knees to her chest as she stares at the moon.*)

                        I've heard rumors, you know. A rumor
you were seeing Wendy.

GUY (*Softly.*)   So what if I am? Look, we had a good run,
you and me. But we're young, you know?

(*GUY pauses a beat and turns to leave.*)

GIRL (*Desperately.*)   Don't go.

(*GUY continues to walk. HE is almost offstage.*)

GIRL   I'll die without you.

(GUY *abruptly stops walking. He turns around to face her.*)

GUY   Don't talk crazy.

(GIRL *starts to cry. GUY sits back down next to her.*)

      You deserve someone who really cares
      about you.

GIRL   I remember the first time we got together.
      You told me that I was special . . . that
      you had never felt like this about anyone
      before. That you loved me. Remember?

GUY   I remember.

GIRL   Was it a lie?

GUY   Of course not.

GIRL   When you first broke up with me I was so
      devastated, I couldn't sleep. I couldn't
      eat . . . I couldn't do anything. And then
      I thought . . . I'll be okay as long as he
      doesn't date anyone else. As long as I
      know his heart still belongs to me. When
      I heard that you and Wendy were

hanging out, I told myself that you guys were just friends. And last night, when you saw me talking to that guy, I could see the pain in your eyes and I knew you were jealous. I knew you still cared about me. And then you touched my arm. Remember? "I miss you," you said.

(GUY looks away. GIRL begins caressing his arm.)

You still love me.

GUY

But that doesn't change how I feel about us. I can't . . . I don't want a relationship right now.

GIRL

So we won't call it a relationship. It's just about what feels good. And this feels good.

(THEY kiss long and slow. Suddenly, HE breaks away, jumping to his feet.)

GUY

No!

GIRL *(Standing up to face him.)*

Why not?

GUY   Because I don't want this . . . us!

GIRL   But you love me . . .

GUY   Look, this . . . us, it's not love. It's
something else . . .

GIRL   You're wrong. It is love for me. I've always
loved you. From that first moment I saw
you.

GUY   Don't say that. It's not love . . .

*(GIRL kisses him with all her might. HE resists before responding in
spite of himself.)*

GUY   I'm not denying that you're hot. I've
always thought that. But what happened
last night . . . it's not going to happen
again. We had too much to drink. The
moon, the beach . . . we're only human . . .

GIRL   Have you slept with her?

GUY   This conversation is over.

GIRL   Do you . . . do you love her?

GUY   No.

(GIRL sits down and looks back up at the moon.)

GIRL   Are you going to tell her about
last night?

GUY   I'm hoping I don't have to.

(GIRL pulls out her phone and dials a number.)

GUY   What are you doing?

GIRL   I'm calling Wendy.

GUY   No!

GIRL *(furious)*   She needs to know the truth, that you
and I belong to each other. Otherwise last
night never would have happened.

GUY   We don't belong together! We never did!
For God's sake, you don't even really
know me.

GIRL   I know that you're the type of guy who says
hello to people everyone else ignores. I

know you're the type of guy who never makes fun of people less fortunate than you. I know that you like blueberries on your cereal and that you wear boxers not briefs and that you have a birthmark right . . .

GUY
I'm the type of guy who has sex with another girl when my girlfriend is on vacation with her family.

GIRL (*Stunned.*)
What? What are you talking about?

GUY
Over Christmas break when you guys were in Jamaica, I hooked up with a girl I met at a party.

GIRL (*Upset.*)
No. You called me every night. You told me you were just staying home and watching TV.

GUY
I lied.

GIRL
Who . . . who was she?

GUY
Just some girl. A friend of a friend.

GIRL
What happened to her?

GUY	She went back to college and, well, you came home.
GIRL (*Weakly.*)	No. I don't believe it.
GUY	I could have gotten away with it. You never would have known. I'm just telling you now to, well, to make things easier for you.

GIRL (*SHE looks back at the moon.*)

You see? I was right. There was a monster in this park. And it was right in front of my eyes the whole time.

(*GUY pauses a beat before turning and walking to the back of the stage. He is still visible although covered in darkness.*)

(*SHE takes the necklace off her neck and looks at it. She sets it on the bench and looks back up at the moon before leaving the necklace and walking away.*)

FINIS